Praise for *Mrs. Witherspoon Goes to War*

"Wartime creates heroes in unlikely
WASPs go wheels-up on a covert rescue
Plenty. But in Mary Davis's typical st
beneath their wings, Mrs. Witherspo
through."

—Kristen Heitzmann, bestselling and Christy Award-Winning
author of numerous books, including *Secrets* and *The Breath of Dawn*

"If you're looking for a WWII story where troops are storming Normandy, world leaders are contemplating their nuclear options, or paradise is decimated, look elsewhere. *Mrs. Witherspoon Goes to War* shows the softer-yet just as powerful-depiction of that time in history we must never forget. Mary Davis does a spectacular job telling the women's story, the WASP, the Women Airforce Service Pilots. We follow a soldier with a mother's heart, who puts soccer moms to shame as she strives to take matters in her own hands and win the war, one POW at a time."

—Kathleen E. Kovach, award-winning author
of *Titanic: Legacy of Betrayal*

"*Mrs. Witherspoon Goes to War* is a fun adventure. It really gives the feel of being a female pilot in WWII."

—Suzanne Norquist, author of *A Song for Rose*
and *Mending Sarah's Heart.*

"…I love this story… I appreciated the detail about the planes that to me balances important information with avoiding the glazed-eye effect on non-aviation enthusiasts."

—Becky Durost Fish, freelance editor

HEROINES OF WWII

Mrs. Witherspoon
GOES TO WAR

MARY DAVIS

BARBOUR
PUBLISHING

Mrs. Witherspoon Goes to War ©2022 by Mary Davis

Print ISBN 978-1-63609-156-3

eBook Editions:
Adobe Digital Edition (.epub) 978-1-63609-158-7

All scripture quotations, unless otherwise noted, are taken from the King James Version of the Bible.

This book is a work of fiction. Names, characters, places, and incidents are either products of the author's imagination or used fictitiously. Any similarity to actual people, organizations, and/or events is purely coincidental.

Cover image: Sandra Cunningham/Trevillion Images

Published by Barbour Publishing, Inc., 1810 Barbour Drive, Uhrichsville, Ohio 44683, www.barbourbooks.com

Our mission is to inspire the world with the life-changing message of the Bible.

ecpa Member of the
Evangelical Christian
Publishers Association

Printed in the United States of America

DEDICATION

Dedicated to my stepdad, Allen (US army).
You would have loved this one, Dad!

I also dedicate this story to all the military people in my life.

My husband, Chip (Ret. Colonel US Air Force) Thanks for helping
me get a majority of the military stuff mostly correct. There was
only so much you could do before I had to make stuff up. =0)

My brother, Jim (Ret. US Navy)

My brother-in-law, Dennis (Ret. US Navy)

My brother-in-law, John (Forest Fire Fighter and Smoke Jumper)

And to all the men and women who fight to serve and
protect the United States of America and the people in it.

A special thanks to my critique partners Kathy & Suzanne
for helping me make this story soar to life and fly high.

Also a shout-out to my dolly friend Jolene.

To every thing there is a season,
and a time to every purpose
under the heaven: . . .a time to love,
and a time to hate; a time of war,
and a time of peace.

—ECCLESIASTES 3:1, 8

ᚎ PROLOGUE ᚎ

Washington State, 1927

Seventeen-year-old Margaret Deny opened an old cookie tin and handed over a bulk of her savings from working various jobs the past three years.

The burly man squinted and rubbed the back of his neck. "I'm not sure if I should take your money, little lady."

Margaret straightened. "I'm not a little lady. I'm going to be a pilot."

"I doubt that." He thumbed toward the tattered and faded JN-4 biplane. "You know this doesn't fly. It's been busted for years."

The Curtiss Jenny with a Rolls-Royce Merlin engine—even not working—was a great find. "I know. I'll fix her up."

He squinted at her. "Who's going to do that for you?"

"No one." Margaret stretched to her full five foot two and jammed a finger to her shoulder. "I'm going to do it and make her fly." The JN-4 was just the machine to help her soar into the air.

She didn't have enough money to pay for fancy lessons or buy a functioning aircraft. But there was a pilot from the Great War in her town who said if she had a working plane, he would teach her to fly it. She had the first half. Now she needed to get the Jenny home and make it run.

Two weeks later, sitting on the floor of her grandparents' barn where she kept her biplane, Margaret still couldn't believe she owned an aircraft. Soon she would be able to take flight. With her legs crossed, she leaned against the landing gear and had the mechanics manual open on her lap. Men sure didn't know how to write directions very well. No matter, she would figure it out. After having read the entire book from front to back, she sort of understood how an engine worked. Tinkering would help her to figure out what was wrong so she could repair it.

"Hello?" a male voice called from near the open doorway.

Margaret looked up from the volume and peered around the landing gear struts.

George Witherspoon sauntered into the barn, his hands deep in the pockets of his trousers. He must have wandered in here by mistake.

She jumped to her feet, brushed dust off her overalls, and patted her hair. She must look atrocious. "Hello. You need something?"

His mouth broke into the best smile she'd ever seen. "I'm George Witherspoon."

"Oh, I know who you are. Everyone knows who *you* are." The most handsome boy in school. Or at least he had been until he graduated last year. Now he was the most handsome man in town. There wasn't a girl who didn't dream about him asking her out. "My grandfather's not here. He went over to help a neighbor. If that's who you're looking for."

He chuckled. "I'm not. I think I'm looking for you. I presume you're Margaret Deny."

He knew her name? "I am. Call me Peggy. Everyone does."

He rested a hand on the wing of her Jenny. "And this is your JN-4?"

"It is."

He shook his head in what appeared to be either disbelief or awe. "When I heard a girl bought an airplane, I had to see for myself. Does it work?"

Peggy straightened. "Not yet, but I'm going to get her working."

His mouth pulled to one side. "Don't tell me you know how to repair engines."

She wouldn't let her lack of knowledge stop her. "I'm learning."

"You're learning?" He grinned. "Do you want some help?"

"You know about engines? Aircraft engines?" She doubted it. Not many people had experience with flying machines.

"Most engines work pretty much the same. I bet together we could figure it out."

"Thanks!" She would likely get her Jenny into the air sooner with his help, *and* she'd get to see George Witherspoon often. That was better than him asking her out.

He tilted his head. "However, when we get this thing ready to fly, will you let me give it a go? I've always wanted to pilot an airplane."

"Sure, but I get to fly her first."

He thrust out his arm. "Deal."

Her hand trembled with excitement as she reached to shake his and nearly melted at his touch.

Get yourself together, Peggy.

First she needed to get the Jenny in the air; then she could enjoy the boy on the ground.

The best of both worlds.

⫶ CHAPTER I ⫶

15 August 1944, 0600 GMT (Greenwich Mean Time)

Operation Dragoon: Allied forces mount invasion and land troops in the Provence region of southern France, along the Côte d'Azur. The landing force consists of three infantry divisions: the Third, Thirty-sixth, and Forty-fifth.

Late Summer, 1944

Peggy Witherspoon sailed through the atmosphere in the twin engine Douglas C-47 Skytrain aircraft. Her mission as a WASP, or member of the Women Airforce Service Pilots, was a short ferrying trip from Connecticut back to DC. She loved being in the air and the freedom up here.

Soaring through the clouds used to make her feel close to God, but not anymore. He had turned a deaf ear to her pleas for the safe return of her husband, George, who had been killed in the skies over Germany when his Mustang fighter plane was shot down. So she had become complacent about spending time in prayer. She merely went through the motions of going to church for the sake of her daughters. Each Sunday when she wasn't working, she sat in a pew like a hollow shell.

This trip was almost over, and soon enough she would be tethered back on the ground.

The Skytrain normally had a crew of four: pilot, co-pilot, radio operator, and navigator. Today, Peggy flew alone. The Connecticut base mechanics had rigged a radio up front so she could handle the aircraft on her own. Risky but manageable.

She drew in a deep breath.

What was that?

She sniffed and sniffed again.

Was that smoke?

She glanced at engine number one and then toward number two, which she couldn't see from the pilot's seat. That was silly. If one had caught fire, she wouldn't be smelling smoke inside the cockpit. Besides, they both felt fine, responsive and not lagging.

At least for now.

Nonetheless, she definitely smelled smoke.

And now, she *saw* smoke. Small tendrils drifted out from her control panel. *Not good.* Smoke meant fire, and fire was never good a few thousand feet in the air.

She snagged the radio mike. "This is Mama Bird calling Bolling Airfield. Mama Bird to Bolling Field. Come in, Bolling Field."

The radio crackled. "This is Bolling Field, Mama Bird. We weren't expecting contact for another fifteen minutes."

"Bolling Field, Mama Bird has a situation up here. Smoke is coming out of my instrument panel." Peggy waved a hand in front of her to move some of the smoke aside. The action was futile, but a reflex nonetheless.

"Mama Bird, stand by for instructions."

What else could she do? Peggy coughed on the smoke. The acrid smell of hot wires burned her nostrils. She pulled her pilot's neck scarf up over her mouth. If this had been a regular mission, she would have been supplied with an air mask.

She descended to twenty-five hundred feet and slid open the side window for fresh air.

A second voice came over the radio. "This is Major Berg. What is your status, Mama Bird?"

She couldn't believe he asked that after she had just told those on the ground her predicament. Had he not heard her? "Smoke is pouring out of the instrument panel. Cockpit is filling up. Mama Bird is having trouble seeing. Visibility is getting poor." Maybe not filling up, but it soon would if this continued. And she wasn't having too much trouble seeing.

Yet.

It would only be a matter of time before it *did* inhibit her ability to see the terrain outside. She might have to depend solely on her instruments. She couldn't wait for someone else to take their time making a decision. Major Berg needed to know it was urgent he make a determination fast.

"Bail out, Mama Bird. Bail out."

That's what she wanted to hear. She liked the decisiveness of the new Army Air Corps officer in charge of the Women Airforce Service Pilots.

"Mama Bird, do you copy?"

She scanned the horizon. Where would the plane crash?

Her eyes burned and watered from the smoke. She blinked to clear her vision.

"Mama Bird, bail out. *Do you copy?*"

She peered out the open side window at the terrain below. Buildings of towns and neighborhoods lay in front of her in all directions. No place for the plane to safely crash. Besides, she'd never lost a plane yet and now wasn't a good time to start by causing numerous civilian casualties.

"Mama Bird? Do—you—copy? Bail out! Bail out!"

"Negative, Bolling Field. Too much population."

"Aim it for the ocean and bail out." The major's voice turned gruff. "That's an order!"

She checked the responsiveness of the yoke. The aircraft obeyed her maneuvers. "I can do this. Clear the landing strip."

The major's brusque voice boomed through the radio. "Negative! It's not worth the risk! Bail out!"

She *could* do this. If she were a man, she would likely be given a different order. "I can land this plane. Over and out." Men thought women were less capable than them. Not true. Peggy knew dozens of excellent female pilots. The Women Airforce Service Pilots only employed the best. Better than the best.

"Negative! Negati—" The radio went silent from the other end.

What had happened? Why was he cut off?

The calm voice of her fellow WASP Jolene, call sign Nightingale, crackled over the radio. "Peggy, think of Wendy and Junie."

Her daughters' faces flashed in her mind. Jolene used her real name rather than her call sign. That cut through to her. She took a deep breath.

"They have already lost their father. Don't orphan them, Peggy."

No, she didn't want to orphan her girls. She must bail out even with the danger of using a too large parachute designed for men. She glanced out each of her windows. With quick mental calculation of range and airspeed, every direction was too populated to aim an unpiloted aircraft toward. Even if she could point it toward a less populated area, there would be no way to tell if an air current would pop the craft up or down, causing it to land in a neighborhood or worse. . .a school.

"Peggy, bail out. The aircraft isn't worth it." As Jolene spoke, the major grumbled in the background.

She couldn't risk the lives of hundreds of others by abandoning the C-47. It was too huge to allow it to crash anywhere. The destruction would be devastating.

"Negative."

"Think of your girls."

"I am." How could she look her daughters in the eyes when she might orphan someone else's children? "I have no safe place to ditch the plane."

Major Berg came back on the radio. "Bail out. That's an order."

Funny thing was, she couldn't be court marshaled for her disobedience as the army refused military status to the WASP program, but she could still be in a lot of trouble. *Lord, I know we're not on the best of terms, but whether I come out of this alive or not, please protect those on the ground.* God couldn't fault her for praying for innocent bystanders. She hoped this prayer didn't fall on deaf ears as all her others had.

"Clear the runway." Peace about the decision washed over her.

She banked to head toward the airfield. The least populated place in the vicinity.

Guide my wings to the ground.

Air turbulence shook the plane. Or at least that was what she told herself. To think it was the craft falling apart might paralyze her into inaction. With a snap and a spark, her instruments went dark. That's what she got for praying. This was all on her now. She needed to fly by her wits.

She looked out of her side window to the terrain below and descended to one thousand feet. Without her instruments to guide her, that was a guess from the last reading on her altimeter, but it felt about right. She had logged enough flying hours to have a sense of her airspeed and altitude. Her instruments generally confirmed what she already knew.

Jolene's voice came over the radio again. "What you're doing is foolish. I see you on radar."

Good. Jolene could talk her down. "Bad news. My instruments are dark. I'm flying blind up here."

"Roger that. I'll be your gauges. Air speed looks good. You're at 1,050 feet. You're too high. Ease her down a little bit."

Peggy tipped the aircraft's nose down.

"Mama Bird—"

Then scratching sounds came over the radio.

"Hand over the radio." Major Berg's voice.

Then Jolene. "I've got this."

This wasn't helping Peggy. "The mike is open." She needed them to stop arguing and guide her down.

With a click, the radio went silent.

Peggy's heart stilled for a beat in the silence, and she felt very alone. She would rather have her friend talk her down, so she pressed the radio button. "Nightingale knows what she is doing. I trust her."

After a moment, Jolene's calm voice drifted over the airwaves. "Eight hundred feet. You're coming down too fast. Level off, Mama Bird."

Peggy did as instructed. Then her gut tightened. If she didn't have instruments, could she engage the landing gear? She needed to try while she still had time to pull up. She worked the lever. The clunk of the landing gear doors opening and then the air drag on the tires reverberated through the plane. Though the light to indicate they were down wasn't lit, Peggy was sure they had engaged and locked. If they hadn't, she would need to head out to sea and ditch the plane in open water. If she could make it that far.

"Visual contact for a moment then you disappeared behind some trees. You were looking good."

After a minute, Nightingale spoke again. "Five hundred feet. Can you see the runway?"

Peggy came over the top of the trees. The tarmac stretched out up ahead. "Roger. The air strip is in sight."

"I don't see any flames or smoke. Ease on down." The fact Jolene couldn't see any visible damage was comforting.

"Nightingale, would you check my landing gear?"

After a moment, the radio crackled. "Landing gear is down."

But that didn't mean it was locked in place. She prayed it was, or the wheels would buckle as soon as they touched down.

"Three hundred feet."

Major Berg came on the radio again. "You're coming in too fast, ease back on the throttle and engage flaps."

Again, Peggy did as directed. She felt the drag of the flaps but glanced out the side window. "Flaps are engaged."

Jolene again. "Two hundred feet. Your air speed is good."

She thought so. She could feel it.

Close enough now that the plane wouldn't crash in the middle of the Capitol or a neighborhood.

"One hundred feet. Ease back on the throttle."

Peggy did.

The plane drifted down and down.

She pulled back slightly on the yoke to keep from hitting the fence before the leading edge of the runway.

Dare she pray for a safe landing? God hadn't been in the mood to listen to her prayers lately. *Please.* Maybe that would be enough but not too much to make God turn away from her.

Once she cleared the fence, she pushed the yoke forward and throttled back.

She held her breath as she anticipated the ground grabbing at the wheels.

When she could hold her breath no longer, the wheels tapped the ground with a screech.

Thank You.

She cut the throttle and engaged the toe-operated hydraulic brakes. The tires squealed. Gravity and braking pressed her into the seat as though she had a hundred-pound sack of flour on her lap. Not her best landing, but she was alive.

Red emergency-vehicle lights flashed up ahead.

Other than the smoke and no instruments, this felt like any other landing.

She slowed to a smooth stop.

After releasing her harness straps, she scrambled to the back of the aircraft and opened the rear door. She sat on the floor with her legs dangling out and jumped to the ground a few feet below. Just because Nightingale hadn't seen flames or smoke didn't mean there weren't any. She hustled away from the craft.

The emergency crew sped toward the C-47 Skytrain to inspect it for danger.

A Jeep raced up faster than the emergency vehicles. Jolene was at the wheel. An irate-looking army officer sat in the passenger seat. That must be Major Berg.

Jolene barely got the vehicle stopped when the major climbed out with his cane and hobbled over.

He seemed much too young for a cane, but then Peggy remembered hearing that their new commander had been injured in combat. Perhaps he'd even received a battlefield promotion. He'd been stationed at Bolling Field while his wounds continued to heal.

He marched up to her as much as he could march, cane-hobbling. "What were you thinking, soldier?" His hat snugged on his brown hair, and his gray eyes sparked with fury.

Soldier? He should be thanking her. Peggy straightened and squared her shoulders. "I saved a very expensive aircraft and didn't risk the lives of innocent civilians."

"You risked your own life."

That's what he was worried about? "I made a judgement call. The smoke didn't smell like a fuel fire. It smelled more like the pungent aroma of hot wires and their insulation. The yoke was still responsive.

I believed I could safely land. I couldn't, in good conscience, allow an unmanned airplane to crash just any old place."

"This is why women shouldn't fly. It's too risky."

That raised her hackles. "If WASPs weren't stuck with old, worn-out planes—some that barely get off the ground—we wouldn't be risking our lives so much." She hated that her fellow pilots were put in danger by being assigned the worst airplanes the army had to offer.

"I doubt that. Don't let your insubordination happen again, soldier."

She wasn't normally insubordinate, but this officer was out of line. "I'm not technically a soldier." Though she felt like one. "The army doesn't believe WASPs are good enough to be military."

"This is why women shouldn't be in the military. They can't follow orders, and it's too dangerous."

"Men risk their lives all the time for their families and country, why shouldn't women do the same?" Though she should, she wouldn't back down to him or any other man who believed women didn't belong in the air.

He studied her a long time. "Because women shouldn't be put in that kind of danger. Don't let it happen again. I'll see you in my office later when I put a formal reprimand in your file." He did an about-face and returned to the Jeep. His bark might feel a bit more threatening if he didn't have the cane.

Jolene mouthed, "Formal reprimand?"

Peggy merely shook her head.

Jolene scrambled into the driver's seat.

Peggy stayed behind with the aircraft and the crew that was assessing it. The army *did* give the women the old buckets of bolts that the military didn't think were fit for combat or other necessary duties. Regardless, the WASPs excelled at all their jobs.

She spoke with the crew chief, Sergeant Kent, and explained what had happened.

Once the initial assessment determined there was no active fire, Peggy climbed back into the cockpit and taxied it to the hangar.

Now it was her job to figure out what happened.

Sergeant Kent worked alongside her. "If you ask me—and I know you didn't—you made the right call. You're the pilot, and only you could assess the flight worthiness and risk. That's what being a pilot is all about."

"The call to bail out was a good one. I probably would have if there had been a decent place to let the plane crash. I couldn't risk innocent civilians."

The sergeant raised his eyebrows. "As you told the major, you *are* a civilian."

"That's different. I have a duty to uphold to protect lives." Though ferrying aircraft from one place to another didn't seem like much, it freed up a man to go into combat who could save lives and make a real difference. Therefore, she was saving lives by association.

"Don't worry about the major. Once he sees how well you WASPs perform, he'll come around."

"Thanks, Kent." She hoped the major didn't have her terminated as a WASP.

≡ CHAPTER 2 ≡

Major Howie Berg hobbled into his office, shut the door, and tossed his cane on the floor. The stupid thing. It made him look weak and made people not take him seriously. It didn't bode well for him to have his first official act since he'd been injured be met with insubordination. It wasn't the pilot's refusal to obey his orders, but the fact a woman had been in harm's way. He had been raised to protect and cherish ladies. Not carelessly put them in danger.

What irked him the most was that if the pilot had been male, he wouldn't have hesitated to allow the man to land the plane. He probably would have insisted upon it. Would have chided the pilot if he contemplated bailing. Berg himself had refused to bail and landed a plane in worse shape. But the idea of a lady at risk had made his blood run cold.

An hour later, WASP Margaret "Peggy" Witherspoon, call sign Mama Bird, sat across the desk from him. How could she have been so reckless with two children at home?

Barbara Poole, Witherspoon's WASP superior, also sat across from him. Both women sat straight and confidently held his gaze.

He knew a lot of male soldiers who wouldn't be so bold or brave. He addressed the higher ranking of the two ladies. "When I give an order, I need to know your WASPs will follow my commands."

"When my Women Airforce Service Pilots feel innocent civilians are in danger, they have the liberty to act as they see fit. WASP Witherspoon was within her rights and did just that."

"What if the plane exploded? She could have been killed."

"WASP Witherspoon is a seasoned pilot. She has logged no less than three hundred hours in a C-47 and more than two thousand flight hours over her fifteen years as a licensed pilot."

That was more hours in the air than Berg had racked up. It still didn't excuse her for her actions. "So you trust her?"

"Implicitly. I would travel in any aircraft she was piloting without question."

He was getting nowhere. "I can't have individuals under my command ignoring my direct orders." It was a recipe for chaos.

"As I said, WASP Witherspoon was well within her rights."

How could he get these women to see they needed to play things safe? They should be home baking and taking care of their children. Nevertheless, they were also right to be here, ferrying aircraft, which freed up men for more dangerous jobs. "I admit the jobs you WASPs do are important and are helping to win the war. Is there anything I can say to get you to follow my orders without question?"

Poole inclined her head slightly. "Give orders that make sense and give my pilots credit for knowing what they're doing."

He supposed that was the best he was going to get for now. On to the next topic. He shifted his attention to WASP Witherspoon. "Did the maintenance crew discover the cause of the fire?"

"It was only smoke, sir, and yes, I discovered the source. Old wires behind the instrument panel were frayed. Wires that were checked off as assessed to be safe and in good order. Obviously, that wasn't the case. Sloppy records could cost someone their life."

He could tell Witherspoon knew she was saying more than she should, but he let it slide. This time.

Poole narrowed her eyes. "My WASPs regularly get put in buckets of bolts that need to be retired, but instead they are given to the female pilots."

"That can't be true."

"Check the records. You'll see women get poor quality, worn out, and ill-maintained aircraft far more often than men do."

That couldn't be true. If so, that was an outrage. He would look into it, and if it was true, he would see to it changes were made. "WASP

Commander Poole, I would like you to create a report, with evidence and statistics, about the disproportionate number of defective and broken-down aircraft the WASPs are assigned compared to the men."

Poole raised her eyebrows in what might be surprise, but then settled back to disbelief. "Will do, sir."

"That will be all."

The two ladies rose and headed for the door.

"Witherspoon."

She turned back to face him. "Yes, sir."

"I'm glad you're safe."

"Thank you, sir." Witherspoon continued out after Poole.

She was one daring lady. He prayed her recklessness didn't turn her children into orphans.

———— ≋ ————

Babs, Commander Poole, crooked her finger. "Come to my office."

Peggy followed.

Babs rounded her desk. "Close the door."

Peggy did but didn't sit as she hadn't been invited to.

Babs leaned forward with her palms pressed onto her desk. "WASP Witherspoon, what am I going to do with you?"

Oh, dear. She had used Peggy's designation and last name rather than her first or her call sign.

"I don't know what you were thinking."

"The—"

"I didn't tell you to speak. You are to listen only."

Peggy had been going to say that the aircraft was too valuable and the areas it might have crashed into would have resulted in civilian casualties. But her commander already knew that.

"You have put this whole organization at risk today. If Major Berg decides to give you and the WASPs an unfavorable report for your actions, the WASP program could be in jeopardy."

But if she had allowed a plane of any size to crash just anywhere, the public outcry could mean the end for the WASP program as well. Most people—military and civilian, male *and* female alike—didn't believe women should be flying and certainly not flying military aircraft.

Peggy wanted to argue with Poole, but that would do no good. Besides, her commander already knew every argument Peggy had. She appreciated her superior standing up for her in front of Major Berg, so she could take Poole's tongue lashing. Peggy wouldn't change a thing. She had made the right decision.

"What do you have to say for yourself?"

Now Peggy could speak. So many insubordinate things rose to her lips, but she pushed them all back. "No excuse for endangering the organization, ma'am."

Poole studied her for a long moment. "There are a few other things you'd like to say to me about your actions, aren't there?"

Definitely. But none of them would do any good and only make matters worse. "No, ma'am."

"Can I trust you, Witherspoon?"

"Yes, ma'am."

"Good." Pushing off her desk, Poole straightened and took the gruff edge out of her voice. "Now as for the events of today. You made the right call. I would have done the same. The Skytrain is one whopper of a beast."

That it was. Some pilots referred to it as the smaller flying truck— the four-engine Liberator being the other flying truck. It hauled like a truck and flew like a truck. A beast indeed.

"In time, Major Berg will understand that without the WASPs, the male pilots couldn't do their jobs. We know we are the ones who really run the military airplane fleet, training, ferrying, and such. He doesn't understand how things work yet. Give him a little time, and the WASPs will get him broken in."

The major probably wouldn't appreciate being discussed in such a manner.

"Yes, ma'am."

"You can drop the ma'am now."

Peggy relaxed her stance.

"Dismissed."

Peggy did an about-face and opened the door.

"And Peggy, stay out of the major's way for a few days to let him cool off."

Peggy would do just that.

She would arrive home after her girls had gone to bed. She was bone tired from the train ride up to Connecticut, then ferrying the cargo plane back, and then having it nearly go up in smoke. Then having to diagnose the plane and begin repairs. WASPs did every job presented to them. From the outside, it would seem cruel to make the women do all the jobs associated with aircraft while their male counterparts specialized in one or two areas. Peggy would argue that by doing every job, she knew each plane she flew better than if she didn't. And experience with so many different aircraft in every aspect not only made her a better pilot but also enabled her to diagnose an issue or potential problem before it happened. Because of her broad experience, she was able to recognize that the in-flight issue wasn't likely detrimental to her life, leading to an inevitable crash.

Not only was she glad to have saved the airplane, but she hated bailing out of a perfectly good aircraft. The sensation of drifting on the air current suspended from a silk sheet. Being at the mercy of any light wind to get her safely to the ground scared her more than flying a damaged plane. No control. At the whim of any breeze and so exposed. Though she never flew over enemy territory, it would terrify her to drift aimlessly over an area, knowing guns could be pointing straight at her. Floating ever so slowly to the ground, waiting for shooting to start. Was that how her husband had felt?

Though Major Berg had felt she had been risking her life by not bailing out, in fact, she had been a lot safer than any of the GIs overseas. Her husband included. He'd gotten shot down over Germany.

She parked her '37 Ford in the detached garage of her Oxen Hill home and entered by way of the back kitchen door.

Her mother greeted her from where she stood scrubbing the stove. "You worked late. I hope everything is all right."

"It was a long day." Peggy couldn't wait to crawl into bed.

Her mom squinted. "You smell like smoke."

"Don't worry. I haven't taken up the habit. It's just from some of the other ladies who do." Peggy's husband had been a smoker before they married, but she had refused to go out with him because of it. He quit just to get her to go to a motion picture with him. She had figured he must like her an awful lot to do that. He'd said numerous times he'd made the right choice.

"It's not that kind of smoke smell."

Before Peggy could respond and tell her about what happened on the challenging flight, her daughters ran in from the other room. Both dressed in their cotton nightgowns. "Mommy!"

Peggy leaned forward and hugged her girls. "What are you two doing out of bed?"

The oldest, ten years old, answered. "We were worried about you."

"I'm home now, so off to bed."

Five-year-old Junie grabbed her hand and tugged Peggy along behind her. "Come tuck us in and say prayers with us."

"Didn't Grandma say prayers with you?"

Her youngest poked out her bottom lip. "But I want you to say prayers with me."

"Let's go." Peggy preferred for her mother to pray with the girls, so she didn't feel so much like a fraud. Just because she had a strained relationship with the Lord didn't mean she should pass that down to her daughters.

In their bedroom, both girls knelt beside their beds and recited the same prayer they said every night. At the end, each girl added a thank-you to God for something good that day and asked God to bless others they listed by name. When her youngest daughter started calling out random names of people Peggy was sure her daughter didn't know, it was time to intervene. "Thank You, God. Amen." Her daughter had likely been trying to make prayer time last as long as possible. A ploy she'd attempted before.

Peggy pulled back the covers on Junie's bed. "Hop in."

Her baby did, lying stiff as a board on her back with her arms pressed at her sides. "Tuck me in tight, Mommy."

She pulled the covers up to her daughter's chin and pushed the edges of the blanket under the mattress then kissed her on the forehead.

Peggy turned to her other daughter.

Ten-year-old Wendy wriggled into her covers. "Mommy, can I be a pilot like you when I grow up?"

Peggy tugged Wendy's blankets around her. "Of course, you can."

Her eldest's expression turned stern. "Good. I want to fly over to the bad people and shoot them down like they did to Daddy."

Her poor jaded daughter was about the same age Peggy had been when Peggy had lost her own father and her brother in the First World War. "By the time you would be old enough, the war will be over." At least, Peggy hoped so, unable to imagine this going on for years and years. Though she would enjoy flying the military aircraft for as long as the military would allow her to. "There are plenty of good guys making sure the bad guys stop doing bad things." She kissed her daughter on the forehead.

"Sleep tight, my precious angels." After crossing the room, she pulled the door until it was open only a couple of inches. Leaving the hall light on for them, she retreated to the living room where her mother waited.

"They were worried about you. From the smoke smell, I suspect they had good reason to."

"It's nothing to be concerned about. I was flying a C-47 Skytrain from Connecticut. A wire behind the instrument panel was worn and caused a little fire. The cockpit filled with smoke."

Her mother's eyes widened. "Did you bail out?"

"It wasn't that bad. I landed safely." Her mother didn't need to know she had been ordered to bail out or that Jolene had to be her instruments and talk her down. That would only worry her mother more than she needed to be. "I met the new Army Air Corps major who is over the WASPs."

Mom gave her a look to say she knew Peggy was changing the subject. "Is he going to be trouble for you ladies?"

"I'm not sure yet. Time will tell." Peggy couldn't quite discern if he was more upset at women flying planes, like most of the military men, or that she had potentially been in danger.

"You know I'm proud of you, don't you?"

"Yes, Mom." Her mother had always been generous with praise. "I appreciate you looking after the girls."

"You are serving our country, and by watching after my grand-daughters, I feel as though I'm serving our country too."

"You are, Mom. I'm proud of you as well." Peggy couldn't do her job without her mother's help.

≣ CHAPTER 3 ≣

16 August 1944, 0800 GMT

German forces in France retreat north.

The next day, Howie rode in a military Jeep with Private Russell driving him. He hated that he wasn't allowed to drive himself around. His right leg had taken the brunt of his brush with death. Though his other injuries had mostly healed, his femur had a pin in it. Fortunately he hadn't lost his leg completely. In less than a year, the pin would be removed. Though he was still healing from the latest surgery on his leg, he would soon be able to drive himself around and get rid of the cane, his constant companion.

The private drove across the tarmac toward the hangar housing the C-47 Skytrain that had nearly gone up in flames yesterday. He had been grateful his first official duty as supervisor to the Women Airforce Service Pilots hadn't resulted in losing an expensive aircraft. He was still sore about the pilot not following his orders. Thankfully she had landed safely. Had it been a man, he wouldn't have questioned the decision to land the plane. But a woman? A woman being in danger had frightened him.

The driver stopped at the huge opening to the hangar.

Howie climbed out and steadied himself on his cane. He was depending on it less and less. He wished he didn't need it at all. But the cane had been a stipulation of him remaining on active duty. The Army Air Corps had wanted to force him out with a medical separation, but he knew he could still be a useful asset to the military. If there hadn't been a war going on, he likely wouldn't have gotten his way. Being grounded wouldn't suit him, but at least he hadn't been put out to pasture.

Concentrating on using his cane as little as possible, he meandered into the hangar, taking note of the sign stating, NO SALUTING AND NO COMING TO ATTENTION AREA. Mechanics couldn't stop riveting or drop whatever tool they were using to come to attention and salute. It would be foolish, waste everyone's time, and someone could get injured popping to attention in the middle of a maintenance procedure.

As he strolled up to a sergeant standing at a tool cart, the man straightened but didn't come to a full attention. "Major."

"At ease, Sergeant Kent. Are you the mechanic in charge of diagnosing and repairing this craft?" The Skytrain didn't have any visible exterior damage. Good. That meant it would likely fly again.

The sergeant pointed with a wrench toward the aircraft. "The lead mechanic is in the cockpit, sir."

"Thank you." Howie turned toward the C-47. A set of flight steps sat at the rear door. He wished he didn't have to take them since they were still a challenge to maneuver without looking as though he were having trouble. He managed to walk fairly normally with only a slight noticeable dependence on his cane, but stairs were another matter. If he relied on the handrail, he might not appear so crippled.

Gripping the railing, he ascended. Not too bad. If the sergeant was watching, he wouldn't have noticed Howie having any trouble. He'd never flown a Skytrain. He'd mostly been in fighter planes, the P-51 Mustang and the P-47 Thunderbolt. He walked to the cockpit.

The whole front panel of the control console had been removed and leaned forward on the pilot's and co-pilot's chairs. Wires bridged from it to under the dashboard. The smell of smoke still lingered in the air. It probably clung to every surface.

A pair of mechanic's coveralls stuck out from under the instrument panel and the jumble of wires. Just the boots and the legs were visible. "How is it looking under there? Have you determined the cause?"

The person stilled.

Was the mechanic going to emerge?

The legs moved. Then the body shimmied out and sat up.

A woman? Not just any woman, the pilot who had flown this aircraft and landed it without instruments. A highly-skilled pilot. What was she doing here? Had she been put in charge of the repairs? "I thought you were a pilot, not a mechanic."

She rested her arms on her bent knees. "I'm both and more. We WASPs repair and pilot aircraft, are flight instructors, ferry planes, tow targets, and any other job that needs to be done."

He'd heard about that, but he thought a single WASP specialized in one area rather than performing all those duties. Now wasn't the time to veer off onto that topic. Nor would he bring up her insubordination the previous day. "What can you tell me about the cause of the fire?"

She rubbed her chin with the back of her greasy hand, leaving an adorable smudge. "Apparently the last mechanic to check this plane didn't think a bare wire was worth replacing. It took out all the other ones nearby while it was at it."

"And almost took you out as well." He should have bit his tongue, but she needed to understand she had put herself in unnecessary danger.

"It was all bark, no bite."

How could she be so cavalier about her life being in peril? He knew what it was to stare death in the face. She needed to take the incident seriously, but irritating her again wouldn't gain him any headway in being sure she took her safety seriously. "Any structural damage? Will it fly again?"

"It's all relatively minor. Burned wires and black soot under the instrument panel."

"How long do you estimate the repair will take?"

"I'll have the rewiring completed in under an hour. I should have the soot cleaned off and the panel back in place by lunch. Then we'll test out the entire dashboard and do preflight checks all the way around the craft. If everything passes, I'll taxi her around to assess if there is any other damage. If there is still daylight after that, I'll take her for a test flight."

"*You're* going to test fly it?"

She nodded. "One of my jobs."

"But this plane almost killed you."

"Correction, carelessness on the part of the previous mechanic nearly killed me." She gave her head a shake. "Not actually. They just made it difficult to fly and land."

Was this woman completely unflappable?

"I wouldn't think you would want to go up in it again after what happened."

"I'm the most qualified person to test her in the air. I flew her from Connecticut. I'm familiar with how she handles. No one else is. Besides, I'm the one who's doing the repairs. I'm not going to do a shoddy job if I'm the one to go up in her. I'll make sure that not only the wires are all good in the instrument panel but throughout the craft. This girl will be as good as new when I'm through."

"You think you can get all that done by yourself?"

She pointed with a screwdriver. "Nightingale and Brownie are helping too. I trust their abilities."

Howie turned around to face two other female pilots in coveralls. He hadn't heard them enter the plane.

They each lifted a hand in greeting. One was the WASP who had fought him for control of the mike when the Skytrain was smoking in the air.

"So just the three of you ladies? No men?"

The taller of the two newcomers, Nightingale, folded her arms across her chest. "If we can't fix it, it needs to be junked."

"Are all you female pilots so. . .brazen about your abilities?"

The other newcomer widened her eyes. "Nothing brazen about it. Just stating facts."

WASP Witherspoon wiped her hands on a grease rag. "As women, we have to be twice as good at everything just so we are allowed to do our jobs. We are as capable as any man. We understand our presence threatens some men's pride, but that's not our purpose. We merely want to do our jobs to the best of our abilities, like anyone else serving this great country of ours. But men don't like the idea of us serving. I know a lot of the WASPs would go into combat if we were allowed.

Female pilots in Russia are fighting in battles right now. But if we aren't allowed in warfare, we can certainly do our part for all our soldiers in the air, on the ground, and at sea to be able to do their part."

The ladies' patriotism surprised him. They didn't cower from duty or treat it like this was some sort of social event. They each wore dirty coveralls and had their hair tied up in turban-style scarves.

"If that's all, we have work to do if we're going to get this completed by lunch."

He hesitated a moment, feeling as though he should say something more but didn't know what. "Carry on." He headed for the exit but stopped in the doorway. "When this bird is ready to be test flown, I want to ride along with you."

Witherspoon raised her eyebrows. "If you want to."

He did. He made his way down the steps. Descending was worse than going up, but he made it without too much trouble. Thankfully, he didn't make a fool of himself by tumbling to the bottom.

Sergeant Kent met him. "You don't have to worry. Those ladies could run circles around some of the male mechanics and pilots. They know what they're doing."

Howie hoped so. "Good to know. Carry on." He walked to the Jeep. His driver lay across the front seats with his eyes closed. Howie couldn't imagine the women he just left doing the same. "Didn't get enough sleep last night, Private?"

The soldier's eyes popped open, and he scrambled to sit up then stand with a salute. "Yes, sir—no, sir. I uh. . .I didn't want to leave the vehicle for when you returned, sir. I thought it would be good to rest my eyes. It won't happen again, sir."

The ladies had exuded more confidence than this trained soldier.

"Take me back to my office."

The private still held his salute. He was required to until the ranking officer returned his salute. "Yes, sir."

Howie saluted back and climbed in. This wasn't the same army as when the war started.

The private climbed in and drove to Bolling Airfield Headquarters.

As Howie approached his office, he addressed the sergeant who served as his aide and admin. "Would you get me all the files on the WASPs stationed here?"

"Yes, sir."

Howie entered his office and sat behind the desk.

Twenty minutes later, Sergeant Miller returned with the requested files. "Thank you. That will be all for now."

Howie dug through the stack until he found Witherspoon's at the bottom since they were alphabetical. What kind of pilot and person—and woman—was she? She was one with grit, and one he'd like to get to know. No. He couldn't think that way. She was a member of the Women Airforce Service Pilots, and he was an Army Air Corps officer. Fraternizing was definitely frowned upon. But there would be nothing wrong with getting to know her better in the work environment.

———— ≈ ————

Peggy sat in the cockpit of the Skytrain as it was towed out of the hangar. All system checks had been good. Next task was to test the engines to make sure nothing shorted between the instrument panel and the engine ignitions.

Brownie sat in the copilot seat, and Jolene in the navigator's seat. Jolene spoke. "Are you really going to have the major go on the test run with you?"

"If he wants to, I have no choice."

His presence would change nothing. The aircraft had been repaired the same as if he wouldn't be along, and the plane was safe to fly.

Brownie turned in the seat to better face Peggy. "Do you think he's going to try to ground you?"

That was a definite possibility, but Peggy hoped not. "He would be a fool if he did. The army needs all the trained pilots they can get to win this war. Unlike other wars, this one will be won or lost in the air."

. Once the plane was in a safe location, Brownie popped to her feet. "I best get to my copilot duties." She exited the aircraft to remove the wooden wedges that locked the ailerons and rudder in place, as well as other preflight exterior tasks.

Peggy had already wired shut the oleo legs, tires, and fuel drain cocks. But she drew comfort knowing they would be checked again.

Even on a short test flight, one of those nuts could vibrate loose. One could never be too safe.

After the outside checks were completed, Brownie returned to her copilot seat. "Everything's shipshape, Captain." She grabbed the cockpit checklist and went through the drill. "Intercom on?"

Peggy maneuvered the switch. "Check."

"Generator on?"

"Check."

Brakes on, master switch off, George the autopilot off, and cross-feed off?

All checked. Peggy then set the battery switch to ON and placed fuel on Main Tanks. They were full as reported earlier. Her excitement rose as she opened the throttles an inch, set the mixture to Idle Cut-out, propeller pitch to Fine, and carburetor to Cold. She opened the "gills" and turned the individual master and ignition switches on. She set the port booster pump switch to ON and switched on the energizer.

A high whine came from the engine and the propeller slowly turned over. After several loud bangs, sputters, and a cough of smoke from the exhaust pipe, the propeller accelerated. One down one to go. She repeated the process with the starboard engine.

The beautiful beast purred like a huge jungle cat.

The radio crackled. A fellow WASP had helped guide the airplane to the correct spot and still stood in front of the aircraft where Peggy could see her. "The fox is approaching the hen house. I repeat—"

"Roger. No need to repeat." Peggy understood Major Berg was about to board the transport plane. She listened for a set of steps to be rolled up to the back hatch which still hung open. Then she anticipated his light foot fall followed by a heavier one due to his limp and cane. And there it was.

She'd learned that he'd been shot down over German-occupied France, receiving several broken bones, including his femur. The army would never let him fly for them again because of those injuries. He could be jaded enough to take it out on her. Peggy didn't like the thought of being grounded. If he tried it, she would appeal to her own superior, Barbara Poole. Babs did all she could to fight for her WASP members to get fair treatment. If Peggy had done something to truly deserve being grounded, she would accept that decision. But she hadn't. She had protected lives and saved a very large aircraft. She wouldn't say she should be commended for her actions, but she also shouldn't be punished.

Brownie and Jolene shot to their feet and stood stiff.

They were all under cover, having the roof of the aircraft over them, so there was no need to come to attention or salute. But since they had, she should stand as well, so she removed the headphones and got to her feet but kept an eye on the controls with the engines going.

Major Berg limped aboard with his cane. "At ease. That's not necessary inside the aircraft."

Pleased to hear him say that, Peggy retook her place in the pilot's seat. Some of the male officers liked to force the issue just to be difficult.

The major turned his attention on Peggy. "You weren't planning to fly this bird without me, were you?"

"No, sir. Merely assessing the engines and then taxiing it around to see if everything was up to snuff. Didn't think you would be interested in all that boring stuff."

"Since I'm here, I might as well go along. If it goes well, we can take off for the test flight. Where shall I sit?"

Jolene and Brownie scooted toward the exit, and Jolene spoke. "That's our cue to disembark." The door latched with a click behind her fellow WASPs. She wasn't sure if she would have preferred to have them along, or if it was best to not have an audience if the major decided to give her a dressing-down or even ground her.

Peggy latched her harness straps around her and pointed to the other seat. "I guess you'll be my copilot. Strap in."

Once the hydraulic pressure reached 825–875 pounds, oil temperature to 40^0, and the cylinder heads to 120^0, Peggy settled the earphones on her head, and retrieved the radio mike. "This is Mama Bird requesting permission to taxi to test out maintenance. Over."

"Mama Bird, you are go for taxi test on runway three. Over."

"Roger. If this goes well, Mama Bird would like to take this bird up. Over."

"Affirmative, Mama Bird. Wait at the end of three for clearance to take off. Over."

"Roger." Since the control tower already knew she would be assessing this aircraft, they were prepared to give her clearance. She glanced at her copilot.

The major had strapped in.

She double-checked that all systems were ready, trim to neutral, mixture to auto-rich, pitch to fully fine, flaps up, gills to trail, and set gyros. She stuck her left hand out the side window creating a circle with her thumb and index finger, then pulled her right index finger out of the circle to indicate the chocks could be removed from the tires.

After a moment, Jolene held up two fingers in a V, to indicate the wheels were free.

Peggy opened the engines once to clear the plugs of oil from idling. Then she throttled forward, and the aircraft inched along the tarmac. Everything seemed fine. No indications of trouble so far. She gave it more gas and accelerated. Still good. "Hold on." She gave it maximum throttle. The acceleration pressed her into the seat. She glanced at Major Berg to see his reaction.

She couldn't quite read how he was taking this. He was either vexed with her or pleased with the prospect of being in the air again.

The engines rumbled steadily. She throttled back, engaged flaps, and eased on the brakes to a stop. Though she'd like to go full out for longer, the runway wouldn't allow it without taking off.

The radio crackled. "Mama Bird, this is control tower. That acceleration looked good. No issues visible from up here. Over."

Good to know. "Roger, tower. Mama Bird is ready for test flight. Over."

"Swing around and hold until given the go ahead. Over."

"Roger." She wheeled the craft around to takeoff position then set the tail wheel lock until given permission to go.

"What does your husband think of you flying military aircraft?"

"He was all for it." George had been very supportive. He'd said he felt safer going over *there*, meaning Europe, knowing experienced pilots stateside were looking after the aircraft and training his fellow flyboys.

"Was?"

She preferred not to talk to strangers about her late husband. "Shot down over Germany fifteen months ago."

"Prisoner of war?"

She shook her head. "Nope." Tears burned her eyes.

"I'm sorry. What squadron was he with? Maybe I met him."

She really didn't want to talk about this. "The 132nd."

"I was in the seventy-ninth."

The radio crackled. "Mama Bird, this is control tower. You are cleared for takeoff."

She blinked to remove the haze from her vision as she took the hand mike. "Roger. Mama Bird taking off." She checked her levers and gauges one final time. After releasing the tail brake, she jammed the throttle forward. The engines roared loudly, and the aircraft shot forward, pressing her into the seat. She didn't normally start so fast, but she didn't want give the major time to ask any more questions.

Once the wheels lifted off the tarmac, she gave it a little right rudder.

Up, up, up, until she leveled off at a cruising altitude. "I need to put this craft through its paces with some hard banks and a controlled stall. Would you like me to put you on the ground first?" Even seasoned pilots could get sick with g-forces when not the one flying the craft.

"I'm a combat pilot. I can handle it."

"Roger. I'm going to bank port first." If a passenger was prepared, the chance of them becoming ill was lessened. She'd just gotten this cockpit cleaned up from the smoke; she didn't need another mess. She turned the yoke, not banking as hard as she would if she were alone or with one of the WASPs she flew with regularly.

Major Berg had an expression she interpreted as pleasure, but it could just as easily be irritation.

She leveled out. *Let's see what you're made of, Major.* She banked hard to the right.

His eyes were bright with delight. She leveled out and immediately went into a steep climb.

Up.

Up.

Up.

Into the clouds until the craft broke free above them. She loved being up here, away from the cares of the world.

She wasn't showing off. She needed to see if the C-47 was in the best working order it could be. She had to push the craft to its limits.

The major had a slight smile.

That boded well for her. She leveled out at ten thousand feet.

Above the clouds was so peaceful. Her youngest daughter asked her if she could see God when she flew this high. God was no more visible up in the sky than down on the ground. Her older daughter's words from last night about wanting to fight in this war played in her head. Peggy wouldn't let her. She couldn't lose her daughter too. Besides, the army would never allow women in combat. But high above the earth, if God was going to hear a prayer from her, this would be as likely as any place. Because, wasn't she closer to Him up here? *Please let this war end soon, and don't let my little girl ever go to war.* She shook off her melancholy.

Time for the stall. "Ready?"

"Roger." He obviously knew why she'd climbed so high.

She throttled back and cut engine one, then number two. For a fraction of a second, in the peace and quiet, it felt as though she were floating, as though the hand of God were holding her up. In reality, the forward motion slowed, and the craft was sinking slowly. *Just like with God, make her feel safe and calm, then let her down.* As the aircraft descended faster, she angled the nose toward earth. It would do no good to spin out of control tail first.

When her husband was MIA for those weeks, she wondered if she should have told her daughters instead of protecting them from the news. Maybe if they'd had a chance to pray for their father's safe return, God would have listened to them where He hadn't listened to Peggy's prayers.

Major Berg's hands lifted as though he wanted to take control of the yoke. Did he question her abilities? He fisted his hands and returned them to his lap. Hopefully, it was merely a pilot's instinct.

Down the C-47 went into the clouds. Visibility now zero. The descent continued. She watched the altimeter closely to make sure she didn't get too low. The craft dropped out of the clouds at five thousand feet. At four thousand, she pressed the ignition to restart the engines. She could go lower, but the major might appreciate her not cutting it too close. The stall had been sufficient to learn what she needed to as well as to test the aircraft. The engines whirred back to life without issue.

The major drew in a deep breath.

That had been exhilarating being the pilot, but for the passenger it could be scary, knowing someone else held your life in their hands. His adrenaline was probably pumping harder than hers.

Peggy glanced over at him. "What aircraft have you flown?"

"Mostly fighters. I've logged the majority of my hours in the P-51 Mustang. Also, the P-47 Thunderbolt, and a few hours in the Curtiss P-36 Hawk.

"Anything larger? Anything with multiple engines?"

"A twin-engine P-38 Lightning and a P-61 Black Widow."

The major had sufficient experience.

"You want to fly this bird?"

His eyes widened, and a smile pulled at his mouth as he took the copilot's yoke.

"Watch out for the starboard engine. It's a bit stronger than the left but easily compensated for."

He took to the plane as though he'd been flying one his whole life.

After ten minutes, she made a hand motion. "Time to bring her back and land."

Berg nodded and released his control.

She gripped the yoke and brought the aircraft down. Much easier landing than the last time. She taxied and parked the craft near the hangar.

Berg unstrapped. "You and the other WASPs did a great job repairing this airplane."

Peggy removed her headphones. "Thank you."

"And thank you for letting me fly her."

As a pilot, she understood the need to be back in the air and would hate to be grounded for as long as the major had been.

No sooner had he exited the aircraft, than Jolene and Brownie climbed aboard.

Brownie pinned Peggy with a hard stare. "He looked happy. Did he ground you?"

Peggy shook her head. "No. Not even a scolding."

"Then why did he almost have a smile?"

Peggy shrugged. "I guess because I let him take the controls while we were up there."

Brownie scrunched her eyebrows together. "You did?"

Jolene's mouth curved up. "Cunning move."

Peggy could see how it might look that way, but she'd had no other motive than perceiving a need and giving the major an opportunity to fulfill that need.

≣ CHAPTER 4 ≣

21 August 1944, 2342 GMT

German U-boat spotted heading west through the
Strait of Gibraltar, fleeing Allied forces.

Five days later, Howie had his driver take him to the hangar. With his
folder, he entered the building.

Sergeant Kent lay on his back under the front corner of a Jeep.
He scooted out and sat up, evidently seeing Howie approach. "What
can I do for you, Major?"

"I'm looking for WASP Witherspoon. I was told she would be
here."

The sergeant pointed with the screwdriver in his hand. "In the
corner at the desk."

"Thank you." Howie went around the vehicle and skirted a smaller
aircraft in the building before he could see the desk.

Sure enough, Witherspoon sat there with paperwork in front of her.

He crossed to her. "Witherspoon."

She stood. "Sir."

"At ease. Retake your seat."

She did.

He sat in the chair next to the desk. "WASP Poole says you regularly create the female pilots' flying rosters."

"Yes, sir. She approves them of course. I was just about to get
started on next week's schedule."

When Poole had told him this, he'd decided to take a closer look—in the interest of learning the full scope of his duties. One of which was overseeing all aspects of the WASP duties and activities. He wanted to know how everything worked.

He held out his folder to her. "I've come to make your job easier."

Her eyebrows looked as though she couldn't decide whether to raise them or furrow them. She slowly opened the folder. Her eyes narrowed. "What's this?"

"I studied each WASP's file and devised a schedule to best utilize each pilot's strengths and skills." This would have the WASPs stationed at Bolling Airfield performing their very best, as well as saving Witherspoon considerable time. Time she could spend with her children.

She eyed him. "Did Poole approve this?"

"Not yet. I didn't want her to think you were derelict in your duties, so I thought it best if you turned it in to her."

"You've scheduled Brownie and Princess to fly as tow pilots at the same time." She pointed to a spot on the schedule. "That's an inadvisable combination."

"Princess?"

"Ginger Fleming's call sign. She doesn't get along with Brownie." She tapped another line on the paper. "Likewise, you don't want Frog and Dizzy flying together on this transport mission. Put Princess with Dizzy, and I'll fly tows with Brownie."

He mentally sighed. This was why men didn't think women should fly. They were too emotional. "We can't always choose whom we work with. This is war, and we all need to work with people we might not get along with all the time."

She swung her gaze to him. "But why make life more difficult for everyone when you don't have to?"

"I'm here to see that the WASP program at Bolling functions at peak proficiency." He'd created many such schedules overseas and knew how to make the most of the people available. "These combinations will be the most efficient use of personnel."

Witherspoon shook her head. "These pairings will ensure they don't work efficiently. Isn't the sign of a good leader one who considers the experience of others who have been around longer?"

He refused to be manipulated. "Your objection is duly noted. Let's try it for this cycle of the schedule."

"Is that an order, sir?"

He didn't like it to sound so stringent and stood. "Please see that WASP Poole receives this draft of the schedule."

Witherspoon stood and snapped a stiff right hand to her eyebrow. "Yes, sir."

It hit him odd to have her salute him for some reason. He'd felt a connection to her when she'd allowed him to fly the C-47 Skytrain. She didn't need to salute him indoors, but it was acceptable. He saluted back before leaving.

———— ≈ ————

Peggy had stared at the major's schedule for twenty minutes, wondering what to do. She couldn't simply discard it. He expected this one to be followed. Some of her fellow WASPs would be irritated with her when they found out whom they would be paired with. Feeling stuck, she went to Babs's office.

She entered and stood at attention until addressed. "Ma'am."

Her superior looked up. "What is it? Do you have next week's schedule?"

"It's right here, ma'am." Peggy pulled the sheet of paper from her folder and held it out.

Babs pointed to the metal tray on the corner of her desk. "I'm sure it's fine as always. Leave it there."

"Ma'am, I'll wait until you've had a chance to give it a cursory look." Peggy hoped her superior felt the same way she did.

Poole's eyes narrowed as she reached for the paper. As she read, her eyebrows lifted. "What's going on, Peggy? I can't believe you scheduled some of these pilots together."

Peggy gave a mental sigh of relief. "I didn't, ma'am. Major Berg was trying to be helpful." Peggy hated to tattle on a comrade, but what else could she do? "I sincerely believe he meant well."

"Why didn't you tell him some of these ladies don't work well together?"

"He said we don't always have a choice in whom we work with and need to get along with everyone. That this was the most efficient use of the personnel."

"He obviously doesn't know these ladies. I'll take care of this. In the meantime, work up an alternate schedule."

Peggy withdrew another sheet of paper from her folder. "The revised schedule, ma'am."

Babs chuckled. "This is why I put you in charge of scheduling. I never have to worry about it."

Peggy appreciated the confidence Babs placed in her and didn't take it lightly. She hoped the major would understand.

An hour after Howie had returned to his office from speaking with Witherspoon, his desk sergeant knocked and entered. "What do you need?"

"General Hawkins wants to see you at once, sir."

Howie set the papers aside that were in front of him and pushed his chair back from the desk. "Is he in his office?"

"He's at his Pentagon office."

Howie had been inside the new facility but once. It had only been dedicated a little over a year and half ago. Though the distance was short in miles, he didn't look forward to the serpentine trip. "Call Private Russell to drive me."

"I'll have him meet you in front." Sergeant Miller did an about-face and exited.

Forty-five minutes later, Howie walked along a corridor of the middle ring of the huge Pentagon structure. It still smelled of fresh paint. At the general's outer office, he gave his name to the sergeant there and took a seat. A half an hour passed before Howie was called into General Hawkins's office. He stood at attention. "You wanted to see me, sir?"

"Are you having a good day, Major?"

What a strange question. "I suppose so, sir."

"That's about to change." The general scowled. "I got chewed out by Jacqueline Cochran. Do you know who she is?"

"Yes, sir. Founder and head of the Women Airforce Service Pilots." That was an odd question.

"Do you know why she's unhappy?"

He had no idea but figured it must have something to do with him, or else he wouldn't be standing before the general now. "No, sir."

"Because of you." The general handed Howie a piece of paper. "Did you write up that WASP schedule?"

Howie's insides recoiled as though antiaircraft artillery had hit his plane. "Yes, sir." Had Witherspoon turned him in?

"Did you ignore WASP Witherspoon's advice on this schedule?"

He hadn't meant to cause a problem. He had only been trying to make the whole organization run better. "My goal was to learn more about the WASP program and make it more efficient, sir."

"This is not the way to do that. These women have honed their abilities and the way everything works together into a finely oiled machine." The general handed him a second paper. "Here is the revised schedule. See to it WASP Poole receives this immediately."

Poole was Witherspoon's boss. She must have been the one to veto his schedule and started this chain of events. No, Howie's stubbornness had put this all into motion. He should have heeded Witherspoon's warning. "I'll see she receives this straightaway."

"Good. I don't want Cochran coming to me with trivial things like this again. Is that understood?"

"Yes, sir."

"Dismissed."

Howie departed and hightailed it to Poole's office. He didn't have to wait before she granted him access. "Ma'am, here is the WASP schedule."

She took it and studied it a moment. "This looks good. Thank you. I'll see that Witherspoon gets this."

Even though she wasn't his superior, out of courtesy and to make amends for his faux pas he asked, "Ma'am, may I speak freely?"

She leaned back into her chair and narrowed her eyes slightly. "You may."

"I realize I should have taken Witherspoon's WASP recommendations under advisement. It won't happen again."

"I'm glad to hear that. I wouldn't depend on just anyone to draw up the schedule. I trust Witherspoon. She has a level head on her shoulders. We are fortunate to have her."

"I can see that. I would appreciate the opportunity to deliver the schedule to her myself." He owed her that.

Poole held out the paper. "She believed you were well intentioned in your actions."

He was pleased to hear that, but he still owed her an apology. He accepted the paper and left.

He found Witherspoon at the hangar, in the same place he'd left her this morning when he'd initiated today's debacle. He swallowed hard and approached.

When she noticed him, she jerked out of her chair and stood at attention. "Sir."

"At ease. I came to deliver the schedule—the schedule *you* created."

"I'm sorry, sir. I never intended to cause you any difficulties."

He hadn't meant to cause trouble either. "Everything is well. Any flak I received is my fault. I should have listened to your advice. I thought I knew better, but I don't. You were right. I don't know these women the way you do and which work best together. I won't make that mistake again."

≡ CHAPTER 5 ≡

Cargo ship sunk in the middle of the Atlantic by German U-boat.

In a remote location an hour west of Washington, DC, Howie gazed up into the sky. A Mustang—his preferred combat plane—and a Brewster F2A Buffalo towed long fabric-tube drogue for ground soldiers to use as target practice. One of those pilots was WASP Witherspoon. He'd heard she was in the Buffalo. Marines called it a flying coffin. Both pilots were connected into the headphone sets that he and Second Lieutenant Rosbach wore. The lower-ranking officer was in charge of this training. Howie's only duty today was to observe. A couple of WASPs and other soldiers looked on from the ground as well.

As the pair of target tugs flew overhead, the soldiers on the ground fired at them with the M1A2 tank. Not them directly, but in their proximity at the long, sleeve-like drogues they towed. Howie knew these antiaircraft guns by their other name—the Colt 37mm, so designated because the Colt Company produced them. It was one thing to have ammunition shot at a flapping target in a pilot's general vicinity in friendly skies. Something altogether different to have an enemy hunting a person down with the intent to eliminate them from the human race.

The sound of the familiar gunfire jolted Howie's nerves, not having been this close to it since he'd been shot down. The chatter over the radio agitated him further, so he turned down the volume and removed the headset, letting it hang around his neck. His mind raced back, uninvited, to himself in the air with enemy fire exploding all around. His pulse pounded. Sweat broke out over his face. His hands shook. Benson was hit, his Mustang on fire. Another in his squadron shot and heading toward the ground with a trail of smoke. And another.

Then his turn.

Spiraling down.

And down.

He'd wanted to bail out but didn't dare. He would be an easy target for any artillery guns in the vicinity, as he would drift ever so slowly to the ground. No, he would be dead for sure. He stood a better chance staying in his aircraft. Though the engine was gone and half the tail shot off, he could still glide it to the ground. More or less. He had never hurt so badly as on that day when his damaged Mustang careened to the ground and collided with a tree. Then the blackness.

Three days later, he'd woken up in a French field hospital. There had been talk of amputating his leg. He hadn't prayed against something so hard in his life. Fortunately the Lord had spared his leg. It would likely give him trouble for as long as he lived, but he still had two legs to stand on.

He shook off the haunting memories, thanking God he was alive and had all of his limbs. He refocused his attention on the drama playing out in today's sky.

The targets weren't as riddled as he thought they should be. Aiming at a stationary object was far easier than a moving one, and a moving one in the sky was even harder to hit.

A new pair of gunners replaced the previous two.

The tow planes banked around for another pass. The firing began again, shredding his nerves. He tried to shut out the sound and focus on the sky.

The flashes of the bullets blinked in streams against the blue.

One of the gunman's aim was atrocious. Was he blind?

The second lieutenant in charge didn't seem to be advising him on how to correct his aim.

The bullets flew straight toward the aircraft rather than the flapping canvas drogues. Smoke rose from the Mustang. It had been hit!

The Buffalo rolled and banked.

Howie reseated his headset and turned up the volume.

Witherspoon's voice came over the com. "Brownie, bank left. I'll go right."

Another female voice. "That will put you in the line of fire."

"Do it!"

Both planes banked and rolled.

Howie hobbled over to the gunmen. "Cease fire! Cease fire!"

The Colt 37 mm guns went silent, but not before the Buffalo appeared to be hit as well.

Howie grabbed the communication mike. "Brownie, what is the status of your aircraft?" He wanted to ask about Witherspoon first, but the other plane was smoking.

"Engine is sputtering and controls are sluggish."

"And you?"

"I'm. . .fine."

Was she? He would be surprised considering the number of rounds her craft took. "Release your drogue and land immediately."

"Roger. Brownie coming in for a landing. It might be a little rough." Amazingly, she didn't sound panicked.

"We'll be here to meet you." Howie shifted his attention to the other pilot in the air. "Mama Bird, what's your status?"

No response.

"Mama Bird, come in." *Lord, please let her be all right.* "Mama Bird?"

The WASP whose call sign was Nightingale spoke next to him. "She's fine."

He glanced at her. "How can you possibly know?"

Jolene pointed toward the sky. "By the way she's maneuvering."

He watched the Buffalo. She did appear to be flying fine, almost protectively of her fellow WASP. He pressed the talk button on the side of the hand mike. "Mama Bird, I need confirmation that you and your aircraft are all right."

"I am *not* all right. I'm seething mad. This never should have happened. *Never.*"

Howie agreed. This was intolerable. "Release your drogue and land right after WASP Brown."

"Roger." Her single word response, likely through gritted teeth, conveyed her displeasure.

He knew her aggravation was over the incident and not his request for her to land. He spoke to the wide-eyed trainee soldiers. "Everyone on the tarmac. Prepare for two crash landings. Emergency protocols. Mobilize, soldiers!"

The men scurried around, all except Second Lieutenant Rosbach who smirked before sauntering after the others.

Brownie's landing would be rough at best. *Lord, please bring her down safely.* Mama Bird's could be rough too. Her plane had likely been hit as well. *Keep them both safe.*

He climbed into his assigned Jeep and gave orders to his driver. "Get on the edge of the tarmac. Follow behind the planes after they land."

Private Russell saluted and jumped into the driver's seat. He raced toward the tarmac and positioned the vehicle to be ready when the first airplane landed.

The Mustang released its drogue that fluttered toward the ground. The aircraft wobbled as it came in. The engine sputtered then went silent. Brownie was coming in too high and at too steep of a descent. After clearing the end of the runway, the plane leveled off and then almost seemed to drop. The wheels screeched on the tarmac and then lifted. Three more bounces before the wheels remained on the ground.

The Buffalo circled once—probably checking to make sure the first aircraft wasn't going to burst into flames and block the runway. Its drogue already gone, Mama Bird quickly touched down as well.

Howie pointed. "Catch up to the first aircraft." He needed to ensure the pilot was indeed all right. The Jeep stopped about the same time as the Mustang. The Buffalo stopped soon after.

The canopy on the Mustang slid back, and Brownie swiped off her leather helmet. That meant the pilot was well enough. He glanced at the Buffalo. Mama Bird's canopy jerked open, and Witherspoon popped out. She scrambled down the side of her bird. He breathed a sigh of relief. She was obviously not injured. She reached the Mustang at the same time Howie did.

Being more agile, she climbed up onto the wing and to the cockpit.

"Halt!" What was Mama Bird doing? "The plane could burst into flames." Why hadn't Brownie exited her smoking aircraft?

Witherspoon reached in and assisted her fellow WASP. Why did she need to do that?

"What's wrong with her?"

Mama Bird glared over her shoulder as she got Brownie onto the wing. "She's been shot in the foot."

What? "But she said she was fine." He dropped his cane and reached up to help the injured pilot down.

Brownie slid along the curve of the wing and landed on her good foot but held onto him for balance.

He probably wasn't the best option to be supporting an injured person, but there was no way he was going to allow her fall. He called to his driver. "Help her to the Jeep."

As Russell draped Brownie's arm over his shoulder, Mama Bird took Brownie's other side, freeing Howie to retrieve his cane and make his way to the vehicle.

Blood drops left a path to the Jeep.

At the vehicle, Mama Bird unlaced Brownie's boot and eased it off.

Brownie sucked in air through clenched teeth.

Mama Bird removed the silk flying scarf from her neck, wrapped it around the bleeding foot, and tied it securely. She glanced at him over her shoulder. "Not the first time this has happened to a WASP."

Unbelievable. Howie spoke to the driver. "Take them to the hospital ASAP."

"What about you, sir?" the private asked.

"You can come back for me. Now go." Then he spoke to Mama Bird. "Go with her, and have yourself checked out as well. No arguments. Go."

She nodded and climbed in. She probably would have gone anyway, even if he hadn't ordered her.

If one WASP could claim to be fine after being shot—*shot!*—then the other could be injured as well and refusing to admit it or trying to cover it up. Those women were amazing.

The Jeep raced away.

Now that Brownie was off to the hospital, Howie made a cursory inspection of the two aircraft while the trainee soldiers and the second lieutenant looked on. The Mustang had several holes in it, but the smoke was diminishing. WASP Brown was fortunate to be alive with nothing more than a hole in her foot. The Buffalo had a couple of bullet holes in the tail section as well but nothing critical. Witherspoon had flown into danger to protect her fellow WASP. The kind of pilot he wanted in the air with him in a dogfight.

She seemed so calm on the ground, like being shot at was normal, all in a day's work.

Both behaved unlike any ladies he'd met before. They were strong, tough women.

Now for the trainees and the second lieutenant. He gave them all a good dressing-down for more than ten minutes. He hadn't disciplined troops in a while and needed to stop before he lost his voice, diminishing the impact of his anger. "All of you back to Bolling Field. I expect you to be on the parade grounds at attention when I arrive."

Without a word, they scrambled into the transport truck. Second Lieutenant Rosbach sauntered over to his own issued Jeep.

"Not so fast, *Second Lieutenant*." Howie made his way to the vehicle.

Rosbach stopped.

"In the vehicle with the others. I'm taking the Jeep."

The second lieutenant glared at him and made the soldier in the passenger seat of the truck get in the back, and he climbed in the front.

Howie watched the truck drive away. Now he was in a pickle. He hadn't been given clearance by a doctor to drive, but he had no choice and settled himself into the driver's seat. He pressed in the clutch with his good leg, turned over the engine, moved the gearshift to first, and eased on the gas. He took it slow. If he was careful, he would be able to drive.

His right leg was stiff and a little difficult to maneuver the pedals with. Though the process was a bit herky-jerky and took him a while, he managed to get himself to the headquarters building and park. As he approached his office, Sergeant Miller stood at attention. "Sir."

"At ease."

The sergeant relaxed. "I heard there was a bit of trouble out on the practice range."

The news had traveled fast—well at least faster than Howie could drive. It had been more than trouble. It had been stupidity at its finest. "Fortunately the pilots were able to land safely. WASPs Witherspoon and Brown were taken to the hospital. Get me an update."

"Yes, sir. Were they injured?"

"Witherspoon appeared fine but is getting checked out to make sure. Brown was shot in the foot." Howie still couldn't believe that had occurred. "I don't think she had any other injuries."

"I've heard of that happening."

Howie hadn't. How inconceivable. "I want all the reports you can get your hands on of target tug incidents where WASPs have been shot or injured. Also I want to see Privates Jones and Horowitz and Second Lieutenant Rosbach. They should be on the parade grounds. Anyone not at attention, make them stay there. Otherwise, they may be dismissed."

From behind him a man spoke. "I'll do that, sir."

Howie spun around to face Captain Cooper who stood rigid. There was an eagerness in the captain's eyes.

"Very well."

With a formal turn, Captain Cooper about-faced and marched away.

"I'll be in my office when you get those reports." Howie entered and sat behind his desk, relieved to get off his bum leg. He leaned his cane against the side of the desk and rubbed his thigh. Driving had exercised muscles he hadn't used in a while.

A short time later, Captain Cooper's voice filtered through the door. "Stand at attention right there until the major is ready to see you." Then came a knock.

"Come."

The captain entered, closed the door, and stood stiff.

"At ease."

Cooper relaxed his stance. "Permission to speak freely, sir?"

"Granted."

"I believe the two privates were just plain pea-brained."

Howie agreed. "And Second Lieutenant Rosbach?"

"He's a bully. He's drunk on power and likes to push his weight around. You need to watch that one."

"What is his position on the WASP program?"

"Mouths off all the time about how they don't belong, they shouldn't be flying, and that they are a nuisance."

Good to know it wasn't just his own interpretation.

"Sir, mind if I ask what he did?"

Howie's blood boiled at the events of earlier. "Nothing. He did *nothing* to stop two privates from shooting at the actual aircraft rather than the drogues. One WASP was shot in the foot."

The captain cursed under his breath, then straightened to attention. "Sorry for my foul language, sir."

Howie understood, and the man's outburst let him know how the captain felt about the whole situation. "Don't let it happen again."

"Yes, sir. Request, sir?"

"What is it?"

"Request permission to be present when you speak to Rosbach."

It wasn't a bad idea to have another officer present. "Affirmative. Would you send the privates in first?"

The captain opened the door. "Jones. Horowitz. Inside."

The two privates marched in and stood at attention, both had beads of sweat on their upper lips and foreheads.

The captain stood off to the side, feet apart, hands behind his back, a flame in his gaze that could have reduced the two offenders to cinders if palpable.

After the two soldiers bumbled through their explanations of what happened and promised it would never happen again, Howie dismissed them.

The captain said, "Those two really are pea-brains. How did we ever let them in the army?"

Howie felt the same. "Wartime. They'll let any knucklehead in."

"What about Rosbach?"

"I need to go to the hospital to see about my two WASPs first." Howie grabbed his cane and exited. He glared at the second lieutenant. "I expect you to be right there when I return." He continued down the corridor with Captain Cooper.

Once out of earshot, the captain spoke. "Are you really going to make him stay there while you go all the way to Bethesda and back."

"Yes. A small price to pay for nearly costing a pilot her life." The soldier deserved a lot worse for endangering those ladies' lives.

"I'm going to like having you here. Would you let me know when you return so I can witness Rosbach's downfall?"

Howie was going to like working with this captain as well. "I'll let you know."

≣ CHAPTER 6 ≣

Howie traversed the corridor of the hospital. His insides tangled with what could have happened today.

He inquired at the nurses' desk where WASP Brown's room was located, but as he glanced down the corridor, he could have guessed. Private Jones hesitated outside a door, cracking his knuckles nervously and muttering to himself.

He caught up to the private. "Go on in."

The wide-eyed soldier resembled young men on the battlefield who knew they were going to die. "But I shot her. Those WASPs are intimidating. They are always so confident."

That they were. Howie clasped the younger man on the shoulder. "I'm sure she'll appreciate your contriteness."

Pulling a chocolate bar from his breast pocket and holding it in front of him like a protective shield, Jones swallowed hard and entered Brownie's hospital room.

Howie held a pair of small bouquets of carnations as he followed the private into the hospital room.

Witherspoon sat in a chair next to Brownie's bed. Howie's gut disentangled at the sight of Witherspoon well and unharmed. Though she had scrambled to help her fellow pilot out of her plane, she could have been hiding an injury.

Around the room stood four other WASPs, including Nightingale. The five uninjured women snapped to attention.

"At ease." None of them needed to do that here.

Brownie's foot sat propped on a mountain of pillows, wrapped up to three times its normal size.

The private handed the candy to the WASP laid up in the bed. "I know how hard it is to get chocolate with the rationing, so I thought you might like this."

Brownie snatched the bar. "I love chocolate. I haven't had any in ever so long."

"I'm terribly sorry. I never meant to shoot you. I thought we were supposed to target the planes. You could be my sister."

Brownie's eyelids drooped a little. "You're not the first soldier to aim at the wrong target. It can be mighty stressful firing an M1A2. It's a *big* gun."

"You're awfully nice about this whole thing."

She waved a hand in the air across the front of her. "I've got a kid brother."

Howie stepped forward and handed a bundle of flowers to her and one to Mama Bird. Brownie smelled them. "Thanks."

Witherspoon merely held hers. "Thanks." An unenthusiastic response.

He had hoped for more appreciation from her.

The others in the room looked at him oddly. He sensed he'd done something wrong but couldn't guess what. He would figure it out later. "WASP Brown, what's your status?"

She grinned with a dopey smile. "I got shot, but I don't feel it. They gave me happy medicine. It works."

He could tell.

Witherspoon scrutinized him as though she wasn't sure what to make of him. "Miraculously, the bullet missed the bones and went all the way through. They cleaned the wound and stitched her foot. She needs to stay off it for a couple of weeks but should recover well."

"I'm glad to hear that."

Brownie chimed in again. "I got shot." She swung her head back and forth. "But I don't feel it."

He smiled. "I'm glad you aren't in any pain. I merely wanted to stop by and see how you two were getting on." He turned his attention back to Mama Bird. "Did you have a doctor check you over?"

"Yes. Sir."

"Any injuries?"

"No, sir."

"Glad to hear." Very glad. He sensed his presence was making those in the room uncomfortable. "I'll leave you all to your visit." He exited.

Witherspoon followed him out and held up the bouquet. "What were these for?"

Didn't she like them? "It's customary to bring flowers when one is in the hospital. I felt terrible the pair of you were shot at. Is there a problem?"

She narrowed her eyes slightly. "Yes, there is. Would you bring flowers to a wounded or 'shot at' male soldier?"

"Wh–what? No."

"So why for us WASPs? We are doing the same jobs as men." Though she spoke the words kindly, they still cut. "If the WASPs ever hope to be looked at as equals, we need to be treated as such."

"I never thought of it that way. I was raised to behave toward ladies in a certain way. They should be protected and cared for, not put in danger."

"That's all well and good, but this is war. If we are mollycoddled, then how can we help our men overseas? What we do here matters."

"I agree. My mistake." He straightened. "I was still thinking of you WASPs as ladies rather than fellow soldiers. I appreciate everything you women do. You made it possible for us to fight in combat in the air, on land, and at sea. This war would have already been lost if not for all the efforts of women in so many areas from factories, hospitals, aircraft, and so much more. Thank you." He snapped a salute to her as a sign of honor and held it.

Her eyebrows pulled together as she returned his salute.

He lowered his hand. "I was going to give you a couple of days leave, but since I wouldn't do that for one of the male soldiers, I'll expect you to be at your duty post tomorrow."

She squared her shoulders as though not being given time off was an honor. "I will, sir."

"I will be reprimanding Second Lieutenant Rosbach for his actions today."

"Thank you, sir."

"Dismissed." He walked away.

He'd been a fool to treat the ladies differently. They did the same work as the men, most did it better. It would be hard to undo his whole upbringing and treat ladies like he did the men, but out of respect for them and all they were doing and all they were sacrificing, he needed to.

First, the women were given defective aircraft and now they were being shot at and injured. What other atrocities had they been subjected to?

When Howie returned to his office and informed Captain Cooper, he brought the junior officer with him. They passed Second Lieutenant Rosbach still standing at attention in the corridor. "I'll be with you in a minute." He and the captain entered Howie's office.

General Hawkins sat behind Howie's desk.

He snapped to attention, as did the captain. "What can I do for you, sir?"

"Close the door."

Captain Cooper did.

The general steepled his hands. "I understand you have left Lieutenant Rosbach standing in the corridor for some time."

"Yes, sir." Was Howie in trouble? "Permission to speak candidly, sir?"

"Granted."

"Second Lieutenant Rosbach's actions today nearly got a pilot killed."

The general's expression darkened. "Go on."

"A WASP tow pilot, sir. The gunnery soldiers shot at the planes rather than the drogues." The thought still sent a chill through Howie. "The lieutenant did nothing to stop them. He stood there and let it continue. I had to order the soldiers to cease fire. Rosbach told me that them getting shot was proof women shouldn't be flying. Both aircraft were hit. One seriously. One of the pilots injured. Shot in the foot."

"How is she?"

"She's in the hospital recovering. She'll be fine. The other WASP by the name of Witherspoon flew her aircraft in the line of fire to protect the already smoking aircraft of her comrade."

"He didn't order the gunners to halt? Could he have possibly not realized what was happening?"

"He knew exactly what was happening." And had smirked about it.

The general's nostrils flared. "Rosbach! Get in here!" He cocked his head to Howie and the captain.

He and Cooper stepped to the side of the room.

Rosbach entered.

The general spent the next twenty minutes chewing out the lieu-tenant at a volume that could likely be heard halfway down the cor-ridor. Then assigned him to cleaning the latrines with his toothbrush for a month.

Dismissed, Rosbach did an about-face and left.

Though Howie'd been slightly disappointed he hadn't been the one to chew out the derelict lieutenant, witnessing the general do it had been extremely satisfying. "Sir, I'd like to recommend both WASPs for commendations."

"They aren't military. We can't do that."

"Is there anything they can receive?"

"I'll speak to Cochran and see what she can do for her pilots."

"I'd appreciate that."

"Carry on." The general left.

———≈———

Peggy pulled into her driveway and parked. She lifted the bouquet of carnations to her nose and sniffed. Peggy had been so moved by the gift, she had almost cried. It had been all she could do to hold back the tears. The major had been sweet to bring them flowers. She'd wished they had meant more than him being sorry she and Brownie had gotten shot at. Just the same, they were special to her. Even though she had given him an earful.

It had been a very long time since a man had given her flowers.

When she entered the house, her mother stood at the stove, cook-ing supper. Wendy and Junie sat on the living-room floor, playing with Shirley Temple paper dolls. Her girls jumped up and ran to her.

Peggy wrapped her arms around them and squeezed. "I love you both so much." Her heart tightened at the thought they could have lost their mother today.

Her oldest daughter touched the bouquet in her hand. "You have flowers."

Her younger one said, "They are prettiful."

"I thought these carnations would look nice on our table." It wouldn't be wise to admit they came from her superior. "What do you think?"

They chorused, "Yes."

Peggy handed them to her oldest daughter. "Would you put them in vase with water?"

As her daughters skipped away, her mother stepped next to her and raised an eyebrow. "Look nice on the table?"

She never could get anything past her mom. "It's been a challenging day." She didn't want to confess to her mother that she'd almost been shot down—by one of their own! Even so, her mother deserved the truth. "I was a tow pilot today."

"I hate it when you have to do that job."

Peggy lowered her voice so her daughters couldn't hear. "The gunners were confused as to what to shoot at."

Her mother's eyebrows rose in understanding. "Mercy. Are you all right?"

"I'm fine. My fellow WASP wasn't so fortunate. She got shot in the foot. She's going to be fine too. The new major felt bad for us and brought us flowers at the hospital."

Her mother crinkled her eyebrows. "Would he do that if you two had been men?"

"I asked him the same thing." And he'd seemed quite contrite. She had probably overreacted, but it had been in front of her fellow WASPs who razzed her afterward. It wouldn't be good if she was seen as a favorite of the major's. Though the thought of him viewing her favorably was appealing.

She shook her head. It would do no good thinking that way. But why not? She was a warm-blooded human. Everyone needed somebody.

"Why are you shaking your head at me?"

"Not you. The major."

With one hand on her hip, Mom cocked her head. "You want to know what I think?"

"No. Don't start in."

"It wouldn't hurt to consider another man. George told you before he shipped out that if anything happened to him, he wanted you to find someone else. He told me that too. He didn't want you shriveling up and becoming bitter."

Peggy remembered. In spite of his warning, she *had* shriveled up inside to a degree, as well as become bitter. Why did she have to have so many losses in her life when others had none? She wanted to feel whole and alive again. Glancing at the flowers on the table, she realized she had a glimpse of those feelings when she was around Major Berg. She looked forward to the next time she would see him.

And the next.

"Mom, I'm not ready to think that way. There's a war going on."

"I would say more than one."

Peggy would say so as well. How long should one wait after the death of a spouse before it was acceptable to be interested in another? A part of her never wanted to care for anyone else. She wanted to hold on to her feelings for her deceased husband.

How would her daughters take to a new man? No, she couldn't risk their little hearts. Besides, the major likely didn't consider her beyond her duties as a WASP.

After the girls went to bed and her mother had turned in for the night, Peggy would normally sit up in bed, reading for a while. Instead, she took a carnation from the vase. She had done her best to downplay the flowers in front of her mother.

Why did these flowers touch her so deeply when they didn't really mean anything? The major had only brought them out of some sort of habit. Regardless, they had broken through a place in her soul that had been walled off for years—ever since her husband had shipped off to Europe for the war. Her heart had done all it could to safeguard itself. Could it ever be truly safe? No. It was shriveling up from lack of nourishment and love. Starving. If she let down her guard, she could be hurt. Would she survive another painful loss? Could she risk being too broken to function? What would become of her daughters? They needed her. Disregarding herself, she couldn't allow her daughters to be hurt.

So why had she flown between Brownie and the artillery fire?

She had needed to protect the younger WASP. It had been instinct. Peggy was already broken inside. Brownie didn't need to be too. She also knew if her aircraft was hit badly, she had more flying experience and would have a better chance of landing safely.

She brought the flower to her nose. It smelled sweet. Wandering into her backyard, she plucked at the carnation petals, tearing pieces off. She went around and around the flower until only a few shreds of the petals remained.

This was her. A sad flower with only tattered bits left. Only God could fix a flower this damaged.

In the middle somewhere were the seeds clustered together. They would grow into new flowers if planted. Like her daughters blooming into flowers.

Some plants could have a shoot snipped off. Then that cutting could sprout roots and grow into a new healthy plant. Could she?

For some reason the major came to mind.

———— ≈ ————

Howie sat in his Transient Living Facility quarters, watching the hands on the clock move ever so slowly.

Had Witherspoon kept the flowers or pitched them? He hoped she'd kept them. Did it even matter? They hadn't meant anything. Not really. Not to her. They had been a reminder that as a WASP most viewed her as less than her male counterpart, but she wasn't.

He picked up the prescription bottle of sleeping medication. He should take one before the night was over and sunrise was upon him. He didn't like the way they made him feel. Like he was no longer in control. Drugged.

Setting the bottle aside, he climbed into bed and stared at the ceiling. If he couldn't sleep, he could at least rest.

Witherspoon weighed heavy on his heart, so he turned his mind to prayer. He thanked God she and Brownie hadn't been killed or injured worse. He prayed mostly for Witherspoon. He felt she needed it. Not because of the incident, but for some deeper reason.

≣ CHAPTER 7 ≣

Two days later, Peggy had the engine compartment open on the Mustang which had been damaged during the target towing operation. It had been set aside to be repaired—or scrapped—at some date in the future. A beautiful craft like this should never be discarded. With a little tender-loving care, she would fly again.

The bullets had pierced the radiator, battery, and oil lines. The battery would need to be replaced. No salvaging it. Fortunately, she found a used one from a previously decommissioned plane and hooked it up to charge.

She'd already replaced the punctured oil hose as well as the fuel line while she was at it. In case there was damage to any of the belts, all of those would be replaced too. The radiator was another matter. She'd removed the parts and set about to repair the liquid cooling system, which was a difficult task. There wasn't a spare she could use to simply replace it. It had been tough to get permission to attempt any kind of repair on this aircraft.

She wasn't allowed to work on it during her normal duty hours, so she set about tinkering little by little on her lunch breaks and now this evening. She'd let her mother know she would be late. Her daughters would be in bed by the time she arrived home.

So why had she chosen to spend her time with an aircraft instead of her daughters? Something inside her had a drive to fix things. It helped occupy her mind. Kept her from thinking too much about the people she'd lost, that God had turned His back on her, and a certain major who invaded her thoughts. Working on the Mustang would keep images of him at bay.

The places where the shell of the airplane had been pierced by the 37mm ammunition rounds needed to be sheet welded. Peggy geared up in the heavy leather apron that hung down nearly to the floor, the leather gloves that came up to her elbows, and the welding helmet. She lit the welding torch and aimed it toward the metal.

Welding provided a cathartic release for her, the glow of the flame and the sparks from touching the metal. Taking something as hard as metal that was torn or damaged in some way and repairing so it could be used again. It wasn't like new but still useful once more. Much like the human heart. It could get damaged and over time be mended, but it too would never be like new. Forever altered, but able to function again.

The metal glowed as she worked.

Her own heart still harbored the war wounds from her husband's death. It had already been scarred from losing her father and older brother in the First World War. She wished she could remove her heart and weld it. Only God could accomplish that, but He'd been the one to tear it apart by turning away from her.

She slowly knit the rips and punctures in the fuselage together.

Once the damage was fixed, she turned off the torch and lifted the helmet's visor.

"Looks good."

At the unexpected voice, Peggy sucked in a breath and spun around as she jumped back.

Major Berg stood in front of her with wide eyes the color of polished steel. "I'm sorry. I didn't want to startle you, so I waited until you were done before speaking."

She drew in a deep breath. "I wasn't expecting anyone." How long had he been standing there?

"I've never seen someone weld before. It's fascinating."

She found it fascinating as well and pointed toward the plane. "I was given permission to work on this aircraft in my off hours." She relished the challenge of bringing back to life something everyone else had considered unsalvageable and never usable again.

"I'm aware. That's why I'm here." He motioned toward a paper bag. "I brought supper. I figured you hadn't eaten."

He was right, and her stomach had been telling her to feed it for a while now. "That was kind of you."

"Let's sit and eat, and you can update me on the progress of this Mustang."

She removed the too big welding helmet, the too large gloves, and the too heavy leather apron. She placed them all on the welding cart of tools. She rolled a stool over for the major to sit on near a sawhorse she would use.

He pointed to the sawhorse. "I can't let you sit on that. You take the stool."

She tilted her head.

He held his hands up in surrender. "If I wouldn't capitulate to a man, I shouldn't for you, but I sit on this stool in protest."

It was nice having a man consider her comfort. The sawhorse was rather uncomfortable. "I appreciate the gesture, but I'll be fine here. Next time, I'll capitulate."

"Deal." He sat and opened the bag. "Hoagie sandwiches from Sam's Deli. Ham or Beef?"

"Ham."

He handed her a paper-wrapped sandwich and put the other one on his lap. He passed her a small bag of potato chips and poured coffee from a thermos into a ceramic mug which he gave to her as well. "It's decaffeinated. I wasn't sure whether you could drink caffeine this late or if it would keep you awake."

She didn't need anything else adding to her sleeplessness. "This is fine." She lifted the cup and took a sip of the hot brew. It slid down her throat, comforting her like an old friend. "Does caffeine keep you awake?"

He shook his head. "When I can't sleep, it has nothing to do with caffeine."

He likely had battle terrors in the night. As did many soldiers who had experienced combat. Some were tormented by their experiences. Even knowing that, men willingly went to war. She respected them for their courage.

She slipped a potato chip piece between the bread roll halves and then took a bite. The crunch and saltiness added to the flavor and experience of the sandwich.

He chuckled. "I do the same thing." He tucked a chip into his sandwich. "The key is to add the chips one bite at a time. If you put them all in at once, they become soggy half way through."

She brightened. "Exactly."

The image of the welding torch mending the metal came to her mind. Was God using this man's simple considerate actions to aid in welding her heart back together? Did she even want Him to?

After finishing his hoagie, Howie drained the coffee in the cup and screwed it back on the thermos. He'd feared Mama Bird would reject his offer of food. He had no ulterior motives other than seeing to the welfare of one of the people under his command. If asked, he would have to admit he wouldn't have done the same for one of the men. He would have ordered the soldier to leave and get food. At the very most, drop off something to eat but not stay. He'd been pleased she hadn't turned him away.

"How did you earn the call sign Mama Bird? Is it because you are protective of the other WASPs?" He'd seen it when Brownie had been shot.

"I would die for any one of my fellow WASPs, but that's not why I'm called Mama Bird. Bird because I fly in the sky with the birds, and Mama because I have two little girls, Wendy and Junie."

The poor woman had lost her husband and now had to raise her children on her own. Another thing to admire her for. "Would you fill me in on the repairs?"

She brushed the crumbs from her hands and hopped off the saw-horse. She moved a little stiffly. It *had* been uncomfortable. He knew it would be, but he feared if he pressed the issue to be the one to sit on it, she would have refused to eat with him altogether. Also if he'd sat on it, his injuries would be causing him a whole lot more pain than normal. Maybe that was the reason she had insisted upon sitting on the hunk of wood. Next time, he would make sure there was a second stool.

Next time? Would she still agree to a next time?

She went over to the workbench where various engine parts lay. She explained the damage and what would be involved in the repairs.

It sounded tedious. He didn't enjoy fixing things. He preferred to spend his time in the air rather than earthbound, tinkering. But this lady made the ground more tolerable.

He'd dated from time to time, but moving around in the Army Air Corps didn't seem like the kind of life he wanted to foist upon a wife. Because of that, he'd remained a bachelor, which had suited him fine most of the time, but now he wondered if it might not anymore.

"Can you really fix that as good as new?"

"Nothing is ever as good as new."

Like him.

"But it will be strong and function well."

The doctors had repaired as much damage within him as they could, and now his body had to finish the rest. He would function like normal in time but never as good as new.

She took him to the engine compartment and explained the damage there and what she'd done.

"I am in awe of people who can repair mechanical things the way you do. I have a rudimentary knowledge, but fixing stuff like this doesn't interest me much. I trust you mechanics every time I climb into an airplane."

"Mechanics appreciate pilots trusting them." She gifted him with a smile, warming him inside.

"I suppose it's easy for you to trust your mechanic." He gave her a cheeky grin.

She put one hand on the hip of her ill-fitting zoot suit. "Some days I do, and some days I don't."

He raised his eyebrows. He knew she was teasing, because how could she not trust her own work? "Well, you better have a strong talk with your mechanic to get up to snuff with her repair work."

She laughed then, and so did he. It felt good to laugh. He hadn't done much of that since crashing. Maybe this lady would help mend him.

≣ CHAPTER 8 ≣

4 September 1944, 0430 GMT

A Venezuelan freighter reported spotting the fleeing German
U-boat heading for the United States East Coast.

Howie's desk sergeant knocked on his open door. "Sir, General Hawkins wants to see you in his Bolling office." The general had an office at both the Pentagon and here at the airfield.

"Right away?"

"Yes, sir. His aide said it was urgent."

"I'm on my way." Howie snatched his cane and headed upstairs.

Once in the general's outer office, Howie approached the aide's desk.

A sergeant looked up from his work. "He's talking to one of the Joint Chiefs of Staff on the telephone. He'll be with you soon."

A joint chief? Something must have come up. "Should I return at a more convenient time?"

The sergeant gave a tight smile. "No. He needs to speak with you now. You can take one of the chairs."

Howie sat in the nearest one. Ten minutes passed.

The phone rang, and the sergeant picked it up. "Yes, sir." He hung up and stood. "The general will see you now, sir."

Howie got to his feet and followed the aide the few feet to the office door.

The sergeant opened it. "Sir, Major Berg."

"Send him in."

The aide stepped aside.

Howie moved inside and stood at attention. The door clicked shut behind him.

General Hawkins flipped through papers in a folder. "Your service record is exemplary."

Why did he have Howie's records? "Thank you, sir. I'm proud to serve my country."

"That's obvious from your insistence to remain in service when you could have been honorably discharged for medical reasons."

He was injured, not inept. "I felt there was still much I could contribute for my country. Once my leg heals fully, I would be honored to climb back into the cockpit." If the general put in a good word for him, he could be granted a waiver to pilot military airplanes again.

"I appreciate your enthusiasm. At ease. Do you need to take a seat?" The general focused on Howie's cane.

"No, sir." Though sitting was usually preferred, he didn't want to show any kind of weakness in front of the general. He stood at rest with his feet apart and his free hand at the small of his back.

"Several WASPs will be traveling to Texas by train. They will test-fly an aircraft and bring it back here. You will accompany them."

Howie's spine stiffened. "Am I to understand I'm to play babysitter to highly skilled pilots?"

"I wouldn't call it that."

Howie would. "From what I have seen of these women, they are more than capable to do this mission without supervision."

"As far as the women—or anyone else—will know, that is exactly what you are doing. No one will question it. A Colonel Watson will make contact once you are there."

"Is this a covert mission, sir?"

He nodded. "Jackie Cochran herself has hand-chosen the ladies."

The mastermind behind the development of the WASP and its subsequent head? Must be something important.

The general leaned forward. "No one will suspect you of anything more than escorting the WASPs."

"Yes, sir. May I speak frankly, sir?"

Though his superior looked a little annoyed, he agreed.

"These women are highly capable. Having me along to keep watch of them will insult them."

"As you well know, Major, some in the military don't believe women belong in aircraft regardless of their capabilities and have the propensity to treat them poorly."

Howie had been learning that and wished it wasn't that way. "Even so, the ladies will be insulted."

"I suspect you have another idea."

Howie did. "Put it on me. We tell them I'm accompanying them so I can gain a better understanding of what they do."

"I like that. Anything to deflect from the real purpose of the mission."

"When do we leave, sir?"

"At 0700 tomorrow."

Howie was pleased to be honored with such an important task. "Is there anything I'm to tell Colonel Watson?"

"Negatory. He will give you something to bring back on the flight. You are *not* to tell the women about it. Do you understand?"

"Yes, sir. May I ask a question, sir?"

"Go ahead."

"Does this have anything to do with the German U-boat spotted on this side of the Atlantic? Or the cargo ship that mysteriously disappeared in the middle of the ocean?"

The general scowled. "Where did you hear those things?"

"People talk when they believe no one else is present. As though voices don't carry around corners. They think they are being cryptic on the telephone, but when enough seemingly unrelated pieces are fitted together, things start adding up." The ditty *Loose Lips Sink Ships* came to mind.

General Hawkins remained silent.

Had Howie overstepped? Should he have kept this to himself? He wanted to help if at all possible. He could better offer that help if the general knew Howie already possessed information.

"You are to keep what you think you know to yourself. Is that understood?"

"Yes, sir. I would never speak of it to anyone else. If there is something more I can do, I am ready and willing to assist in any way I can."

The general narrowed his eyes. "Colonel Watson has some documents you are to bring back. We need the utmost security on this."

"Are these documents about the U-boat?"

"That and German movements throughout the Atlantic."

"Sir, I won't fail you or these great United States." This responsibility was an honor. Maybe this was the sole reason the Lord had allowed Howie to be shot down and live: so he could be placed stateside at this time for this mission.

"You mustn't tell anyone: not your sergeant administrator and definitely not the women you will be traveling with."

"The WASPs are very patriotic. I'm sure the ones Cochran has chosen are trustworthy." Howie knew of one he wouldn't mind taking part in this mission.

"No one. Is that clear?"

"Clear, sir. Does that mean the WASPs believe they are retrieving an aircraft and nothing more?"

The general folded his hands on his desk. "It will appear like dozens of other missions they have gone on."

"Except I'll be along for the ride."

"Will you have any trouble getting them to believe you are merely along to oversee this mission?"

"No, sir." Howie would hopefully get them to think he believed his presence wasn't necessary, but orders were orders.

———— ≈ ————

On the westbound passenger train, Howie sat across the aisle from Mama Bird, Brownie, and Nightingale. Did these three always travel and work together? The hard bench—even though padded—made his hip ache where the pin had been put down his leg to hold it together while it healed. A revolutionary method born in the field hospitals of Europe. He, for one, was glad for the invention. If not for it, he might still be in a nearly full body cast.

He had his legs stretched out and his head leaned back. He would will the pain away.

Mama Bird shuffled a deck of cards. The rhythm of them swishing together repeatedly soothed him. As though it drew his discomfort away.

Why had Brownie been chosen for this trip? Wasn't she still healing from being shot in the foot? This was a strange first mission for her.

Though the women spoke softly across the aisle, their voices carried. Their conversation centered around not being trusted as female pilots, why men thought they needed a babysitter, and when would they ever be trusted. Indignation in every syllable of every comment.

Time for him to speak up, but he kept his eyes closed. He could picture them surprised he could hear them. "This isn't about you three or the WASP program in general. This is about me needing to learn more about the various tasks you ladies perform."

One of them, probably Nightingale, whispered, "He can hear us?"

"Yes, I can." At this point, he opened his eyes and sat up straight. "I simply need to get a better understanding of all the things you ladies contribute to the war effort."

Brownie squared her shoulders. "You're not trying to find fault with us?"

Nightingale glared at Brownie. "You shouldn't talk to him like that."

No, she shouldn't as Howie was her superior, but it was a legitimate question. "No. Even if I were, I doubt there would be any to find." And his true mission had nothing to do with them. He glanced toward Mama Bird and made eye contact to get a read on how she felt about this topic.

She held his steady gaze. Did her expression convey pleasure that he didn't have it in for them? Or was that his wishful hoping?

Why did this woman get under his skin when no other had?

He inclined his head toward Peggy as the cards flipped through her fingers, tapping together against each other. "You planning to play solitaire or gin rummy with those?"

Mama Bird shook her head as she bent them into an arch and let them slide flat into each other. "They're pinochle cards." She held up the deck. "Do you play?"

He had always enjoyed the game. Many of the men overseas played incessantly during their off time. There wasn't much else to do most of the time. "I do."

Her expression brightened. "We could use a fourth."

The other two women brightened as well.

Fraternizing with subordinates, especially female ones, was frowned upon. But if these were male pilots, he wouldn't hesitate.

"We still have two days of travel. Need to fill the time somehow."

Good point. "Sure."

They drew for partners. He rejoiced internally when he got paired with Mama Bird. They lost the first game but won the second.

Later, Nightingale sat with her back to the window and her feet up on the bench, reading a book. Brownie, next to Mama Bird, had set her knitting aside and tried to tuck her feet up under her while leaning on the window, blackened by the night.

Mama Bird indicated the bench across from Howie with the book she was reading. "You mind if I move across from you so Brownie can stretch out?"

"Not at all."

As she stood, Mama Bird patted Brownie's calf. "You can lie all the way down on the bench."

Sleepily, Brownie replied, "Thanks." She scooched down and laid curled on the barely padded seat.

He longed to stretch out in the berth the army paid for him but felt it unfair to the women. If they could ride three days on uncomfortable seats, so could he. So he had given his sleeping compartment to a young mother traveling alone with a baby.

Mama Bird sat across from him. "Thank you. These cross-country trips can be long, and we try to get sleep when we can."

His heartbeat rushed. Why did he have that schoolboy reaction to her sitting with him? As though this were the cafeteria and the most popular and prettiest girl in school were gifting him with her presence. *Settle down, Howie.*

"Thanks for playing pinochle with us earlier. We don't usually have trouble rounding up four players."

"It has been a while. Haven't had much chance since lying around in the hospital after I was shot down."

Her face muscles twitched to a momentary frown. "Does your leg hurt a lot?"

"Not like it did when I first stopped taking the pain medication. Some days are better than others, but I manage."

"I'm sure these train benches don't help."

"They aren't as bad as one would imagine. It's remaining stagnant that causes the most trouble. Makes it stiff and slow to move." After a moment, he asked her a question. "When did you know you wanted to be a pilot?"

"When I was eleven. My father and brother were both killed during the First Great War, so it was just me and my mom. I had become despondent and moody. We were a close family. The loss of Dad and Keith left a huge hole inside me. Mom took me to the state fair. When she saw how I lit up at the Curtiss JN-4 Jenny biplane that flew overhead, she scraped together the money to pay for a ride for me."

"I'm surprised the pilot would take you up because you were so young."

"He balked at first, but Mom told him her husband and son both gave their lives in the war this man had returned from. He refused Mom's money and took me up. Mom brought him a meatloaf sandwich and two dozen oatmeal cookies to thank him in spite of the fact I threw up after landing."

He couldn't believe she'd just told him that. "You did? So you didn't like flying? Why become a pilot then?"

"When the pilot first took off, I loved being up in the air and flying. Then I wondered what would happen if the pilot made a mistake, and I was suddenly terrified. When he landed and I got out of the Jenny, I threw up because I had let my fear tie my stomach into knots. I knew then that I wanted to be the one in control of the airplane."

"Even being so terrified, you wanted to go up again? Is that why you became a pilot? To get over your fear?"

"You could view it that way. I looked at it as not letting Tommy Higgins be in control."

"Tommy Higgins?"

"Winter of 1916. I was six, and the neighbor boy was eleven. He taunted me and said I was too afraid to go down the hill on the sled with him. Called me chicken."

"So you took the challenge."

"I did, but Tommy didn't steer the sled correctly. He veered off the path, and we went down an embankment. The crash broke my arm. Tommy broke a leg, a wrist, and his collar bone. My brother said it was a good thing 'that neighbor boy' was in the hospital, or he would punch him in the nose for hurting his baby sister."

Because of that event, she liked to be in control. Good to know.

She continued her story. "When I started taking flying lessons, I felt free up in the air, as though I could do anything."

"Did you get your pilot's license before you became a WASP?"

"Long before. More than fifteen years."

That put a chink in his thinking. She had been a licensed pilot twice as long as he had.

"I didn't fly much after having my first baby."

"Did your husband disapprove of you being a pilot?" A lot of men would.

"No. We had an airplane business, ferrying people and parcels. I was so in love with my baby daughter, I didn't want to leave her. I decided I would teach her to fly when she was old enough. Then another baby came along and then this war. I still want to encourage her to get her pilot's license if that's what she still wants to do."

The more Howie got to know this woman, the more incredible she was.

"What about you? Did you always want to be a pilot?"

"No. I was afraid of heights." He didn't normally divulge that to people, but since she had admitted to throwing up, he should reciprocate the trust. "I was in the army and was assigned to train as a pilot. I felt I had no choice. Once I learned to fly and was up in the air, I didn't like returning to earth."

"Did it cure your fear of heights?"

"Surprisingly, no. I know I'm much farther from the ground than even the tallest building I could climb, but being in an aircraft doesn't trigger it. Don't ask me to climb a ladder though." He chuckled at the silliness of it. "It makes no sense to me."

"It might defy logic, but it does make sense."

He couldn't imagine his fellow male pilots being so understanding. They would harass him about it.

She studied him with an intense gaze as though she were trying to figure him out.

"What's on your mind?"

She pressed her lips together. "I was wondering what your call sign is. Does it have anything to do with your fear? I know some pilots have given others dreadful call signs. My husband's wasn't bad. It was Spooner because of his last name, and also he liked to switch the beginning letters of words around when speaking."

Howie would have liked her husband. "Mine's not terrible either. Iceman. Last name Berg, which is short for Iceberg, which in turn became Iceman."

"I can see that."

He liked having her so focused on him. "You won't tell anyone about my fear, will you?"

"I won't."

He knew he could trust her.

From across the aisle, a voice rose. "I won't tell either."

"Nor I."

He glanced across to the two other WASPs. He should have known they could hear him if he could hear them earlier.

≡ CHAPTER 9 ≡

Peggy stretched her arms over her head as the train pulled into the station in Texas at 0657 on Monday. She disliked the long train rides to reach factories and bases they were sent to. During a brief layover yesterday at a station, she had been able to call home and talk to her mom and daughters. She missed them so much when she had to travel.

When the train stopped, the major stood. "There will be a car waiting to take us to the base."

Peggy glanced toward her fellow WASPs and raised her eyebrows. Jolene and Brownie shrugged.

Normally, when WASPs traveled to various locations, they paid their own way and had to make arrangements once they arrived for transportation to the base or factory. Having a major along was nice. She would not be the one to question it and retrieved her small suitcase without a word. The other two did the same.

Did the major know the army didn't usually pay for any of the WASPs' transportation expenses? Now wasn't the time to inform him.

Peggy, Jolene, and Brownie piled into the back of the military car, and the major climbed into the front.

At the base, the car drove directly to the hangar on the edge of the tarmac. Nearby sat the Lockheed B-34 Lexington, a medium bomber. Presumably the aircraft the WASPs had been sent to test, make any repairs necessary, and fly back to Bolling Field in DC.

Depending on the type and duration of the tests needed and subsequent adjustments and repairs would determine how long the layover here would be. Hopefully not more than a day or two.

Peggy, the other WASPS, and the major climbed out of the vehicle and strode into the cavernous building.

Captain Billingsly saluted Major Berg. The major saluted back. In case the captain expected to be saluted, Peggy snapped her right hand up to the corner of her eyebrow. Jolene and Brownie followed suit. The captain saluted back. After the formalities were over, everyone seemed to relax a little.

Captain Billingsly addressed Peggy. "The B-34 isn't ready for you ladies yet. We'll let you know when we need you."

In other words, go away. "How long do you expect it will be, sir?"

"Hard to tell. We'll let you know."

She could tell a subtle dismissal when faced with one. "May we go inspect the exterior?" It was better to do something rather than sit around bored.

The captain frowned. "I don't care."

Peggy turned to the major for approval.

He nodded.

Peggy and her comrades headed for the Lexington. "Shouldn't someone be working on this aircraft to prepare it to be test flown?"

Brownie heaved a sigh. "You would think so."

Jolene shook her head. "I get so tired of being brushed aside simply because I'm a woman."

Peggy was weary of it too. "We all feel the same. Eventually, they will realize how much we contribute and recognize us for it."

Jolene blurted out a laugh. "I doubt that."

Peggy chose to believe the way things worked now would change and improve. "We can at least do a preflight check of the exterior. If we find any issues, maybe they'll allow us to work on it while we wait. Maybe Major Berg will convince the captain to let us get to it."

A vehicle pulled up to the hangar, but not the same one that had brought them from the train station.

Jolene pointed to the car. "I wonder who that is."

Maybe someone to tell the hangar crew to let the WASPs do their jobs.

Peggy stared as Major Berg climbed into the car and left.

Jolene waved her hand toward the retreating vehicle. "How is he supposed to babysit and learn about our jobs if he's gone?"

How indeed?

Three hours later, Peggy, along with her friends, sat in the shade on the side of the hangar, with her head back against the exterior of the building. They had not been allowed to do anything more than a cursory check of the outside of the B-34 Lexington. Then they were told to go find something to do until the maintenance crew was ready for them. Where had the major gone?

Jolene spoke from beside her. "This is stupid. Why have us travel all this way on a less than comfortable train and not let us do anything? I think they do these kinds of things to us just to waste our time and humiliate us."

Peggy couldn't argue with that most of the time, but she didn't think Major Berg would do that to them. Then again, he wasn't the one to arrange this mission. "They'll give us something to do soon." They always did when they reached a point when they realized the WASPs weren't going anywhere.

A military vehicle pulled up to the open hangar door. The major climbed out with a briefcase and a small wooden crate with paper sacks lined up in it. When he looked at the ladies sitting there, he furrowed his eyebrows and strode toward them.

Peggy scrambled to her feet as did the other two and saluted. "Sir."

The major had the crate in his saluting hand. He scowled as though he wished he didn't need to return the salute.

Holding her hand in the proper position, Peggy stepped forward and gripped the small crate with her free hand.

"Thank you." He quickly saluted them. "At ease." He retrieved the crate.

Peggy could smell what she'd been trying not to think about. Food.

"What are you three doing out here?"

She poked her thumb toward the large open wall of the hangar. "We weren't wanted in there, and no one would give us a task to do. They wouldn't allow us inside the airplane to complete any checks.

We have no idea what will be involved to get this craft ready to fly."

The major shook his head. "We'll get that sorted out. In the meantime, I'm starved, so I figured you ladies were too."

Brownie shifted from one foot to the other and cringed, likely from her still healing foot. "I'm famished."

"Sandwiches and colas." He tilted his head toward the gaping door. "Let's see if there's someplace inside to sit."

A table off to one side had several chairs and made a good place to eat. All four quickly consumed their food.

Peggy crumpled her paper sack. "We would like to get started on the Lexington. Let me be honest. As WASPs we have often been made to wait for no reason." As much as she hated to make this request, she had little choice. "Would you see if they'll tell you what the holdup is?"

Major Berg stood. "I wish this wasn't the case, but some people are slow to accept the changes we face today. I'll see to it we get into that aircraft and assess how long it will take. Hopefully, we can leave later today or tomorrow." He retrieved the briefcase he'd returned with that he hadn't had on the train and crossed to the sergeant.

What was up with that briefcase?

Jolene swigged the last of her cola. "Do you think he'll be successful?"

"I hope so. I don't appreciate sitting around."

Brownie swallowed her final bite. "Me either. I want to be productive."

Berg returned. "He says he doesn't know but is contacting the deputy commander for maintenance."

Five minutes later, an army Jeep pulled up. A colonel climbed out, spoke to the sergeant, then approached the table. He must be the DCM.

Peggy and her fellow WASPs stood and saluted. Major Berg saluted as well.

Colonel Cox returned the salute. "As you were."

Berg lowered his hand. "Sir—"

"Major, you and these WASPs are cleared to depart immediately."

Peggy couldn't keep quiet. "But the Lockheed B-34 hasn't been checked or prepped. We have no idea what kind of condition that aircraft is in. Sir."

Cox fixed his gaze on Peggy. "You will find the plane is in fine shape with no issues."

Then what were she and her comrades doing here? She opened her mouth to give a retort but stopped when Major Berg lifted his hand to indicate it would be best not to rebut the colonel.

"Thank you, Colonel Cox. As soon as WASPs Witherspoon, Nightingale, and Brownie complete their preflight checks, we'll be on our way."

"Sergeant Hill will see you have anything you need." Colonel Cox strode back to the Jeep and drove off.

Major Berg turned to Peggy. "Let's preflight this bird and head home."

Peggy, the other WASPS, and the major collected their travel bags from the corner of the hangar and loaded them onto the Lexington. The preflight was completed quickly and without any issues. Why couldn't the men in the hangar have simply told them the Lockheed B-34 was in perfect working order? Why make them wait for nothing? Why make them think they were an annoyance and in the way?

Jolene flew as pilot, Peggy as the co, and Brownie as navigator. The major manned the radio. The course of the flight was uneventful.

Upon landing at Bolling Field, Major Berg addressed the three WASPs. "You are all free for the rest of the day."

Brownie squinted a bit. "This was the strangest trip I've ever been on. I can't figure out why we were even sent. Sure, we flew back a plane, but it was an odd trip."

Jolene echoed the sentiment.

It wouldn't be good for them to put too much thought into it or start asking questions. Best to let it drift into the past. "Who knows why the army does anything? I'll catch up with you two in a minute." Peggy held back to speak to the major.

Once the others were out of earshot, she indicated the attaché case the major hadn't let more than a few inches away from himself since it first appeared. "Sir, this wasn't about a standard WASP mission. We were nothing more than a cover for whatever you have in that briefcase."

He neither confirmed nor denied her conclusion and gave her a pointed look. "It's best not to talk that way. Don't mention this to anyone. Is that understood?" He didn't speak in a threatening way but a cautionary one.

"Yes, sir." That didn't stop her curiosity from wanting to know what was inside. Though she'd ventured to pray during the flight, she hadn't gotten the impression the major was doing anything nefarious. "I'm pleased to be a part of whatever mission the army needs me for, sir." She saluted him.

He saluted back. "The army is fortunate to have people like you. Even so, it's best no one knows you suspect anything. Put this all out of your mind."

She knew not to say anything and tilted her head slightly. "Suspect anything about what?" She winked.

He chuckled. "Exactly. I'll see you tomorrow." He strode off.

She watched him go and felt a loss at his parting. She longed for more time with him. Though she'd initially been annoyed he'd been sent on this trip to babysit the WASPs, it had ended too soon.

Howie headed to Brigadier General Hawkins's office in the Pentagon. He'd been glad Witherspoon hadn't pressed the matter about the briefcase. Before he reached the desk sergeant, the enlisted man stood.

"He's waiting for you, sir." The sergeant crossed to the door and opened it.

Howie had never been ushered into a superior's office so quickly. "Thank you." Inside, he stood at attention. The door shut behind him.

"At ease. Take a seat." General Hawkins held his gaze.

Howie sat.

"Any trouble?"

"No, sir." Howie lifted the briefcase onto his lap and opened it. "Here are the documents Colonel Watson gave me to give to you." He handed over two files.

The general glanced through them. "Did Watson brief you on what is in these?"

MRS. WITHERSPOON GOES TO WAR

"He did, sir. If they were destroyed along the way for some reason, I was a sort of back up copy."

"Understood. The ladies don't know what was in here, do they?"

"No, sir." It wasn't important to mention Witherspoon had been curious. If asked directly, he'd tell the general. "Sir, why wasn't this information relayed over a secure telephone line or dispatched by courier from there. Either would have been faster."

"There are those who believe we might have some leaks. No one would suspect WASPs of transporting anything of importance. It is vital that no one suspects we know a German U-boat is headed our way."

Surprise was always a good tactic. Unless, of course, one were sneaking up on an intriguing WASP.

◣ CHAPTER 10 ◢

12 September 1944, 2115 GMT

US Navy thwarts German U-boat's
attempt to attack the Panama Canal.
U-boat slips through Navy blockade and escapes.

Peggy stood outside Babs's office. For the past four days, she hadn't been able to get the Texas trip off her mind. She kept telling herself Major Berg was a good man and officer who would never do anything to intentionally harm the United States. Which she truly believed. So why did a little voice within repeatedly whisper, *But what if he's not so good? What if he's been fooling you and everyone? What if he's a traitor and you said nothing?*

With apprehension, she had prayed about what to do, which surprised her. Talking to God seemed natural for the first time in a long time, and it comforted her. Maybe the lingering stalemate was coming to an end. Or was it merely a temporary armistice? Either way, she relished the reprieve for as long as it would last.

That praying had brought her here to her superior's office. She wanted to put to rest the questions tumbling around inside her.

Once invited in, she stood before a woman of integrity she highly respected. "Ma'am."

Babs shuffled the papers before her. "Ma'am is it? Something must be bothering you."

"Yes, ma'am. It's about the Texas trip."

"I didn't think there were any problems. I read your mission report as well as Nightingale's and Brownie's. Nothing in them mentioned anything out of the ordinary."

Uncertainty about her decision to come to her superior pressed in on her. Could she respectfully back out of this? She didn't want to needlessly throw suspicion on Major Berg and cause him trouble.

"Out with it, Peggy."

She had gone too far to retreat now. "I have debated whether or not to bring this to you. If an Army Air Corps officer tells you not to mention something, but you don't even know what that something is, would it be disobeying an order to say something?"

"Because you mentioned Texas, I'll assume the officer in question is Major Berg. Since you're bothered, tell me what this is about."

"I—we were under the impression that. . .the officer had come along to gain a better understanding of what the WASPs do." It might be best not to use his name just in case. "We were there for only a few minutes when a car came and took the officer away. He returned over three hours later with a briefcase he hadn't had before. When I asked him about it, he said I shouldn't mention it. I don't believe he was doing or would do anything wrong, but I felt derelict in my duties not to mention it. I don't want to get him into any kind of trouble."

Babs remained silent for several heartbeats. "I told Jackie when she handpicked the three of you, that at least one of you would notice something."

"Jackie Cochran? Handpicked me?" Peggy had no idea the head of the WASP even knew of her.

"Yes. I can assure you that the reasons for Major Berg to be in Texas go up to the highest clearances. You have nothing to worry about. Did you voice your concerns to Nightingale or Brownie?"

"No, ma'am."

"Do you believe they suspected anything?"

"Neither of them acted as though they did. Should I have not brought this up? Should I have let this go?"

"We all need to let our consciences be our guides. One of the things I appreciate about you is your honesty and your compassion for others."

Comforted after her talk with Babs, Peggy headed back to the hangar. She couldn't believe that Jackie Cochran even knew her name, let alone thought so highly of her as to recommend her for such an important mission.

Peggy entered the hangar where Jolene had removed the engine cover of the Brewster F2A Buffalo and worked inside the compartment. After the tow target debacle, the Buffalo had seemed fine. Not all of the damage had revealed itself right away. "How does it look in there?"

Jolene removed her head from inside the craft. "Not too bad. I would guess that it was partially from fatigue, and the maneuvers required during the flight, which hastened its demise. Would you hand me a three-eighths wrench?"

Peggy passed her the tool. "That means, the tow incident wasn't the downfall of this craft. Things wear out. It's good to have caught it now rather than have it fail in the air."

Jolene waggled the wrench. "Incident? Stupidity is more like it."

Peggy had to agree but being too disparaging and keeping the incident fresh in everyone's mind would only serve to widen the divide between the WASPs and their male army counterparts. No one would benefit from that. "I'm just grateful no one was hurt worse and things turned out all right."

Brownie approached. "I'm worried about Edith." Edith was one of the youngest WASPs.

Peggy gave Brownie her full attention. "What's wrong?"

"I think she's going to drop out of the WASP program."

Jolene stopped her work. "She can't do that."

"Why would she want to quit?" Peggy had noticed the young woman was a bit melancholy.

"She's terribly homesick and cries most nights."

Jolene nodded. "I've heard her too."

The poor kid. For some of the WASPs, this was the first time they had been away from home. Many were far, far from their loved ones. Unlike Peggy and her husband, who had been able to move her mom and their daughters to the greater DC area. "I would hate to see her quit. She's an excellent pilot."

Jolene set aside the wrench. "Not to mention the irreparable damage it would do to the WASP reputation."

Brownie tilted her head. "Reputation?"

Jolene thinned her lips. "If she quits, it will look bad on all of us. It will prove everyone's point that we women shouldn't fly."

"I hadn't thought of that." Brownie turned her attention on Peggy for her reaction.

That idea had been forming in Peggy's head as Jolene spoke it. "She probably just misses her family." Homesickness generally passed if given enough time. The key was to hold out until the strong desire to flee melted away. "What if I invite her over this weekend for a get-together. It might help her endure her loneliness. Of course, you two are invited."

Brownie flashed a smile. "That sounds like fun. Should we invite any of the other WASPs?"

With only ten, Peggy didn't want to leave some out. "We'll invite all of them stationed at Bolling." She knew that a couple of them wouldn't come for their own reasons, whether it was family nearby or clashing personalities.

Jolene glanced around the hangar at the various male mechanics working on their projects. "What about the men on the maintenance crew? I know some of them are missing home."

"We'll invite them too. My backyard isn't huge, but I don't think people will mind. A break from our normal routines will be good for morale." The mere thought had already boosted Peggy's.

Brownie shifted her weight to her uninjured foot. "We could have each person bring a different type of food to share."

Jolene's eyes brightened. "Great idea. Do we want to make a list so people don't all bring the same dishes?"

Pleased to have her friends excited, Peggy didn't want to make this complicated with a list. "It might be harder for some to make a dish than others. I think whatever people bring will be fine. If we have all desserts or something, then that tells me we all sort of need a dessert day. We'll enjoy whatever is provided."

Brownie nodded. "We'll let the Lord sort out what people bring."

Didn't God have more important things to worry about?

Jolene pinned Peggy with her gaze. "Can I announce the invitation in here, right now?"

The sooner people knew, the more time they would have to figure out what to bring. "That's fine with me."

Jolene stepped away from the Buffalo she had been working on. "Hey, everyone. Mama Bird is inviting all of you to her backyard for a get-together on Saturday afternoon. All the WASPs and those in the hangar are invited. Bring whatever food you can spare."

Cheers rose from around the room.

Simply being invited was already lifting people's attitudes.

Someone called out, "*Everyone* here is invited?"

"Every—" Jolene halted.

Why? Peggy knew not everyone got along but all were welcome. "Everyone is invited."

That same person pointed. "Even them?"

She didn't want anyone to feel left out. "Of course." Peggy turned to see whom the soldier referred to. Major Berg stood with two captains. He studied her as though he wasn't sure she'd meant it. Enlisted and officers socializing together? Maybe not the best idea, but not unheard of. She couldn't very well take back her invitation. "Yes, they're welcome too." But would they come? Surprisingly, she hoped so.

She held the major's gaze to try to read whether or not he would come.

He gave her a nod before turning his attention back to the two captains with him.

What had that nod meant? Yes, he planned to come? Or was it a nod of approval for inviting people to help boost morale?

Hopefully, both.

≡ CHAPTER II ≡

17 September 1944, 0739 GMT

US Navy Sinks German U-boat attempting
to enter the Gulf of Mexico.

On Saturday, Peggy stood in her kitchen, preparing a couple of dishes to take out into the backyard. Her insides twitched. She couldn't believe the thrill she felt at the prospect Major Berg might come today.

When she had invited the WASPs and maintenance crews to her home, she hadn't realized Major Berg, Captain Cooper, and Captain Lewiston were in the hangar. She couldn't very well withdraw the invitation. Nor did she want to, surprisingly. None of the three had said they would come, but they also didn't decline the invitation. Not that any of them had much of a chance to, given they were dealing with the Great Atlantic Hurricane that had rushed up the Eastern Seaboard. Peggy, along with every able-bodied pilot in the area, had flown the Army Air Corps and US Navy aircraft inland until the risk was over. Fortunately the threat had passed in time to still hold the gathering in her backyard.

The major and Captain Lewiston were both bachelors, and Captain Cooper's wife was out of town. This barbecue was good for morale. Most of the WASPs lived in barracks at Bolling Field. The event would give them a chance for a change of scenery because Peggy lived in Oxen Hill, Maryland, just outside the airfield.

How could she be this nervous? She saw the major all the time at Bolling Field. But he'd never been to her home. She should have spoken to him and told him that she hadn't meant to invite him and the other two officers. He would have understood, wouldn't he? But the truth was a part of her wanted him to come, and if he came, it was best a couple of other officers came as well so it didn't appear as though there was something between herself and the major. Because there wasn't.

WASPs were strongly discouraged from developing romantic entanglements with the army men. It could cause serious issues between the men and women and strain relations between the two organizations, the Army Air Corps and the WASP. It had been a long, hard-fought battle for women to fly military aircraft. No one wanted to jeopardize the state of the organization. Also most of the female pilots were serious about the work they accomplished. They didn't want to risk being dismissed for conduct unbecoming a WASP.

Peggy's daughters ran into the kitchen. Her oldest said, "A bunch of people just came."

Peggy went to the living room and peered out the front window. A bus with Bolling Airfield stenciled on the side sat parked on the street, and over a dozen WASPs and maintenance crew poured out, each carrying some sort of food. Even with ration books, it appeared everyone was generous.

She studied the disembarking occupants of the bus. No Major Berg. Disappointment settled heavily on her. He must have realized it would be best if he and the captains didn't attend. Of course if they decided to come, as officers they wouldn't have ridden the bus but would have requisitioned a car from the motor pool.

She stepped out the front door and pointed to the side. "Go through the gate. Tables are set up in the back."

The gaggle of people chattered as they headed around the house.

Peggy approached Brownie, who limped along. "How did your doctor's appointment go yesterday?"

"Almost better. The doc said to be careful for a couple of more weeks and limited my use of it. I can't wait to be walking normally again."

"I'm glad you're following doctor's orders so you heal properly."

"Has nothing to do with the doctors. Poole threatened to separate me from the WASP program altogether and send me home if I reinjured myself."

Being separated from the program was a mighty deterrent. "I have a chair with a footstool for you in the back."

Jolene gave her a nod. "I'll see that she gets there, and I'll boot anyone off who took her spot."

The WASPs looked out for one another. She liked that about them. They were like a family. Peggy returned to the kitchen, gathered her food offerings, and headed out to the backyard. She shouldn't be this disappointed over the major not showing up. What was it about the man that had tangled him up in her thoughts? A few more soldiers arrived, a couple with their wives and children.

Minutes later, several people stood at attention, and one of them said, "Yard, atten-*hut*." Which caused the remainder of the people, including Peggy, to jolt to attention and snap a salute.

Her heart sped up and her insides smiled at the sight of Major Berg.

The major waved his cane. "None of that today. At ease. I'm just Howie. Same goes for the captains."

Peggy relaxed.

Some smart aleck called out, "Their names are Howie too?"

The major smiled and shook his head.

One captain said, "Joe will do for today."

"I think I prefer Howie to my name," the other captain said. "But that will get confusing, so you may call me *your majesty*." With a wave of his hand, he made a flourishing bow.

Howie shook his head. "He's Elmer."

He glared at his superior sideways. "That's King Elmer."

Someone threw a crumpled napkin at him, and several others laughed.

Peggy breathed deeply of contentment. This was what this gathering was about, allowing everyone to unwind and raise people's spirits.

Major Berg strolled over to her. "I hope you don't mind that we came. I know it's unorthodox, but I thought they could use the change of scenery. Everyone's tense with this war."

"Major, I'm glad you three came." Though her pleasure was mostly for his attendance. "I wanted this to be a morale booster."

"It's Howie for today, and I think you've succeeded."

She didn't know if she should be thinking of him by his first name. Using *major* kept things professional and her heart reined in. "All right." However, she would be careful not to use either *Howie* or *major*.

An hour later, her youngest daughter stood under the large elm tree and wailed, "I want my dolly!" Then she screeched her words: *"I—Want—Penelope!"*

Sergeant Kent's eleven-year-old son had thrown Junie's rag doll up into the tree. The sergeant went over to his son who was taunting Junie and scolded him.

Suddenly her daughter stopped crying.

Major Berg—Howie—stood next to Junie.

Peggy walked over. "Sweetie, it's all right. We'll borrow Mr. Sawyer's ladder later and get her down."

"No, Mommy. Mr. Howie will get my dolly."

Howie gazed right at Peggy. "Do you mind if I try?"

The major wouldn't be able to climb up and get it. Not with his bum leg. "I can't ask you to do that."

"No one asked. I offered." He gazed at her with his molten gray eyes, and she melted.

"Are you sure?"

"Yes, ma'am."

Should she tell him no for his own safety? Or let him try? Certainly, he knew his limitations. "If you're sure, then I guess so." She bit her bottom lip in anticipation of the risk he would be taking.

He pointed to a place in the grass directly below where the doll hung precariously by one foot. "Stand right there."

Junie moved to the spot, her blue eyes wide in expectation.

Howie shifted his weight and balanced on his good leg. Then he lifted his cane into the branches.

Peggy smiled. Smart of him. No climbing necessary.

He spoke to her five-year-old. "Get ready to catch her."

With big round eyes, Junie thrust her arms out wide. Too far apart to have any hope of catching her doll.

Peggy crouched beside her daughter and adjusted her small arms to form a cradle.

Howie angled his cane toward the target. "Ready?"

Her little girl nodded.

He poked at the doll with the tip of his cane.

The foot came free, and dolly dropped into Junie's waiting arms. She hugged it to her chest.

Everyone clapped and cheered.

Howie lowered his cane to the ground and hopped a little to retain his balance, then bowed.

Junie turned to her. "Mommy, he saved Penelope."

Peggy had seen. A regular hero. "I saw. Did you thank him?"

Her little girl ran over to the major. "Thank you for saving Penelope." With the doll in one hand, she threw her arms around his midsection.

Peggy gasped and hoped her daughter didn't knock him over, but he remained steady.

Howie smiled down at the five-year-old. "You are very welcome."

The rest of the afternoon, Junie stayed close to the major, even sitting on his lap. She brought him a book, which he was now reading to her.

Her baby girl missed having her daddy, though Peggy wasn't sure how much her daughter remembered of her father. She'd been three the last time she saw him. It was sweet of the major to be so kind to her daughter.

———— ≈ ————

Howie finished the story and closed the book. "The end."

Junie gazed up at him and blinked. "My daddy died in the war."

What had brought that up? "I know. I'm sorry you lost your daddy, but I'm sure he fought bravely."

The little girl snatched the book, scooted off his lap, and ran inside.

Should he have not said so much to her comment about her father? Or had he done something wrong in how he read the story?

Peggy strolled over. "Thank you for being so kind to her."

He stood as he'd been taught to when a lady was standing. "She's a darling. She's going to break a few hearts when she gets older."

"I'm not ready for her to grow up that fast. She's going to be my little girl until she's thirty."

He chuckled. His own parents had said similar things about his sister until she became a difficult teenager. "Did I do something wrong to make her run away like that?"

Peggy flashed him a beautiful smile. "On the contrary. She loved having you read to her. She delights in any and all attention."

But the child ran away. He didn't understand. "Then what happened?"

"She's getting another book."

How could Peggy know that? He liked thinking of her by her first name.

Junie ran out the back door with three books in her hands. When she reached Howie, she pushed on her mother's thigh. "Move, Mommy. He has to sit down." The blue-eyed imp gazed up at him. Eyes the color of her mother's.

Peggy stepped aside and shrugged as though saying, *I told you*.

He chuckled and sat.

The little girl scurried onto Howie's lap again. "Read this one."

"Junie, did you ask if he wanted to read you another story?"

"Please, Mr. Howie. Read me another story." She blinked rapidly.

Yep, this one was going to break hearts.

"You can refuse. You have already done enough."

Howie smiled at Peggy. "I don't mind. I can read her one more."

Peggy smiled back. "She won't stop at one. You have been warned."

He didn't mind if it caused a smile like that from the courageous pilot.

Peggy's other daughter came over and stood next to the chair as he read.

"Do you want to sit too?"

Wendy shook her head. She seemed a little reticent, so he didn't press her. Instead he focused on the first of the three volumes, *The Velveteen Rabbit*.

After those three storybooks and sometime later, Howie had gone inside the house to use the facilities. On his way back out, when he turned the corner toward the living room, he nearly ran into Peggy.

She gasped, so his presence must have startled her. She stumbled sideways. Her foot caught on the leg of the end table, and her arms circled in the air.

He instinctively reached out and latched his arms around her. His cane clunked to the floor. He hadn't realized he'd let go of it. Now he was in a bit of a pickle. His awkward balance threatened to take him down. If he released her, he might fall. Equally, she still seemed off balance as she held onto him, so she might tumble to the ground. He couldn't have that. He shifted his weight and regained his footing. She seemed to be stable now as well. So why didn't he release her? Neither did she appear to try to free herself.

His pulse raced as he peered into her blue eyes, almost the color of a cloudless sky. He shifted his gaze to her mouth, the shade of ripening raspberries, but not a fraudulent lipstick shade, their natural hue.

She licked her lips.

Did she want him to kiss her? He wanted to kiss her.

Tiny footsteps thumping in from the back door and Junie calling out, "Mr. Howie?" broke the spell. They stepped away from each other.

As the little girl raced into the room, Howie steadied himself on the end table and retrieved his fallen cane. He took a slow breath and straightened. That had been close. He'd almost crossed a forbidden line.

Junie beamed at him. "There you are." She snatched his hand and pulled. "Penelope wants you to come outside. We set up a tea party on the grass."

It was best he and Peggy had been interrupted. He glanced at her. Her cheeks now matched her lips. He hadn't imagined anything could fluster this tough cookie, especially after her calm reaction to being in the line of fire.

More incredible all the time.

———— ≈ ————

That evening, while her daughters got dressed for bed, Peggy stood at the sink, washing dishes. Today had not only been successful but fun. She hadn't realized how much she had needed this break from the routine.

Her mom stood next to her drying a plate. "That major is quite a catch."

Peggy's insides danced at the mention of him. "Mom, please don't." She was having a hard enough time attempting to ignore what almost happened this afternoon—and failing in the effort. Would he have kissed her if Junie hadn't come in? Did she want him to?

"You have to admit he's special and handsome to boot."

That he was on both accounts, but it was too dangerous to admit it.

"All I'm saying is you're still young. You shouldn't spend the rest of your life alone."

Peggy made a half turn to face her mom. "You have. I was about Wendy's age when Daddy was killed in the First World War. You never remarried."

Mom put the plate in the open cupboard. "I never had someone like Howie looking at me the way that man studied you."

He had been looking at her? In some special way? That was beside the point. "WASP and army are not supposed to fraternize. We keep everything professional."

"So what do you call today? I saw a lot of fraternizing."

It could appear that way. "Morale boosting."

Mom gave a disagreeing half grunt and half laugh. "It was still fraternizing even if you don't call it that."

Mom was right, but Peggy would ignore it. It was one afternoon and everyone would return to the order of things before. No harm done.

Except to Peggy's heart. It would take her some time before she would be able to stop thinking about the major almost kissing her. Well, he hadn't *actually* almost kissed her. That thought probably hadn't even crossed his mind. She was the one who had entertained the idea of his lips touching hers. He was merely trying to keep his balance. Though startled, his nearness had been what had knocked *her* off balance. She would do her best to expunge that encounter from her memory.

No matter how hard that would prove to be.

CHAPTER 12

On Monday, Howie sat at his office desk. He'd had a better time than he thought he would at Peggy's—no, WASP Witherspoon's. He'd allowed himself, for one day, to drop rank and formalities, but he couldn't slip at work. Her daughters were so cute. That little one had not only climbed onto his lap, but she might have climbed into his heart as well. Witherspoon and her girls made him want a different life. A life he couldn't have. A life full of hope and promise. They provoked dreams he hadn't realized he'd held before they had been shot down over Europe. Apparently, he hadn't been as content to be a confirmed bachelor as he'd thought.

Captain Cooper knocked on Howie's open office door. "Hello, Romeo."

Howie squinted at him. He liked the captain. Since the man wasn't his direct subordinate, he'd allowed a friendship to develop. "What?"

"You and the lady, Peggy Witherspoon."

"It wasn't like that. We were all there for a break and to blow off a little steam." Howie had barely spent any time with her. Except for that moment in the living room when he'd contemplated kissing her. Fortunately, the little one had come in.

Joe entered all the way and sat in the chair across the desk. "Oh, it was like that. You rescued her daughter's doll and then you let the girl sit on your lap and read her stories. If that wasn't enough, you agreed to attend her other daughter's spelling bee."

"So?" What did any of that have to do with Peggy?

The captain shook his head. "You haven't had children, so you don't understand the bond between a mother and her children. If you hurt one of her children, even just a little bruised feeling, a mother will kill you, and you won't even see it coming. You waltzed in there with your fancy cane and rescued the princess—the doll—from the tower. Then you won the little princess over with stories, and made promises to the other princess. Your actions didn't go unnoticed by the queen. You might as well have given her a bouquet of flowers and a box of chocolates. Though they wouldn't have been nearly as effective."

Howie *had* given Peggy a bouquet of flowers before. Joe didn't need to know that. It had been a mistake. "I am not trying to woo WASP Witherspoon. That sort of thing is frowned upon."

"You saw Sergeant Kent's boy taunting the little girl, and you raced in like a knight in shining armor."

Hardly a knight. If he could equate himself to a knight at all, it would be more like a rusted and dented one. "I was only being nice." Yet the thought of Peggy appreciating his actions *was* pleasing. *Very* pleasing.

"This war won't go on forever, and the Women Airforce Service Pilots will have served their purpose and go back to being housewives."

"But there will still be WASPs. The program will go on." Wouldn't it? He couldn't imagine someone like Mama Bird grounded.

Joe tilted his head and pulled a face. "It'll be like with the First World War. The men will return from overseas, and the women will return to the home."

Howie hadn't thought much about what would happen after the war. Would Peggy and the other WASPs acquiesce to the life they had before? Likely, but he suspected a few would try to remain and continue to fight for the chance to actually be military members in the Army Air Corps. The likelihood of that happening was slim. Men wouldn't easily give up dominance in the air.

If Howie's actions at the get-together could be misinterpreted by Peggy, then he probably shouldn't attend her other daughter's spelling bee competition. People, including Peggy and her family, might get the wrong impression.

He might too.

———— ≈ ————

Two days later, Howie slipped into the back of the Oxen Hill elementary school gymnasium and sat in the last row. The spelling bee proceedings had already started with opening remarks and introductions of the ten students competing. Wendy wore a pleated plaid skirt, a white blouse with small puffed sleeves, and saddle shoes. He had his mother and sister to thank for his female-clothing knowledge.

He hadn't been able to dislodge Witherspoon's daughter Wendy from his thoughts. She had smiled so brightly when her little sister had invited him to her big sister's spelling bee. Wendy had seemed quite pleased when he'd agreed to attend. He'd won a spelling bee or two in his school days.

He probably shouldn't have come because of the way it might appear to some people, but he would keep his promise to the girl. If he could catch her gaze while she was on the stage, she would know he had kept his word. No one else needed to know of his presence.

The room was full of women with only the occasional older man. Presumably, the fathers of these students were entangled in some aspect of the war. Howie searched the backs of heads for Peggy. He shouldn't be looking for her, but he couldn't help himself. Without her flight suit and without her head wrapped in one of those scarf turbans, she could be most any of these women.

Put her out of your mind, Howie, and focus on the sweet girl you came to support.

Of the competing students, seven were boys and three were girls. The odds weren't in favor of a girl winning. How would Wendy do? According to her little sister, she was the best speller in the world. So heartwarming to see siblings who thought the best of each other.

The first two rounds retained all the participants. Round three knocked out one of the boys. Round four eliminated one boy and two of the girls, leaving Wendy as the sole female contestant. He prayed she received words she knew how to spell for the next few rounds, at least.

A grandmotherly woman in the front row stood, blocking his view of Wendy. Even though it wasn't the girl's turn, Howie liked to

MARY DAVIS

watch her face to see her reaction to words other contestants were given. With each one, he detected her lips moving as though silently spelling the words. Now the woman stood in his way.

Please sit down.

She stretched out her arm and a small hand gripped hers, then she moved to the aisle. Peggy's mother, Muriel, and Junie.

His heart swelled with affection for the little poppet. Holding her grandmother's hand, Junie half skipped and half. . . what? Danced? Her doll tucked under one arm. He smiled at the memory of rescuing Penelope. His heart swelled for the little mite.

As the pair headed toward him, he realized they would see him sitting in the aisle seat. He needed to go unnoticed. *Look straight ahead, Howie. Maybe they won't notice you.*

Closer and closer. Almost to him and still no recognition. He wasn't surprised with all the little girl's flapping around.

"Mr. Howie!"

Caught. He turned to the little girl and smiled. In a whisper, he said, "Hello, Junie." He tapped the doll's arm. "Hello, Penelope." He lifted his gaze to the grandmother. "Hello."

The grandmother had the same blue eyes as her daughter. She whispered too. "Good evening, Major Berg. You made it."

"I did."

Junie wiggled. "I have to go to the restroom. That's what they call it at school, but I don't need to rest."

"All right, Junie. Let's go." Muriel guided the little one away.

His mission to go unseen had failed, but it didn't really bother him. Hopefully Peggy wouldn't mind that he'd come.

A few minutes later, Junie stood next to him again and pulled on his hand. "Come sit with us."

"I—um. . ."

With her voice soft, Muriel said, "Junie, you know there aren't any free seats up where we are."

Howie mouthed "Thank you" to the older woman.

She nodded in reply. "Does Peggy know you're here?"

"I doubt it. I didn't arrive until after the event started."

"She'll be glad to know you made it."

That would be nice, but it wasn't likely. "I told Wendy I would come. I'm a man of my word."

Muriel's mouth pulled up at the corners. "I'm sure you are."

There seemed to be more to the woman's simple comment than met the eye, but Howie wasn't quite sure what. Feeling a need to fill them in, he whispered and pointed toward the stage. "The boy in the yellow plaid shirt is out. He misspelled *ruefully*. Wendy was given *tasty* for her word. She spelled it brilliantly."

"That's my girl. A lot of students forget to drop the *e* before adding the *y*. We'll see you after the event." Muriel led Junie up the aisle, but the little girl kept her head swung around toward him and nearly fell twice. If not for her grandmother, she would have landed on the ground.

Howie had planned to slip out as soon as this was over so he didn't cause Peggy any discomfort. No chance of doing that now. He watched where the pair sat and discovered which woman was Peggy. She turned and, upon spying him, smiled. He returned the gesture and gave her a nod. She had seemed pleased he was here. He felt a little foolish for hiding in the back.

Two more rounds of no one missing a word, then the next round knocked out three of the remaining boys. That left Wendy and the boy in the slightly too-small blazer.

This was nerve-racking, almost as stressful as facing the enemy in the unfriendly skies half a world away. Peggy must be tied up in all sorts of knots. Three more turns a piece and both students were still in the competition.

Then blazer boy misspelled *rhythm*, but that didn't make Wendy the winner. She needed to spell her word correctly.

Wendy stepped up to the microphone.

"*Recognition.*"

Howie sucked in air and held it.

"May I hear it used it in a sentence?" Wendy's soft voice drifted through the speakers.

The judge did so, then when requested, gave the definition and word origin.

This was a smart move on the girl's part. It gave her more time to contemplate the spelling.

"*Recognition.* R–e. . .c–o. . ."

Come on, Wendy, you can do it.

". . .g. . .n–i. . .t–i–o–n. *Recognition.*"

Howie expelled his breath. "Yes!"

The older woman on the other side of the two empty chairs eyed him. "Is she your child?"

"No. The daughter of a friend." But if he were to have a daughter, he would be proud to have one like Wendy.

Peggy blew the air out of her lungs. *Recognition* had been a troublesome word for Wendy. Possibly the first time she'd spelled it correctly without help. Only a week ago, her daughter had crumpled into tears at not being able to spell *recognition* along with a handful of other difficult words that were above her grade level. She had her father's determination.

Junie slid off her chair. "Did Wendy win?"

"She did."

"Okay." Junie attempted to scoot past Peggy.

Peggy snagged her little arm. "Where are you off to?"

"To tell Mr. Howie Wendy won."

Peggy lifted her youngest onto her lap. "He could see and knows. Your sister still needs to be given her award, so please sit still." She hadn't needed that reminder to be acutely aware of the major's presence in the large room. Since her daughter had returned from the restroom and informed her he'd come, it was as though he were right beside her.

She had cautioned Wendy that the major might not make it and she shouldn't get her hopes up. Her daughter hadn't heeded her warning, so Peggy's gratitude that Major Berg had been able to come welled within her. Excitement twirled inside her at seeing him in a non-work setting again.

The person in charge of the spelling bee event presented Wendy with her first-place "medal" hanging from a red ribbon. With all metals being used for the war effort, the medallion was a carved wooden disk with *Spelling Bee 1st Place* burned into it. *Oxen Hill Elementary* and *September 19, 1944* had been burned onto the reverse side. Peggy appreciated the school's sensitivity in not using any kind of metal. Some parents had been displeased with the decision.

Once the ceremony portion was completed and the audience dismissed, Peggy stood to meet Wendy at the front, while keeping a firm hold on Junie's hand.

Junie pulled free and headed down the aisle toward the back of the gymnasium. "Excuse me. Please move."

"Junie, come back. Junie?"

"Please move. Please move." Junie wiggled her little form between people.

Mom tapped Peggy on the shoulder. "I'll go after her. We'll meet you in the hallway."

"Thanks, Mom." Peggy would like to go herself to hopefully catch Major Berg before he escaped. She hoped he didn't leave before Wendy could see that he'd come. She would at least tell her daughter he'd made it so she would know.

As she approached Wendy, Junie's request for people to move out of her way still filtered to the front.

Peggy hugged her oldest daughter. "I'm so proud of you."

Wendy held out the award hanging around her neck. "I spelled *recognition.*"

"I know." Her daughter's award had been expertly crafted by the father of one of the teachers. The carving and wood staining he'd done was excellent along with the burning of the lettering. He'd even carved a bumble bee on the front. This was better than anything made out of metal.

Wendy leaned to peer around her mom. "Mr. Howie came. I saw him in the last row."

"I know."

"I want to show him my award." Wendy moved toward the cluster of people. "Do you think he's still here?"

If Junie had anything to do with it, he was, and if he tried to leave, her baby girl would drag him back. "Let's go see." The major certainly made an impression on her daughters.

He'd made an impression on Peggy as well.

The crowd in the gymnasium thinned. No sign of the major, but neither was there any sign of Mom or Junie.

Out in the hallway, Mom stood with Major Berg. At his side, Junie held his hand. He appeared to be completely at ease and so natural standing there with her daughter's hand in his. Anyone passing by, could easily mistake him for Junie's father.

Peggy mentally shook herself. She should not be having thoughts of her commanding officer.

Wendy rushed over to him, holding out her medallion. "Look."

The major leaned his cane against his leg so he would have a free hand and fingered the award. "This is great. You spelled some pretty tough words."

Wendy beamed up at him. "I studied really hard. I never spelled *recognition* right before."

"But you did today when it counted. That's impressive." He released the wooden medal and reached for his cane.

Peggy's heart hurt a little for her daughter drinking in this man's praise. Wendy longed for her father's attention and approval. She remembered her father and missed him.

The willingness of this man to support and interact with her daughters triggered appreciation and respect for him Peggy hadn't expected.

⟩ CHAPTER 13 ⟨

The next day, with her fingertips touching the corner of her right eyebrow, Peggy stood at attention in Brigadier General Hawkins's office on Bolling Airfield. Jackie Cochran sat off to the side.

The general saluted back. "At ease."

Peggy shifted her feet a shoulder's width apart and tucked her hands at the small of her back. What was this meeting about? Why would two of the top military personnel want to see her? Had she done something wrong? She couldn't think of what. Nothing to do but simply wait it out until they told her.

The general steepled his hands. "Do you know why you are here?"

"No, sir."

"You recently went on a mission to Texas."

This was about that? Was she in trouble? Or was Major Berg? "Yes, sir."

"I understand you suspected something was amiss with the trip."

Peggy stood silent. She hadn't been directly asked a question and wasn't sure how she should respond.

"Your husband was killed in the line of duty."

Why was he bringing up George? "Yes, sir."

"How does that make you feel about this war and your country, having to raise your daughters without their father?"

"I'm not sure I understand your question, sir."

Cochran spoke up. "Do you resent this war? Do you resent the United States of America for sending your husband to Europe to die?"

"There are people on the other side of the world suffering far worse than me. Governments doing terrible things to their citizens. My husband gladly volunteered to go. Even if he knew ahead of time he would die"—which he seemed to sense—"he still would have gone. I am proud of my husband, proud that he was the kind of man to stand up for others. If I resent anyone, it is Hitler and the other Axis powers for harming so many people. For the individuals who support them. Permission to speak freely, sir, ma'am?"

General Hawkins raised his eyebrows. "I thought you were. Go ahead."

Maybe she should hold her tongue, but when else would she be given the opportunity to say what was on her mind? "I resent that I'm not allowed to do more to serve my country, that so many limits are placed on WASPs, on women. I know a lot of ladies who feel the same. We are more capable than we are given credit for. Russian female pilots fight in combat." She wanted to say more, to bring up the mistreatment of WASPs by some members of the military. For now, this was probably enough.

The general's desk phone rang, and he picked up the receiver. "Have him wait." He hung up.

Cochran addressed the general picking up the conversation before the short interruption. "I told you she was a good egg. That's why I chose her."

The general narrowed his eyes slightly. "Apparently a little too good of an egg."

This was the strangest meeting she'd ever been a part of.

General Hawkins turned his attention back to Peggy. "What specifically made you believe there was something about the Texas trip that was off?"

A direct question she couldn't avoid answering. "We were told we had been sent to test an aircraft, make any changes or repairs necessary to get it flight worthy, and ferry it back here. Once there, we weren't allowed to do anything. Which isn't unusual."

"Not unusual? What did you do while there?"

"We did an exterior assessment of the aircraft we would be flying back but weren't permitted inside. With nothing to do, we stood or sat around."

"And this isn't unusual?" the general asked.

Sadly, true.

General Hawkins motioned with his hand. "Speak freely. I want to know."

Cochran gave Peggy a nod.

"The experience of many WASPs, despite our various skills, is to be left waiting around for no apparent reason."

This time Cochran gave a nod to the general.

"If waiting around is normal, what made you suspicious on this trip?"

Peggy must choose her words carefully. "An officer was sent along with us so he could learn about the duties of WASPs."

"Major Berg?"

Peggy had tried to refrain from using his name so as not to get him in trouble. "Yes, sir."

"So his being assigned to this trip made you suspicious?"

"No. First, a military car came and immediately took him away. If he was there to observe the WASPs, he couldn't do that if he was gone. Second, upon his return several hours later, he carried an attaché case he hadn't had before. He never allowed it to leave his side. Third, we were promptly informed we could take off. We hadn't even been allowed in the B-34. An aircraft we were supposed to assess, make any needed repairs to, and test fly. Without any of that, we were told it was fueled up and ready to go. We did our preflight checks and the aircraft was indeed in excellent working order. That has never happened to us before, even when we've been told a plane was flight ready. Which tells me that aircraft was meticulously serviced for a quick turnaround." Peggy decided it might be best to stop there. She'd given all the relevant information. The rest was merely her mulling it all over during the flight home.

General Hawkins remained silent as did Cochran. Then he said, "What did Major Berg tell you about the dispatch case and his mission?"

"Nothing. He suggested I shouldn't say anything to anyone."

"Yet you told WASP Poole."

"I felt it was my duty—"

"Duty?"

Peggy didn't want to get the major in trouble. "I believe the major to be an honorable man, loyal to this country, but on the off chance I was wrong. . ." She felt duty bound to at least mention it.

"Understood."

However, she'd gotten to know him better since then. "I'm sure Major Berg would never betray the United States. Never." Though she hadn't known him long, she knew because of something intangible deep down. Was that God? She liked to believe it was.

"I concur. For that very reason, he was chosen." The general's commanding expression changed slightly to almost that of a student eager to learn. "Moving forward, what would you recommend to avoid suspicion in instances such as this?"

"Besides having a WASP be the courier?"

The general raised his eyebrows as though the idea were interesting. "Besides that."

"Well, whoever is sent along could feign an injury or illness as a reason for them to be whisked away." She couldn't believe she was being allowed to speak so freely to a general.

"That may work a time or two but not in the long run."

"True. Give the WASPs something to do. If we are busy, we would be less likely to notice the absence of a tag-a-long. We want to work. It is as simple as that."

"WASP Witherspoon, the US Army appreciates your service and your input into this matter. If you think of any other ways these types of missions, with WASP and the army, could be executed without suspicion, contact my desk sergeant and he'll make an appointment for you to come in to see me."

"Thank you, sir. I do have one more thought."

"Go on."

"If the WASPs are given an aircraft to repair, the officer who is there can watch for a bit, then excuse himself to allow the WASPs to do their work. He will have done his job to see how the WASPs operate, fulfilling that role. The WASPs will be grateful to not have someone looking over their shoulders, while the officer goes off and performs his other duty." She would likely be dismissed now. The general did have someone else waiting.

He picked up the receiver from the telephone on his desk. "Send him in."

"Shall I go now, sir?"

"Not yet."

The door opened behind her, and a familiar voice said, "Sir? Ma'am?"

"Come in, Major."

Peggy's insides twirled as she turned to see the officer on her left. Major Berg. She shouldn't be so pleased to see him. He gave her a sideways glance and nod.

General Hawkins leaned forward, pressing into his desk. "Apparently, our plan to have your mission to Texas go unnoticed failed. WASP Witherspoon figured out something was amiss."

Her joy plummeted. Had she gotten the major in trouble? She wanted to speak up but knew that would be out of line.

Major Berg's stance seemed to get stiffer. "Permission to speak freely, sir?"

"Go ahead."

"WASP Witherspoon's loyalty is impeccable. She is trustworthy. The mission was in no way compromised."

"But it was. No one was supposed to know you were there for any reason other than to observe and supervise the WASPs. But that's not why I have you two in here. It's obvious you work well together and look out for each other. Qualities that make good soldiers."

Peggy wasn't technically a soldier, but the compliment was a great praise.

The general went on. "Major Berg, the Army Air Corps needs procedures for missions such as the one you took to Texas to avoid suspicion. Witherspoon has a few ideas. I want the pair of you to work on a set of protocols."

What an honor.

And the chance to work with the handsome major.

☰ CHAPTER 14 ☰

The following day when Howie returned from lunch, his desk sergeant stopped him from going into his office.

"Sir, you have a visitor."

He wasn't expecting anyone. "Who is it?"

"Mrs. Deny."

Though the name sounded vaguely familiar, he couldn't place it. Howie had hoped for Peggy but knew she was on a transport run.

"She has a plate covered with a cloth. Smells like cookies. Sugar if I'm not mistaken."

Who was this woman?

"I hope you don't mind that I let her wait in your office."

"That's fine. Thank you." Time to find out who this mystery woman was. He entered his office. "Mrs. Deny?"

The older woman swiveled in the chair and beamed up at him. "Howie. Or should I call you Major Berg here at your work?"

Peggy's mother? What was she doing here? "Howie's fine." Was this a good visit? Or was he in for a scolding?

"Then you must call me Muriel."

He wasn't sure if that was appropriate, but she seemed to be in a pleasant mood. He rounded his desk, sat, and leaned his cane against the side of it. "What brings you here?"

She reached halfway across the desk with the cloth covered plate. "I brought these for you."

He took the plate. "For me?" What was she up to?

She nodded. "Have one."

He folded back the cloth. Sugar cookies. The sergeant had a good nose. He chose one and took a bite. "Mmm." This was quite a gift, to sacrifice their rationed sugar and butter on him.

Muriel beamed. "It's nice to have a treat every now and then. I reckon you haven't had home-baked cookies in a while."

It had been a long time. "I'm sure you didn't come here merely to tempt me with your baked goods."

"No. Well, actually yes. What are you doing on Sunday?"

"I'm on duty. I volunteer once in a while on weekends so the married men with families can have it off." It was also a slower work day, less goings on.

"That's very thoughtful of you." She beamed at him. "I knew you were a good man. What day do you have off?"

"Tomorrow, but—"

"Tomorrow would be perfect. You must come over for supper."

"Supper?" Did Mama Bird know about this?

"Yes, we're inviting you over for supper."

"We?" Certainly not Peggy.

"The whole family. My girls are taken with you. *All* of them."

He had been taken with them as well. "That's a tempting offer."

"So tomorrow for supper?"

He wanted to, but should he? Since Mama Bird was apparently fine with this and she had seemed pleased he had shown up at Wendy's event, then it would be all right. "Very well. What time?"

"Five o'clock. We'll eat at five thirty."

"I'll be there."

"Wonderful. I'll let you get back to work." She stood.

He walked her to the door and held it for her.

As she left, she waved with wiggling fingers. "Until tomorrow." She sashayed down the corridor.

He knew where Peggy got her beauty and charm from. Not that the WASP had ever behaved that way toward him, nor would he expect her to. It was more her determination, not backing down, and knowing what she wanted.

"Major?"

Howie swung his gaze to his desk sergeant.

"Is everything all right, sir?"

Yes, it was. He was going to supper with an intriguing pilot and her family. "Just fine. You were right, sugar cookies." He headed into his office and sat behind his desk. He would need to check out a car from the motor pool— Wait. He couldn't do that. More like he wouldn't be allowed to. Until he'd been given clearance to drive, he was stuck with a driver. Though there was nothing wrong with him having supper with a nice family, it would be best if others didn't know about it.

He picked up the telephone receiver on his desk and called the sergeant in the outer office.

"Yes, sir."

"Get me an appointment at the medical clinic."

"When would you like that for?"

"Today or tomorrow at the latest."

"Sir?"

"I know it might be a little hard, but make it happen."

"Yes, sir."

Howie hung up. If he didn't get in to see the doctor today or tomorrow, he couldn't get cleared to drive. If he couldn't get cleared to drive, he would have to cancel dinner plans with Peggy and her family. He wasn't about to have word spread around the airfield that he'd had supper with one of the WASPs. He wouldn't embarrass her like that.

The next morning in the medical clinic, Howie sat on the exam table in the doctor's office. Captain Warren worked Howie's leg back and forth and tested its strength. Though the process hurt, Howie didn't let on. He wanted—no, *needed* the doctor to approve him for driving a vehicle. "What's the verdict?"

"You seem to be healing well. I'm surprised all my manipulating of your leg didn't cause more pain." The captain wrote on Howie's chart.

"It feels better and stronger every day. I try to use it more to build strength."

"I can tell, but don't overdo it."

"I'm careful." And he was. He pushed himself to the point of improvement without risking further damage or causing a setback.

"So what was concerning you that prompted you to make an urgent appointment?"

Now for the important question. "I want to be cleared to drive." Though nothing would or could happen between him and Peggy, he didn't need anyone tattling on him. And surprisingly, he honestly looked forward to seeing those two little girls.

"I'd like to wait another week or two."

That wouldn't do. "I drove once, a month ago. It was an emergency situation for a short distance. I had no trouble." Maybe that was a bit of an overstatement, minimal trouble.

Captain Warren narrowed his eyes. "Why can't you soldiers and pilots realize you're not invincible? You could have caused additional damage."

"I was careful. I actually felt better afterward. To do something as simple as driving after being denied it for so long and wondering if I would ever drive again was encouraging."

"You're not going to wait another week or two, are you?"

He didn't want to but also didn't want to be refused. "I can handle it. I *can* drive."

The captain scooted the chair up near the exam table. "Swing your legs over the edge."

Howie did. Excitement bubbled inside him.

The doctor slowly bent his leg until his knee touched his chest. "That hurts, doesn't it?"

"Not bad." More than not bad, but also not excruciating as it had been a few months ago.

"Push against my hand."

Howie pressed his leg forward.

"Harder. Try to move me back."

He pushed. Though the pain increased, surprisingly it wasn't enough to stop him. He'd expected more, but since it wasn't too bad, pushed harder and did indeed displace the doctor a little.

"Okay, stop. Straighten your leg and hold it up, level with the table."

Howie tried, but he couldn't hold it even with the table. It slowly inched downward.

"Good."

"Good? I couldn't hold it up."

"I didn't expect you to, but your leg didn't drop rapidly. It's gaining strength as you said." The doctor put his hands on his knees with his palms facing Howie. "This is the brake and this the accelerator." He lifted one hand and then the other. "Work the invisible clutch with one foot. Now, step on the brake."

Howie put his hands on the table behind him for support and put his right foot on the "brake".

"Now accelerate."

He pressed in the clutch pedal with his left foot and put his other on the gas, easing off the clutch. If he were in a real vehicle, that clutch release would have been jerky.

"Good. Now brake!"

Howie automatically moved both feet, one to the brake and the other to the clutch.

The doctor nodded. "You can relax now." He wrote in the chart again. "You are impatient to drive, aren't you?"

More so since Mrs. Deny's visit and invitation. "Yes."

"I still think you should wait another week or two."

No. He didn't want to. If he couldn't drive, he would need to cancel his supper plans with an intriguing family.

"But I'll sign off on limited use of a car. If you overdo it and end up back here with further damage, sir, you might never drive again."

"No sir, I won't overdo it. I promise."

Captain Warren raised an eyebrow.

It had been unorthodox to call a junior officer *sir*, but he wouldn't retract it. Hopefully, it showed his gratitude.

Warren scrolled on a piece of paper on a yellow legal pad and tore it off. "If anyone questions your approval to drive, show them this. I'll put a more formal letter in your file, both your medical one and your personnel one." He handed it over.

Howie lifted the paper. "Thank you."

"Remember, use caution, or we'll both regret this."

Peggy pulled into her driveway and frowned at the car parked on the street in front of her house. Was someone here? She couldn't imagine who. Her mom must have one of her lady friends over. She wasn't up for company tonight. Perhaps she could slip into her room and read. She shut off the car's engine.

When she opened the car door, her girls burst out the front of the house.

Junie grabbed her hand. "Hurry, Mommy. He's here."

He? "Who's here?" Peggy shifted her gaze to her oldest daughter for the answer.

Wendy smiled but said nothing.

Peggy grabbed her handbag and barely got the car door closed before Junie pulled her toward the front door. She was tired and wanted nothing more than to collapse.

She stopped short inside when she saw Major Berg standing in the kitchen with Mom. Was he slicing tomatoes? In Mom's blue ruffled apron?

"Mr. Howie, Mr. Howie, Mommy's home."

He looked up and smiled.

Suddenly, she wasn't so tired. "What are you doing here?"

Her mom answered. "I invited him for supper."

Why had she done that?

His smile turned shy. "I hope you don't mind."

"Not at all. Let me put my things away and I'll help."

Her mom waved the wooden spoon in her hand. "Nonsense. You've been working all day. We're almost done here. You relax."

Mom was apparently playing matchmaker. "All right. I'm going to change out of my work clothes." She headed to her room. She couldn't relax, not with a handsome man in her kitchen. One who was helping make her supper in a frilly apron.

Well, she wouldn't be wearing her old baggy slack suit she normally wore in the evenings. She rifled through the clothes hanging in her closet. She hadn't bought anything new since the war started.

Before that, very little after the stock market crash. Most of her adult life had been fraught with trials.

She would wear a skirt. The two wool ones would be too hot, and the cotton ones were too worn. She would look like a beggar in them. She pulled out her blue and white print church dress. It wasn't fancy or anything, no adornments, no wide white collar, nothing special about it except the plain buttons down the front. Though she did reserve it for church, it was showing its wear. She had few options. She hadn't been concerned with her appearance at home. Her husband had understood the need to wear clothes until they were almost falling apart. They always put their daughters first. Then when George shipped over to Europe, there had been no one to dress up for. Not that she was dressing up for the major, but she should at least be presentable.

With the dress on, she sat at her vanity dresser to comb her hair. Mercy. What a fright after having been mashed under the scarf turban. She quickly combed it all into place. She still appeared haggard, but it was the best she could do on such short notice. Shoes had been optional in the evenings around the house but not tonight. She put on the shoes she normally wore around town when doing the shopping and such. It felt odd to be dressed like this in her own home, but she was raised to treat company with respect, and with that respect came dressing appropriately.

She stood and smoothed her hands down her dress. Was she nervous? Why? How could she be? She worked with the man and saw him a few times every week. Why did having him in her home unnerve her?

Because this was different. This was personal rather than professional. This actually mattered. She wanted him to like her, but she also didn't want him to. The idea of him being attracted to her was appealing, but that could mean developing a relationship. Was she ready for a *relationship*?

She stepped away from her vanity far enough to see a little more than half of herself in the mirror. Presentable.

Then she heard the echo of the words her husband had whispered in her ear when she'd made this dress. *"You look beautiful. No matter what you wear, you'll always be beautiful."* He'd come up behind her, wrapped his arms around her, and kissed her neck.

She was being foolish. The major wasn't really interested in her. He probably merely appreciated a home-cooked meal. The poor man lived in the Transient Living Facility. Just a normal meal with a coworker.

Then her husband's voice again. *"If I don't come back, I want you to marry again. I don't want you to spend your life alone."*

She'd told him nothing was going to happen to him.

"This is war, darling. People die. If I'm one of them, I want you to know I want you to be happy. I want you to find love again. Find a good man who will treat our girls well. They shouldn't grow up without a father."

She'd hated him talking that way. It was as though he had known he wouldn't return.

Her eyes burned.

"Now, no crying on my account. You are the strongest, bravest woman I know."

She blinked away the sudden tears.

She'd had an A1 life with her husband and wished she could have grown old with him. Unfortunately, that wasn't how life had turned out. No sense wishing what could never be. She did want to be happy again. . .when this war was over. However being happy didn't necessarily mean marrying again.

"Mommy?"

In the mirror, Peggy could see her oldest daughter in the doorway. When had she come in? "Hi, Sweetie." Turning, she held out her arms.

Wendy came to her and wrapped her arms around her waist. She spoke sullenly. "You look pretty."

"Thank you."

Wendy had always been her melancholy girl. Being born during the Great Depression, she seemed to have the weight of the world on her slim little shoulders. This war didn't help.

Peggy was happy. Happy to have her girls. Happy they were all healthy. Happy she had a job as a pilot. She straightened and took a deep breath. "Shall we go out and see if we can help with supper?"

"There's nothing left to do. Grandma is just waiting for it to finish cooking."

"What are we having?" Peggy imagined her mom would have cooked the fanciest thing their ration coupons could get them.

"Chicken pot pie, boiled potatoes, and sliced tomatoes and carrots from our Victory Garden."

"Sounds tasty."

"Mr. Howie brought store-bought cupcakes. One for each of us. Grandma had made some vanilla pudding, but it wasn't very good because she didn't have enough sugar. She didn't tell Mr. Howie though."

"Well, it's a good thing the major brought cupcakes. It was very thoughtful of him. Shall we go out before they send a search party for us?"

Wendy nodded and led the way.

Peggy took another deep breath to remind herself this was an ordinary supper like every other night. Why should it be any different from inviting old man Sawyer to supper?

When Peggy entered the living room and could see into the kitchen where the major—minus the apron—stood smiling with her mother, her insides got all happy again. *Settle down. Nothing special about tonight.*

As they all headed toward the table, Major Berg held up a hand. "Wait. You all must permit me to seat you. I would be no kind of guest or gentleman if I didn't." Then he proceeded to pull out the chair for each of them one at a time. First, Mom, followed by Wendy, then Junie who giggled. Then finally Peggy.

"Thank you."

He gave her a nod. "My pleasure."

His whispered words almost sounded like a declaration and sent a thrill through her.

"Mr. Howie, the next round of the spelling competition is October 20. Will you come? It's the county level."

Peggy attempted to halt her daughter. "Wendy."

At the same time Major Berg said, "I would be honored to attend again."

He glanced to Peggy for approval. She nodded, not wanting to impose upon the major.

The major turned back to Wendy. "Where is it being held?"

Peggy gave him the necessary information. Though sweet of him to say yes, she didn't expect him to come a second time.

After supper and dessert, Peggy walked the major out to his car at his request. "Where's your driver?" She hadn't thought about it until now that he usually had a driver.

"The doctor gave me approval to drive."

"That's wonderful."

"A small step in my recovery."

"No step is too small to appreciate."

"Oh, I appreciate it all right. You have no idea. Being dependent on someone else to get me everywhere I need to go is tiresome."

She could imagine. Her car afforded her blessed independence. If her husband hadn't bought it before the war started, she wouldn't have been able to buy one. Even a used car. This one had been used and seen better days before they purchased it. Thankfully, her mechanical skills had kept the Ford running.

"The reason I asked you to walk me out was, I wanted to apologize for showing up tonight."

Why had he? Was it more than Mom's invitation? "Supper was nice, and the cupcakes were a big hit. Wendy and Junie will be talking about them long into next week."

"That's not what I mean. When your mother came to my office to invite me, I thought it was your idea or that you were at least aware of the arrangement and had sanctioned it. But when you arrived, you were clearly surprised to see me. I appreciate you not making a fuss."

Though surprised, she had been pleased to see him in her home. "I might not have been expecting you, but it was nice to have company at our table." She shouldn't have said that. It would encourage him, and she had no right to do that.

"Thank you. Next time, I'll check with *you* first."

Next time? She shouldn't like that idea, but she did. She also appreciated his consideration.

He shifted as though nervous. "About Wendy's spelling bee, I can come up with an excuse if you would rather I not attend."

Now it was her turn to be uneasy. "Please don't feel as though you have to go. She shouldn't have put you on the spot like that. She knows better."

"I want to go, but I don't want to crowd in on a family event."

"Since everyone involved appears to want you to come, we look forward to having you there." Peggy's insides danced with giddiness at the anticipation of seeing him away from work again a month from now.

He hesitated, opened his mouth as if he had something else to say, and then he closed it promptly.

"Was there something else, sir?"

He gazed at her a long moment. "No, nothing." He lowered himself into the driver seat. "Have a good rest of your evening."

"You too." As he drove away, Peggy pondered on what he might have been going to say.

Or did she even want to know?

⊒ CHAPTER 15 ⊑

The following week, Peggy maneuvered the C-47 Skytrain cargo plane she'd retrieved from Connecticut toward the airfield in Cuba. The craft had performed flawlessly since being repaired last month. She eased the plane down until the wheels barely kissed the runway. Another great landing. In the aircraft with her were two other Women Airforce Service Pilots and three army soldiers who were the load masters for the cargo. She taxied to the designated spot.

A US military supply truck drove up to the cargo plane. The American armed forces presence here in Cuba was to help protect the Gulf of Mexico and the Caribbean. An Axis attack from here could impair the US's ability to help overseas by dividing their focus.

Sergeant Adams moved to the front of the craft. "I know you WASPs are capable, but I must insist you remain inside the aircraft for your protection while the cargo is being unloaded to the truck. The fewer people who know women are onboard the better."

Nightingale stood from her seat. "Once the cargo is gone, are we permitted to walk around?"

He nodded. "While we refuel, then we are back in the air."

After everything was unloaded, Peggy exited the plane to stretch her legs. She crossed the tarmac and entered the hangar.

A pair of US soldiers inside argued on the other side of a P-51 Mustang inside the cavernous building. Even though they were off to the side at a workbench along the wall, she could see enough of their uniforms from under the aircraft to know they were US.

One man said, "We can't abandon our men."

The other replied, "We don't have a choice. We have our orders."

Peggy's insides knotted. She pictured her own husband, as well as Major Berg, shot down and waiting for rescue. She knew she shouldn't speak up, but she couldn't remain silent and so rounded the aircraft and marched up to the pair of sergeants. "We have men abandoned somewhere?"

The higher-ranking staff sergeant tightened his jaw and narrowed his eyes at her. His gaze flickered to the entrance and back to her. "This is none of your concern. Get back on your aircraft and forget you heard anything." He gave a sharp look to his fellow soldier before walking away.

The other sergeant, one rank below, went back to stowing some tools. Should Peggy say anything more?

The sergeant crouched to organize tools and a disarray of things on a lower shelf. He spoke in a whisper. "Three soldiers. Two enlisted, one officer. Held near the western tip of the island."

He was telling her? Yes, but he didn't want anyone to know he was. "Go on," she said softly without moving her mouth while fingering a screwdriver.

"They were taken a little over a week ago. Being held in the hills or by a lake. They might be moving them around." He tapped the shelf, stood, and walked away.

On the marred board sat a crumpled piece of paper along with the tools and such. The paper looked out of place. Had he left that for her?

Jolene came over. "They are done fueling up the Skytrain. Time to go."

"All right." Peggy turned suddenly and knocked off the screwdriver. "Clumsy me." She bent to pick it up and with her other hand retrieved the paper. She hoped this was what she thought it was and tucked her hand into the pocket of her zoot suit as she straightened and replaced the tool to the top of the workbench.

Make haste, the time is nigh, the time is short, like a thief in the night.

Was that God's voice? Though Peggy didn't know quite what it meant, she understood enough and sprang into action. "Let's go."

Please don't let anyone have seen me snatch that paper.

Her stomach churned and knotted all the way across the tarmac to the cargo plane. Her insides told her to run for her life, but her head told her to act normally. How did one act normally? Simply by thinking she had to meant she would be forcing her actions and not quite succeed in being normal. How did undercover people do covert ops and not get caught?

Jolene sat in the pilot's seat.

Peggy stared at her.

Jolene raised an eyebrow. "Remember, I'm flying on the way back?"

Peggy slipped into the copilot's chair. "I remember." But she hadn't because she had been too distracted by her fears.

"Are you all right, Mama Bird?"

This proved her point. "I'm fine." She strapped into the seat so her friend couldn't scrutinize her more.

Soon the bird was blessedly in the air.

Dare she take out the paper? Should she wait until they were away from Cuba? Or wait until they landed at Bolling Field and she could find someplace alone to survey it?

Her curiosity was too great to wait. She slipped the paper out surreptitiously and uncrumpled it.

The handwriting appeared as though it had been hastily scrawled, a set of numbers and what appeared to be three last names.

Jolene turned her direction. "What have you got there?"

"Shh." Peggy glanced over her shoulder and spoke in a low voice. "I think these are the soldiers being held."

Jolene squinted. "What?"

Peggy shook her head. "I'll tell you after we land." She put her index finger to her lips to let her comrade know not to mention it to anyone else.

The other woman nodded.

Peggy breathed a sigh of relief when they had left Cuban airspace and were over open water. The flight home went smoothly.

Upon landing, Major Berg met them. "Any problems?"

Peggy instinctively held her breath. Had someone from Cuba informed him of what the sergeant had done?

Jolene shook her head. "Smooth trip there and back. We didn't even leave the tarmac."

True. The hangar had been on the tarmac.

"Good to hear. Meet in the briefing room for the debriefing."

Peggy released the air held captive in her lungs but knew she wasn't out of the woods yet. It wasn't that she didn't want to tell the major. She simply wanted to know what it was she would tell him first. It would be silly to say she had found a random piece of paper, decided to take it, and discover it was nothing more than a shopping list or something else innocuous. Once she knew exactly what she had, she would inform him if it was relevant.

The debrief went without incident, and everyone filed out of the room except Major Berg. "Witherspoon, could you stay a minute?"

She swallowed hard. "Sure." He must know something.

Jolene gave her a look. "I'll wait for you at the end of the corridor." She left.

Peggy stood at attention. "Yes, sir."

He sighed and shook his head. "At ease."

She shifted to parade rest. Was she still acting *not* normal?

"About the other day."

The other day?

"The gathering at your home. I know the captains and I probably shouldn't have come, but I noticed they both could use morale boosts. I hope you didn't mind too much."

Her get-together? So, he wasn't going to further grill her on the mission. She breathed easier. "It seemed to be good for everyone."

"I wanted to bring this up after supper at your house the other night but wasn't sure how."

She had suspected he was going to say something. Now she was doubly curious. "What is it?"

"About what happened in the living room."

The memory of him holding her in his arms flashed in her mind, and her skin warmed.

"I want to apologize for my actions. I thought I could pretend it didn't happen and avoid talking about it, but I feel I should say something. I was afraid you were going to fall, and then I lost my cane and was off balance. I know it sounds like I'm making excuses."

It did sound that way. So had he not been thinking of kissing her before Junie interrupted? "I appreciate you seeing to my safety. I understand it was nothing more."

He was silent.

"Is that all, sir?"

"No. And no it wasn't nothing for me." He rubbed his hand across his jaw. "I know it should be nothing, and I've tried making it nothing, but there is something there. Between us. I felt it again at Wendy's spelling bee. Also at supper four nights ago. If I'm not mistaken, you have felt it too."

She had. "Anything but professional interaction would be frowned upon. I won't dishonor the Women Airforce Service Pilots program by doing anything that could jeopardize it."

His mouth twitched as though it wanted to smile. "I'm not asking you to. Maybe when this war is over, you might be open to revisiting this topic?"

"I don't know."

He lifted a hand to stop her. "Don't worry about answering now. It's enough you know I'm interested, and that I will do nothing to compromise or threaten your position. The work you do is too important."

"When I first met you, I thought you didn't like the WASP program and didn't think women should fly."

"I can see how I could have come off that way. The truth is, I was terrified for your safety. I was raised to always protect women and to do everything in my power to keep them out of harm's way. And there you were flirting with danger. I actually really admired your bravery, but I'll never get used to women being in danger."

That was really very sweet. She wanted to respond to his declaration of affection. She both wanted to fall head long into it and at the same time rebuff it. Even though her husband had passed away over fifteen months ago, she still felt married. Because it happened way over in Europe, it never seemed quite real. She knew he was gone and that he would never return from war a living, breathing man. Another part of her could picture him still over there.

Though his death had been confirmed, his body hadn't been

returned yet. She, along with her daughters and mother, had a small memorial service in the backyard to allow her daughters to grieve and move on. She had started mourning, then one day, she had stopped. The pain had been too great and so she had thrown herself into her work as a WASP.

"Sir, each day feels like that day the colonel knocked on my door and told me my husband wasn't coming home. I don't know if I'll ever get over the loss." Oddly, a part of her never had. Her loss was the last thing of her husband she had to hold on to. If she held it tightly enough, she somehow still had a piece of him. "And I have my daughters to consider." Although, witnessing the major interacting with them had gone a long way in mending her heart and her daughters' hearts. Still, it was scary. She knew she was probably hiding behind her husband's death, but she needed to for now.

He nodded. "I understand. Know that I expect nothing from you and won't bring this matter up again. I merely wanted to clear the air. I didn't want it hovering over you wondering about it and what it meant. I will wait until the war is over." After a moment, he said softly, "Dismissed."

She left. In the corridor, she leaned against the wall and took controlled breaths. A part of her wanted to fall into his arms and let him take care of her and everything in her life. But that wasn't who she was. To crumble into pieces wouldn't do her or her daughters any good. Nor would it do the major any good. Her late husband would be disappointed in her.

Late husband. Was that the first time she had thought of him as such? It wasn't as though she never had, but it was always the correction after first thinking or speaking of him as her husband, no past tense. He was gone, and she needed to correct her thinking or she would never move on. If her daughters were going to heal and build happy lives, Peggy needed to start building her life again and try to be happy. She needed to stop living in the past.

She wanted to be happy again, and she had been for a couple of brief moments at the get-together. Once when the major had rescued Junie's doll from the tree and read to her. The other was when he'd accidentally held her in his arms. She'd thought that had meant nothing to him. Knowing differently now made her want more. She couldn't afford to want more in her present circumstances. Her daughters came first, and she had the Women Airforce Service Pilots. Her job was important and necessary for the war effort.

Her whole adult life had been hard. The years leading up to the war had been lean, but she and George had made a good life and were happy. At least when he was home. Come to think of it, he hadn't been around much. First with their airplane business before the US got involved in the war. After that, he'd been in military school, then moving from place to place, and him off on military missions, even before the war broke out. Once the war started, he'd joined up and shipped overseas.

And that was the last she'd seen of him.

Knowing his body was still someplace in Europe left her feeling suspended between the past and the future without really being in the present. Even though they'd had their little "funeral," she didn't have the closure other wives and families had who'd been able to bury an actual body.

The major's desk sergeant came down the hallway.

Enough wallowing. Time to move along. Peggy pushed away from the wall and strolled along the corridor. She nodded to the sergeant as she passed him and caught up with Jolene at the designated spot.

Jolene straightened as Peggy approached. "I was getting worried. What did the major want?"

To dredge up too many memories. Peggy wasn't about to tell her comrade about the incident in her living room with the major. "It was nothing."

Jolene narrowed her eyes. She likely didn't believe Peggy. No matter.

Peggy disregarded the topic. She needed to forget about that discussion with the major, forget he ever held her in his arms, and forget her heart longed to go back to him.

———〰———

Howie dropped his face into his hands. He'd said too much. He hadn't meant to tell her how he felt. He'd only wanted to tell her to not worry about the whole situation. Now she probably thought he was going to pursue her. He wasn't. Unless, of course, she was interested in him as well.

He shook his head. What was he thinking? Now was not the time to be considering matters of the heart. There was a war going on. He didn't have time for such things. And she certainly didn't need him complicating her life. Besides, why would she want to be saddled with a half-crippled man?

He had enjoyed reading to Junie, attending Wendy's spelling bee, and having supper with Peggy and her family. He never would have imagined how much joy those events would give him.

Had he botched up everything with the pretty widow?

He had asked the Lord to direct the conversation with her. So maybe it wasn't as bad as he imagined. Or maybe the Lord had other ideas and had directed the conversation along a path neither he nor Peggy was ready to go down.

CHAPTER 16

Peggy walked with Jolene between buildings at Bolling Airfield. Her fellow WASP had gotten called away yesterday before Peggy could show her the paper from Cuba.

The numbers and names scrawled on it had kept her awake half the night. The urgency she'd felt at the hangar in Cuba didn't seem as intense. Almost as though it had settled into a low hum in the background. Had she been wrong? Had the immediacy been nothing more than her own nerves fearful of being caught? But caught doing what? The paper could easily be an old note where someone had scrawled down unrelated items.

Jolene leaned a little closer. "Did you figure out what that piece of paper you had on the cargo plane was?"

Peggy shook her head, feeling foolish for causing even this little fuss about it.

"Where did you get it?"

"Not here." Peggy kept walking. Even though she doubted the validity of the note, something inside told her it would be prudent to use caution.

As a colonel headed their general direction on a trajectory to cross their path, they snapped to attention and saluted. He saluted back and continued on his way.

Peggy let out a breath she hadn't realized she held. "Where can we go that's private?" Not living on Bolling Airfield, she didn't know the complex as well as the other WASPs.

"No one is usually in the barracks this time of day."

"Perfect."

She marched to the building and sat on Jolene's lower bunk with her friend. She pulled the crumpled paper from her pocket. "When I was in the hangar, two sergeants were arguing. One wanted to rescue some soldiers. It sounded as though they were someplace and needed help or something, as though they were being held captive. The other said they couldn't because of relations with Cuba and not wanting to start an international incident. The one sergeant didn't want to abandon the men."

"Are you sure?"

"He said the soldiers were on the west end of the island. The sergeant left this on one of the shelves before he walked away." At least Peggy believed he'd left it. "I think he wanted me to take it."

"Is that why you dropped the screwdriver? So you could grab the paper?"

"How did you know?"

Jolene shrugged. "I didn't at the time, but I put it together. It's what I would have done so no one would suspect. Show me the note."

"It has numbers and names." Peggy unfurled it.

Jolene took it for a closer examination.

Peggy pointed to the numbers. "If I'm not mistaken, those are latitude and longitude."

"I concur. I wish we could consult a detailed map of Cuba to see if these coordinates point to the western tip. And the names? Are those the soldiers?"

"I assume so." Williams, Gillespie, and Nelson.

"What do we do if these are coordinates on the west part of Cuba somewhere?"

Peggy hadn't figured that part out yet. "I don't know. One step at a time. If they point to someplace in the middle of the Atlantic Ocean, then we can forget all about this, and chalk it up to another juvenile joke of army soldiers and my overactive imagination." She would feel pretty silly if this was all for naught, although pleased, knowing soldiers weren't in danger.

"Our first step is to get into the cartography room and consult the maps to locate these coordinates."

From the end of the room, a woman spoke. "What do you need in cartography?"

Peggy jerked her head up as she crammed the paper under her thigh. "Hi, Brownie." Brownie was a good egg, but the fewer people in on her little secret the better. At least, until they knew more and could corroborate what indeed this note contained.

Brownie, still with a limp—though she wouldn't admit it—stopped next to the bunk. "Hi." She deadpanned. "Cartography? What do you need in there?"

Jolene cleared her throat. "We didn't say *cartography*. We said. . . *photography*."

Their fellow WASP made a circling motion with her index finger. "Though large, sound travels way too well in this sparse room. I distinctly heard *cartography*, *maps*, and *coordinates*. Spill."

Brownie might be the answer to this problem. She had a knack for maps and coordinates.

"I was testing Jolene on some coordinates to see if she could tell me where in the world they point to. She thinks someplace in Mexico, and I think they are in the Caribbean."

A grin brightened Brownie's face. "Fun. What are they?"

Hopefully, this was the right thing to do. Her friend would merely think the numbers were chosen at random. Having read them so many times, she didn't even need to reference the paper. "Twenty-two, eleven, fifty-one point zero seven five. And negative eighty-four, twenty-three, fifty-eight point five two four."

Brownie's gaze rolled heavenward. "Could you repeat those coordinates?"

Peggy did so more slowly this time.

Her friend's fingers and lips moved as though counting. "You're both close, but Peggy's closer. I think it's somewhere in Cuba or pretty close."

Peggy glanced at Jolene who gave her a pointed look back.

"Am I right?" Brownie lowered her hands.

The girl knew she was right. It was her forte.

"You got it."

"Didn't you two just get back from a run to Cuba?"

Oops. "We did. Maybe that's why those coordinates popped into my head."

Brownie put her hands on her hips. "Or maybe you two are up to something and it has to do with your trip to Cuba. Spill the beans."

Peggy and Jolene exchanged glances again.

Brownie huffed. "Now, I know something is up."

Jolene shrugged. "You might as well fill her in."

"Yep," their nosy friend answered. "You might as well, because I'm not leaving until you do."

Peggy heaved a sigh. "You can't tell anyone."

"I won't." Brownie gripped the fabric at the hips of her too large zoot suit and hiked it up. Like Peggy, Brownie was small and the coveralls were all made for the much larger male physique.

Peggy handed the paper to Brownie. "A sergeant at the airstrip where we landed gave that to me. Not exactly *gave*. More like left it for me to pick up. He said three soldiers were being held on the west end of the island. I believe these are the men's names and the coordinates of where they are being detained."

"These are definitely latitude and longitude. What did Major Berg say about this?"

"I didn't tell him." Yet. But she likely would. . .eventually. "I need to find out more first. I need to see where exactly this is on a map."

"I'm in. Let me help figure this out. Tomorrow I'll be in the cartography room and can pinch a map of Cuba."

"No. Don't do that. I don't want you to get into trouble."

Brownie stuck the tip of her tongue out from between her pressed lips, thinking. "I could put down pertinent information on a piece of paper and then reconstruct it back here."

"Perfect."

The next day, the trio met in the barracks. Today, three other WASPs were in there as well. Brownie held a rolled-up piece of brown paper clutched in one hand.

Jolene inclined her head toward the other occupants in the room. "This won't do."

Peggy agreed. "Follow me."

She drove them in her Ford to the far side of the tarmac that wasn't part of the active runways, to a place dubbed the Graveyard. The remote location where derelict aircraft that were out of commission for one reason or another sat, waiting to be scrapped or to decay. Few ever left. An occasional plane found this to be merely a temporary resting place until it could be repaired and find its way back into the air. Most had been stripped of anything valuable.

She parked between a pair of larger aircraft so her automobile wouldn't be conspicuously out of place. The nearest aircraft would suit their purposes.

Peggy dragged a nearby crate over and stood on it. She heaved open the creaky door, cringed at the noise, and hoisted herself inside the fuselage of a large cargo plane. It had been gutted and the parts used on other aircraft. The other two came in after her and sat on the floor. Peggy sat as well.

Brownie rolled out her piece of slightly crinkled brown paper.

Jolene squinted at it. "I thought you were going to make a map."

"No, what I said was, I would mark down pertinent information so I could reconstruct it later."

"But there's nothing here." Jolene waved a hand at the blank paper.

Had Peggy made a mistake by bringing Brownie in on this?

Brownie heaved a breath. "You don't think they would just let me walk out of cartography with an actual map, did you?"

"Well, I thought you would at least have something. Even a faint outline."

"But I do."

She pointed to several creases in the paper. "These folds show where Cuba is." With her pencil, she sketched in the island. "This hole in the paper is Havana. This crease on this edge is Florida." The girl kept drawing until all the creases and holes where either connected or labeled. She tucked the pencil behind her ear. "*Voilà*. Your map."

It was indeed a map. . .and appeared to be quite accurate.

Peggy patted her on the shoulder. "You are amazing."

"Thank you." Brownie blew on her pink painted nails and rubbed them on the top of her zoot suit, showing her pride.

"That means, the soldiers are being held somewhere in this area?" Peggy pointed to the western end of Cuba.

Brownie put the tip of her finger where two folds intersected. "*X* marks the spot."

Leaning closer, Peggy studied the map.

Brownie tilted her head. "How do we know these men are actually being held? Cuba *is* part of the Allied Forces."

Peggy just felt it to be so. "The sergeant told me."

"But what if they were trying to trick you? It wouldn't be the first time army soldiers tried to make fools out of us WASPs."

True. "The sergeant seemed genuine in his concern and anger. Also, the argument they were having before they knew I was there seemed real."

Brownie thinned her lips. "They could have seen you coming and set it up so you only thought you were stumbling in on an argument. They could be laughing at you right now, thinking how gullible you are. How gullible all WASPs are."

That could all be true, but her gut told her it was real. The men were real. The danger was real. "WASPs are *not* gullible."

Jolene thinned her lips. "Now what?"

Brownie spoke again. "We need to determine if those three names correspond to actual US Soldiers in Cuba."

"How do we do that?" Jolene sat back from the map.

"We need to somehow get access to records." Though Peggy didn't know how.

"What about Major Berg?" Jolene asked.

The major's face came to mind. No, it wasn't a good idea to involve him. "He would be obligated to report us, and we would get kicked out the WASP."

"Well, he likes you, Mama Bird."

"What?" How could she know that?

Jolene raised her eyebrows. "I saw the way he was looking at you at the gathering in your backyard."

Had she also seen it?

Peggy dared not mention the spelling bee or family dinner.

Brownie nodded. "I saw it too, and the way he paid attention to your daughter. A bachelor wouldn't do that unless he was sweet on the child's mother. Which is you."

Had everybody seen it but her? She couldn't very well deny it since he'd told her as much. "He has a duty. If we tell him, then he'll have to report it. Report us. We'll all be kicked out."

Jolene pinned Peggy with her gaze. "What other way can we get the information to determine if this is real or not?"

Brownie tapped the brown-paper map. "The coordinates are real, so I think it would be safe to say the men are real."

It felt real to Peggy as well, but reluctance to risk her career on an uncertainty welled up within. "Let me sleep on it. If I decide to speak to him about this, I'll go alone. No sense all of us getting in trouble." Pride surged within her at the thought of serving with these brave ladies.

That night at home, Peggy still hadn't decided what to do.

After the girls went to bed, her mom put her hand on Peggy's arm. "You look as though you have the weight of the world on your shoulders."

"I have a difficult decision to make, and I don't know how to make it."

"Prayer is always the best place to start."

Though she knew that, she wasn't confident the Lord would answer her. "What if He doesn't answer in time?"

"You can't put God on a timetable. He will answer in His time."

Peggy had prayed and prayed and patiently waited on the Lord, but it hadn't saved her husband. "But it could be too late, just like it was for George."

Mom's expression turned to concern. "Is someone's life in danger?"

Oh dear, she'd said too much. "I don't know. I need someone with more knowledge than myself to find out."

"Ask that nice major. Howie will help you or at least advise you. He's sweet on you."

Did everyone know? "If I tell him, he would be duty bound to report it." Tears welled in her eyes. "I could be kicked out of the Women Airforce Service Pilots."

"Margaret Louise, what have you gone and done?"

"Nothing. But if I do nothing, it could have disastrous effects."

"Come sit on the couch." Her mom guided her into the living room, and they sat. "Tell me as much as you are able so I can pray properly. You know I won't say a word to anyone."

Peggy took a deep breath. "I overheard something on my trip to Cuba the other day. I don't know if what I heard is real or if it's another one of the practical jokes service men like to play on us WASPs."

"If it's something you overheard, then how could that get you in trouble?"

"I'm not sure. Possibly because I didn't say anything in the debriefing?"

Her mom was silent a moment. "You could say you weren't sure if it was important, but after sleeping on it, you decided to let the major know in case it *was* important."

That sounded reasonable, and it was the truth. She hadn't been sure if it was important or not. She still didn't know.

"Is anyone's life in danger?"

"Maybe."

Her mom hesitated. "Do you feel comfortable telling me what you heard?"

Peggy conveyed the story, including Jolene's and Brownie's involvement. "This is the sort of trick the men would play on one of us."

"I still can't believe good men would do such things, but I'm not so naive to not know it happens." Mom paused. "If lives are in danger, you can't keep quiet. Think if that were George. You would want someone to do everything they could to help."

Peggy felt the same.

Mom patted Peggy's hand. "I will pray about this, but my first feeling is that you should tell Major Berg and let him deal with this. There are some things the men can do because of their access that the WASPs cannot." She stood to leave then stopped. "And maybe you should keep Jolene and Brownie out of it. If it doesn't go well, there's no sense in all of you getting into trouble."

"I've already told them if I talk to him, I'll do it alone for that very reason."

Mom kissed the top of Peggy's head. "I'm heading to bed. You should get some sleep as well."

"I'll go in a few minutes."

"Don't stay up too long." Her mom headed down the hall.

Mom made sense. Peggy wasn't going to figure this out by herself. Jolene and Brownie had helped as much as they could.

She took a deep breath and closed her eyes. Time to start more regular communication with God.

Lord, I don't know if this will do any good, but help me figure out if the information I heard is real.

She continued to pray about the situation and for the men who might be held captive. She found prayer comforting in a way she hadn't for a long time, as though Someone were actually listening. Almost like being welcomed home.

Unless I receive different guidance from You, I'll speak to Major Berg tomorrow and see what he thinks. Please don't let me lose my job over this.

Peggy thought back to the overwhelming impression she had felt in Cuba when she'd taken that paper the sergeant left for her. She had been sure God was speaking to her. She had never experienced direction from above so strongly. Though she'd been sure then, now she wondered if it had been Him because she didn't feel the urgency she had then. If it were from God, surely He would let her know.

She slipped off the davenport, turned, and knelt in front of it.

"Lord, I know I have been derelict in praying and reading the Bible. I have been hurt and hoped to protect myself, I guess. But how could not speaking to You protect me?"

Was she like a petulant child? The image of one of the times an angry Wendy had screamed she was never going to speak to Peggy again and stomped off to her room came to mind. Peggy knew it was a false declaration. The longest her daughter had avoided her had been three days. Sort of. Though she didn't talk directly to Peggy, she did so through Junie. Sometimes with Peggy in the same room, even right next to her. She put an end to Wendy using her little sister as an intermediary, rewarding Junie for not parroting her sister's words. Until Wendy spoke directly to Peggy, she wouldn't get whatever she'd been after.

How much alike were Peggy and her oldest daughter. Guilt for her neglect of God weighed on her. "Forgive me."

Peace filled her followed by an odd joy she hadn't felt before bubbling up inside her. She poured out her concerns as to whether or not the Cuba note was real and whom she should tell. Then she found herself praying for the captured soldiers and their safety. The sensation they were real and were in peril pressed in.

Strangely, she sensed Someone listening, Someone present. Her recent, half-hearted prayers hadn't truly been focused toward anyone, merely thrown out into empty space with an offhand hope they would be heard. Tonight's prayer was almost like a deep sigh wrapped in a warm blanket.

Finally.

≣ CHAPTER 17 ≣

Standing outside Major Berg's office, Peggy straightened the belted jacket of her dress uniform. She would be taken more seriously if she weren't decked out like a clown in her oversized zoot suit. Her disobedience in not disclosing the note she picked up in Cuba would likely change his fondness for her, but this was the right thing to do. If soldiers were in danger, she couldn't sit by doing nothing because her feelings might get hurt.

She held the desk sergeant's gaze. "I'm here to see Major Berg. I don't have an appointment, but it *is* urgent."

With an armload of folders, Sergeant Miller tipped his head. "Go on in. He's expecting you." He headed down the corridor.

She crinkled her eyebrows. *Expecting her?* That couldn't be right. She went to the door and knocked.

"Come in."

She smoothed her hands down her painstakingly pressed wool-gabardine skirt before opening the door.

The major stood from his seat behind the desk. "Come in. Close the door."

Why didn't he seem surprised to see her? Her insides tightened. Did he know? When she turned to shut the door, she saw the reason. Jolene and Brownie sat in chairs off to the side.

Jolene gave a forced smile. "We figured you would try to come without us, so we arrived early."

Brownie nodded.

How had they known when she would come? Irrelevant.

The major motioned toward the chair directly across from his desk. "Please have a seat."

She would rather stand, given the circumstances.

He shifted his weight. "Please."

She remembered his leg injury and sat. Fortunately he hadn't ordered her.

He retook his seat and laced his hands together. "Now tell me what this is all about."

She glanced at her comrades. "They didn't tell you, sir?"

He shook his head. "They said you were the pilot of this presentation. It must be interesting if they don't want to be left out."

Interesting wasn't the word Peggy would use to describe it. "It's *not* a presentation, sir. It might be nothing at all." She hoped it was nothing, because then three men's lives wouldn't be in danger.

"It has to be something, or you wouldn't have come to me, and the three of you wouldn't look as though you'd been caught swiping an extra cookie."

It was slightly more important than a cookie. If it was real. "While in Cuba, I overheard something."

His expression hardened. "And you failed to disclose this information during the debriefing?"

The disappointment in his gray eyes crushed her.

She knew now that concealing this had been the wrong thing to do. "Sir, I wasn't sure it was important. You have to understand, soldiers try to trick the female pilots all the time. If they can make us look bad, humiliate us, or discourage us, they will at every opportunity."

"As Second Lieutenant Rosbach had?"

"That was worse." Her anger flared. "That could have killed WASP Brown." She glanced at her friend. "As it is, she has been banned from flying because of her injury."

"When she heals fully, she'll be in the air again."

"If they let her, sir." More than likely they would use this to permanently ground her.

"I don't think this is what you wanted to speak to me about. You said you overheard something on your last mission. What was it?"

She tamped down her ire with a deep breath. "While the plane was being refueled, I went into the hangar. Two sergeants were arguing. One said, 'We can't abandon those men.' The other said that they didn't have any choice and to drop it."

"What men?"

"US soldiers, sir. When the one sergeant walked away, the other crouched to rummage around on a lower shelf and spoke in a hushed tone. He said there were three soldiers being held on the west end of the island."

Brownie piped up. "Show him the paper."

Major Berg raised his eyebrows.

Peggy dug in her pocket and retrieved the scrawled missive. "When the sergeant stood, he gave me a pointed look and left. On the shelf where he'd been searching was a piece of crumpled paper. He hadn't been *searching* for anything but writing on this paper."

Major Berg held out his hand. "Let me see it."

Peggy handed it over. "Those numbers are latitude and longitude coordinates to a spot on the western end of Cuba, sir."

"How do you know that?"

"Brownie's good with maps. If you give her most any set of coordinates, she can tell you roughly where it is."

His gaze flickered from Peggy to Brownie who nodded then back to Peggy. "And the names? Are they the men who were supposedly taken?"

"We think so, sir, but we have no way to check if they are stationed in Cuba or even in the army. That's where you come in, sir. You can find out if these men are actual US soldiers there."

He gave her an indulgent look when she'd said *where you come in*. "Williams, Gillespie, and Nelson. There aren't any ranks. Maybe these are civilians."

"I suppose they could have borrowed uniforms, but the sergeant distinctly said three soldiers, two enlisted and one officer. He said they were taken nearly two weeks ago now and being held in the hills or by a lake. He wasn't sure. They might even be moving them around."

Jolene spoke up. "Why wouldn't anyone in Cuba try to rescue them?"

The major shifted his gaze to Jolene then to each of them in turn. "International relations. If the military attempts a retrieval operation without authorization from the Cuban government, it could irrevocably damage our relationship with them."

"Isn't their refusal to help locate our men damaging *their* relationship with *us*?"

"It's not that simple." He tapped the paper. "If this is true, the US Government must tread very lightly. We can't do whatever we want to in a sovereign country. They have rules we must follow. We can't afford to make an enemy so close to our coast."

"So you think this has some merit?"

He studied the paper. "It's hard to say. I'll look into it. Anything else you failed to disclose in the debriefing?"

Peggy stiffened her shoulders. "No, sir."

He rubbed his hand across his chin. "You should have brought this to me straight away."

"Yes, sir."

"Who else knows about this besides the three of you?"

"No one, sir."

"Good. Keep it that way."

"Are you going to report me for dereliction of duty, sir?"

He scrutinized her for a long moment, no doubt to make her squirm, a military tactic. "I don't think that's necessary."

An unspoken *but* hung in the air.

She waited.

"But I have no choice but to put a written reprimand in your file."

Both Jolene and Brownie jumped to their feet. "No."

"Take your seats. Unless the pair of you need reprimands in your files as well."

While still sitting at attention, Peggy wiggled a hand in her comrades' direction to get them to sit. No sense all of them getting into trouble. This was the reason she'd wanted to come alone.

The pair of WASPs mutely obeyed.

The major folded his hands on his desk and gave Peggy a hard stare. "The Army Air Corps can't tolerate pilots doing as they please and withholding information. This knowledge might have been vital coupled with other gathered intelligence. This may seem like one small unrelated factor but could be important for the success of a mission you know nothing about."

Peggy hadn't thought of that. "Yes, sir." She appreciated him not treating her any different than her male counterparts, but it also broke her heart. Maybe he didn't care for her as much as he'd led her to believe. "It won't happen again, sir."

"See that it doesn't. You're fortunate to get off with a warning and note in your file."

"Yes, sir."

He sighed. "What am I going to do with you three? Can I trust you?"

"Absolutely, sir."

Jolene scooted to the edge of her chair. "We want to do our jobs—jobs we are good at—and we want to help those soldiers held captive. What can we do, sir?"

He shook his head. "Nothing."

"But we want to help." Brownie leaned forward. "We are capable."

"This is none of your concern now. I'll see to it this is properly investigated. If action is deemed necessary, the Army Air Corps will handle it."

Peggy had heard similar words when some military men planned to ignore WASPs. Her outrage flamed to life again. "Just like the one sergeant down in Cuba. Brush it under the rug." She shot to her feet, causing the major to stand. "There are three men out there scared for their lives, sir." She'd thought he understood.

Major Berg pressed his hands into the surface of the desk and leaned forward. "I'm aware of that. I will *not* brush this under the rug. You three are dismissed before one or more of you becomes insubordinate." His hard military expression left no room for argument. He'd been pushed as far as she dared.

Jolene and Brownie sensed the major's resoluteness too and scuttled out the door.

"Yes, sir." Peggy snapped an unnecessary salute to show her displeasure. When the major returned it, she did an about-face and marched out of the office.

"They never think a WASP knows anything." Jolene continued to sputter her disapproval as she strode down the hallway.

Peggy and Brownie hustled along but, being short, they couldn't keep up with their fellow WASP's longer stride.

Once outside, Jolene stopped and waited for her and Brownie to catch up. She shook her finger. "He didn't believe you. He's not going to do anything. The men in the army are all the same."

Peggy hadn't felt he'd been convinced either. "I'm sure he'll look into it. You heard him. The government has to be careful not to cause more problems than we currently have in this war. Let's give him a chance to investigate this. He can at least inquire about those names belonging to our military soldiers." She prayed he would do the right thing rather than sitting on this information in the hopes she and her fellow WASPs forgot about it.

He was a good man. She needed to trust that.

———— ≈ ————

Howie studied the slip of wrinkled paper. He wished Witherspoon had come to him straight away. He understood the WASPs weren't always treated fairly so didn't completely blame her for not speaking up. Even so, she and the other WASPs needed to understand they shouldn't remain silent on something like this, and that they could trust him.

This was why getting involved with a subordinate was a bad idea—not that they were involved. It made disciplining so much harder. He might have let it slide had the other WASPs not been present. Now she would never believe his declaration of his feelings to be genuine.

He lifted the receiver on his phone. His sergeant didn't pick up the other end. Probably still off filing those records.

Howie went to the outer office and searched Sergeant Miller's desk for the sheet of phone numbers. Finding it, he returned to his own desk and dialed personnel. "I need information on three soldiers stationed in Cuba."

He would get to the bottom of this and repair the strain between him and Witherspoon.

He hoped.

Two days later, Witherspoon, along with Nightingale and Brownie, knocked on Howie's office door. He hadn't given them any updates on the matter of the captive soldiers in Cuba yet.

"Come in." Howie stood. "I can guess what this is about. Have a seat, ladies." He'd been expecting a visit from them.

They sat, and Witherspoon spoke. "We were wondering what you've found out, sir."

He wished she had come alone. Even though everything needed to stay strictly professional, he would have liked it to be just the two of them. He wanted to speak to her about his brusque behavior last time. "Not much. There are three US Soldiers stationed in Cuba by the names of Williams, Gillespie, and Nelson. Williams is a captain. The other two are a sergeant and a private respectively."

Witherspoon's eyes widened. "Then the note wasn't a farce, sir."

"We don't know that. I've been trying to reach any one of the men by telephone, but I have been unsuccessful thus far. Communications to Cuba can be spotty. I also can't get anyone to tell me their where-abouts. I feel as though I'm getting the runaround."

Nightingale narrowed her eyes. "Do you think it's because they've been captured and no one wants to admit it? Or everyone's sworn to secrecy?"

He did, but he needed some sort of confirmation in order to take any action. "I'm going to speak to General Hawkins about this and see if he can get some answers."

Witherspoon shifted to the edge of her seat. "I want to go with you when you talk to the general, sir."

"That's not a good idea. I'll tell you what I learn. I have an appointment with him at 1400 hours."

"But shouldn't I—"

"No." He wanted to give in to her but couldn't trust her not to blurt out whatever came to her mind if she disagreed with the general. Howie appreciated her speaking her mind, but the general's office wasn't the place for it. "Come back at 1600 hours." He should be back by then. "Dismissed. I need to prepare exactly what I'm going tell the general." He rose to his feet.

The three WASPs stood. Two exited. Witherspoon pinned him with a look.

He wanted to ask her to stay, but to do so might cause the others to wonder why. It wouldn't be the first time. He wanted to apologize for his previous harsh tone with her. The last thing either of them needed was to have tongues start wagging. He'd already made the mistake of confessing his feelings to her. He needed to remember his place. It would be best for both of them to keep everything professional, even if that wasn't what his heart wanted. "Was there something else, Witherspoon?"

Silence stretched between them before she spoke. "No, sir." She about-faced and left.

He breathed a sigh of relief as he sank back into his chair. He'd managed to let her go.

≣ CHAPTER 18 ≣

At 1400 hours, Howie entered Brigadier General Hawkins's Bolling Airfield office and stood at attention.

Without looking up, the general spoke. "At ease. Take a seat." He continued to write on the form in front of him.

Howie sat and waited silently.

After a few moments, the general lifted his gaze but kept his pen poised over the papers on his desk. "I hope this won't take long."

This very well could, or it could be a simple relaying of information and a dismissal. "I've stumbled across some intelligence that may or may not have any relevance." Howie handed the note Peggy had retrieved in Cuba to the general. "We believe those are coordinates where three American soldiers are being held in Cuba."

General Hawkins set his pen aside and pinned Howie with a hard stare. "We?"

"One of the WASPs under my command, sir." He relayed Peggy's story and explained how she came about the information but left the other two out of his narrative. For now. If it became imperative to include them, he would. "I contacted personnel in Cuba to confirm whether or not these names relate to actual American soldiers, but no one will tell me much. I was hoping you could loosen some lips."

"Do you realize the likelihood of American troops being held against their will in Cuba is highly remote?"

Howie leaned forward in his chair. "The fact no one will talk to me, tells me something is amiss. Someone is hiding something. If that

147

something is our men, we should do something about it."

The general spoke slowly as though thinking many scenarios through between his words. "If what you are saying is true, this could be tricky. Let me see what I can find out."

"Thank you, sir."

As though suddenly spurred on by a direct order, the general picked up his phone. "Sergeant, have my car brought around." He hung up, shuffled the stack of files from his desk into an attaché case, and stood. "Come with me."

Howie shoved out of the chair and followed the general out of the office. "Where are we going, sir?"

"The Pentagon. This is too sensitive to speak of here." He addressed his desk sergeant again on his way past the enlisted officer's workstation. "Inform General Arnold I'm on my way."

The sergeant nodded, even as he was already on the phone, likely hailing the general's car.

Outside, a government vehicle pulled up with small blue flags exhibiting a single white star flapping from the front fenders. The driver got out and opened the back door for the general.

Howie circled the car and let himself in on the other side. Not sure of the protocol, he remained silent. If the general wished to talk about this matter on the drive to the Pentagon, he would.

Instead, General Hawkins spent the duration of the ride, going through the files he'd brought.

As the car entered the Pentagon parking lot, all military personnel walking along stopped and saluted the vehicle. The driver pulled right up to the main entrance of the building.

Howie had never been able to do that. Having flags on your transportation had its benefits. No parking a block away on the far side of the car lot and hoofing it to the building. This was nice.

At the curb, the driver opened the general's door, which left Howie to fend for himself.

The general marched toward the entrance. The people between the car and the building saluted him and Howie. He returned the gesture as did the general. A soldier near the door opened it with one hand and raised his other to his eyebrow.

The general saluted back. "As you were."

Howie mimicked the action and scurried in after his superior.

General Hawkins marched through the corridors as though he were tasked with an urgent mission on the battlefield. Howie would not slow him down and hurried along, trying to hide that this pace was a bit of a challenge for him. Pushing himself beyond his perceived limits would make him stronger.

Outside a door with the general's name on it, a middle-aged, female clerk pushed out of her chair to stand. "Sir. General Arnold has been notified. He's expecting you."

The general handed his attaché case to her. "Thank you, Mildred." He turned to Howie. "You wait here." He marched off.

While the clerk ducked into the office to deposit the attaché, Howie sat on a chair in the outer area. This might take a while.

Over an hour later, Howie stood and addressed the clerk. "May I use the telephone?"

The woman nodded as she continued to click the typewriter keys.

He lifted the receiver and dialed his own office, reaching Sergeant Miller. "I have a meeting with some WASPs scheduled in a few minutes at 1600 hours. I'm not going to make it back in time. Can you let them know I'll speak with them tomorrow?"

"Yes, sir."

He hadn't imagined being here this long. He hadn't imagined being at the Pentagon at all today. He would miss seeing Witherspoon.

A couple of minutes later, the telephone rang, and the clerk answered it. "Good afternoon, General Hawkins's office. . .He is, sir. . . Yes, sir. . .I'll be right there, sir." She hung up the receiver. Then she gathered some folders from a desk drawer and stood. "The general wants you to continue to wait for him."

Howie stood as well. "Did he say how much longer it might be?"

She tilted her head. "I'm sorry. He didn't. I have to go. The general needs these files. There's a mess hall on the ground floor if you're hungry." She strolled away.

He left a note on the clerk's desk and got himself a sandwich. When he returned, the desk remained vacant, so he sat. He wished he'd brought some sort of work to keep himself busy.

The clerk soon returned, shook her head to indicate the general wasn't coming yet, and resumed her seat.

The clock on the wall showed 1800 hours, and Howie still waited. Had the general gone home and forgotten he had left Howie sitting here? Howie had refrained from engaging the clerk in conversation so he wouldn't hamper her work, but now he hoped to get a little information. "Isn't it after quitting time for you?"

She smiled up at him. "One would think. The general works unconventional hours. I don't really mind. A few late nights are minuscule compared to the sacrifices you boys have made in Europe and the Pacific."

He suspected it was more than a few. This was probably business as usual.

At 1847 hours, General Hawkins marched down the corridor.

Howie stood. "Sir."

The general gave a nod of acknowledgement but spoke to his clerk. "Mildred, do you have the copies of that report made?"

She pulled the paper from her typewriter with a ratcheting sound and tucked it inside the top folder. One by one, the ten folders had been filled with papers she had typed, page after page, each a crisp original. "Right here, sir." She put her hand on the top of the stack. Each one must have contained twenty pages or more.

"Thank you. Would you take them to General Arnold? Then you can go home."

She stood and handed a folder to him not from the stack. "The original." She scooped up the folders and walked off.

General Hawkins motioned to Howie as he entered his office. "Come in. Take a seat."

Howie waited for the general to sit first before he did.

"Thank you for waiting."

Like Howie had much of a choice. "Not a problem, sir." Good thing he'd gotten that sandwich.

The general steepled his hands. "I spoke with the Joint Chiefs of Staff *and* the President of the United States. You can probably guess what I was told."

Howie was afraid of that, and it wasn't as though he could petition to someone higher. Other than God. "Is there nothing that can be done for our men?"

"Cuba's official position is that no US soldiers are being held against their will. President Batista has less than nine days in power, so it is unlikely he will take any action with tensions so high. It's too risky to send in a rescue team. The military personnel in Cuba are being watched carefully. We can't chance an international incident. We have to think of the big picture here. *And* that picture is over in Europe and in the Pacific."

Howie didn't always like the big picture, especially when lives could be in jeopardy, but he understood.

"This is all the information I could learn. There are suspected German sympathizers, and they even believe there are some actual Germans hiding out in Cuba from the U-boat that was sunk in the area two and a half weeks ago. That's who they believe has them." The general showed him the folder. "The coordinates you gave me were confirmed. Those three soldiers have indeed been missing for nearly two weeks. There will be *no* rescue attempt made by US military personnel. Do I make myself clear?"

Howie didn't like this. Not one bit. Had he been left for dead and abandoned, he wouldn't be here. People had risked their own lives to rescue him. Even as he was helpless to drag himself out of his crashed plane, he knew the decision to rescue him or not would be made. He was only one life. It didn't make sense to risk a dozen other men to *maybe* save one who *might* not even be alive. He wouldn't have wanted others to die on his account. A farmer had come to his aid and hidden him in his cellar for two days until it was safe to transport him to a place where the military could retrieve him.

If Howie hadn't been delirious with pain, he would have urged the farmer not to put his own life in peril to save Howie's. Fortunately, the man had gotten Howie to Allied forces, and he'd woken up in a field hospital. They patched him the best they could before transporting him to England. After three surgeries and five months recuperating, he had been shipped back to the States. His military flying career over. That hurt as much as his leg. In another six months, the pin that had been put in his right thigh would be removed, and he would be deemed cured. But he would never be the same. He would likely carry his limp for the rest of his life. And the nightmares still hadn't abated. Would they also haunt him the rest of his life?

"I said do you understand, Major Berg?"

He did even though it made anger burn inside him. "Is there nothing we can do for our soldiers, sir?"

"It's the cost of war, Major." The general seemed resigned to those men's fate. "You know that."

Why did it have to be such a high cost? "We aren't at war with Cuba."

"Nevertheless, we need to do everything we can to keep it that way. After the tenth when President-elect Dr. Ramón Grau takes office, we can approach him."

It could be too late by then. "But our soldiers?"

"I wish it didn't have to be this way, but *my* hands are tied. The US military and its members can do nothing to help those soldiers without the cooperation of the Cuban government."

Howie chafed at the idea of leaving those soldiers to their fate. "Yes, sir."

"You're dismissed."

Howie stood, saluted, and left.

What was he going to tell Peggy—WASP Witherspoon? She would be so disappointed in his failure.

Disappointed in him.

———— ≈ ————

The next day, Peggy went to Major Berg's office, along with Jolene and Brownie. Unfortunately she hadn't heard news of the plight of the US soldiers in Cuba yesterday. Hopefully, the delay meant he had good news. Perhaps even that the men had already been freed.

"I've met with General Hawkins, as you know."

"Have the soldiers been rescued?" Peggy had been praying for their safe return.

His hesitation couldn't be good. "I'm afraid not."

Jolene edged to the front of her seat. "Why?"

"It's complicated. Cuban President Batista has less than eight days in office. The successor he chose didn't win the election. Dr. Ramón Grau did. Tensions are high in Cuba's government with the transfer of power on October 10." Eight days away.

Peggy sensed she wouldn't like where this conversation was heading. "All the more reason Batista would want to help the US. Or would Dr. Grau be more inclined to assist with a rescue?"

The major appeared to want to speak but didn't.

His delay in answering fueled her irritation. "When are our men coming home?"

The major still hesitated. "Our government has been negotiating with both President Batista and Dr. Grau. Batista is busy with last-minute government issues and says now isn't a good time to look for the missing men. He also refuses to allow American troops to search for them."

"And Dr. Grau?"

"He would make no promises one way or another, but his lack of commitment isn't encouraging. He could surprise us after taking office."

Peggy hated politics sometimes. "Our men could be dead by the tenth. What about a covert operation? No one need know a rescue team is there."

"No official operation can be pursued at this time. I know that's hard to hear. Maybe after the transfer of power, we can negotiate with Dr. Grau. Even then, it's doubtful any efforts will be made to retrieve the soldiers."

Peggy disliked all of these politics toying with people's lives and wanted to tell the major as much but knew to do so would be insubordination. Instead, she huffed out a breath to show her displeasure.

He must have read her irritation. "We are in the middle of the biggest war this world has seen. The US needs to focus all its efforts and resources toward winning in Europe and the Pacific. This is not the time to upset things so close to our own boarders."

Unacceptable. Maybe she could petition the Pentagon or speak with General Hawkins herself. He'd assured her she could come to him if she had any other ideas. She pushed to her feet. "Permission to leave, sir?"

Jolene and Brownie stood as did the major.

"Promise me you ladies won't try to do anything."

What could any of them possibly do? "Like what? We are only *women* after all. May we be dismissed, sir?"

He hesitated before answering. "Dismissed."

Peggy about-faced, wrenched the door open, and marched out.

From behind her, Jolene said, "Peggy?"

Peggy didn't stop. She couldn't. She needed to put some distance between her and the military. Once outside, she halted in response to her fellow WASPs' pleas.

Jolene faced her. "I've never seen you so angry."

Peggy's vision blurred, so she blinked away the accumulating moisture. "You both understand there will be no rescue now or in the future, and there is nothing we can do."

Solemnly they both nodded.

"What if those men were one of our loved ones?" She thought of George being shot down. Had the decision to do nothing been made in his case as well? "Would you be all right with the military simply writing them off? Letting them die?"

Jolene gripped Peggy's shoulders. "Of course not, but I don't know what else we can do."

Brownie edged closer. "Maybe we could write to President Roosevelt."

Simple solutions to a difficult problem. A problem easily ignored by bureaucrats. Peggy wished she *could* do something about all this, but she could see no alternative. "As the major said, our government is too focused with a huge war on the other side of the world to bother with three soldiers on a small island in the Caribbean who may or may not be held captive." She slumped her shoulders in defeat.

After a painful silence, Jolene said, "So what are we going to do?"

How could Peggy's comrade not understand? "They won't go rescue them."

"I'll restate. What are *we* going to do?" Jolene folded her arms. "I know you well enough, Mama Bird. Now that you know for certain this is real and there are indeed soldiers held captive, you won't sit around doing nothing."

Jolene was right. She had poked at Peggy's maternal instinct.

If only Peggy could fly there herself and rescue those men. She just didn't have the means and couldn't figure out how to do it. However, if she came up with a viable solution, there was no way she would involve her fellow Women Airforce Service Pilots. She wouldn't risk their careers and lives.

Brownie gave a deliberate nod. "I'm in."

Jolene echoed, "Me too."

Had Peggy missed something? "In for what?"

Brownie planted her hands on her hips. "Whatever you're planning to do to rescue those men. They don't deserve to sit over there, thinking we all have abandoned them."

No, they didn't. "But they *do* expect they could be casualties of war. That's what they signed up for."

Jolene tilted her head and held up her index finger. "True, they would expect others not to risk their lives if they were over in Europe, but Cuba is an ally. On this side of the ocean, they *would* expect someone to come and free them. So as I said before, I'm in."

Peggy appreciated their enthusiasm. Unfortunately, there was nothing to be *in* for. "Unless either of you have an aircraft or a boat lying around we could use, I don't see how to get to Cuba, let alone free our boys from hostile adversaries and return home without getting captured or killed."

Her fellow WASPs' shoulders drooped, obviously feeling the defeat as much as Peggy.

≡ CHAPTER 19 ≡

The next day, Peggy stood in the front of her oldest daughter's classroom. She had been invited along with a few other parents and grandparents to talk about their jobs. She explained the various tasks she performed, then invited questions.

A boy named Marvin raised his hand. "Ladies can't fly airplanes."

Typical.

Mrs. Livingston spoke before Peggy had a chance to refute the boy. "They most certainly can. There have been women flying airplanes for more than twenty years."

Marvin folded his arms in a huff. "It's not right. My father says so. He says—"

"That's enough, Marvin." Mrs. Livingston gave Peggy an apologetic glance.

Peggy understood. The boy wasn't the first person to criticize her for flying. What surprised her most was the number of *women* who were against women flying.

Mrs. Livingston moved to the front of the room. "Let's thank all our special guests for coming." She led the class in applause. Most clapped normally. Wendy did so energetically, while Marvin didn't at all.

Peggy walked to her daughter's desk. "I'll be waiting by the car when school lets out." It would only be another ten minutes. She left and headed outside.

As she exited the building, someone was calling, "Miss? Miss?" She doubted they were hailing her but turned anyway.

A woman hurried up to her. "You're that pilot lady who's in the army, aren't you?"

"I'm not technically in the Army Air Corps but work with them." It was hard to explain the nature of the relationship between the military and the WASP to civilians.

"You have to help me. My husband is in the army, and he's missing. No one will tell me anything."

Peggy's heart broke for this woman. She pictured her own husband shot down over Germany and remembered the helpless feeling of not knowing for the longest time what had happened to him. "Like I said, I'm not in the army." Civilians didn't understand.

"But you know people. You could talk to someone." The anguish in the woman's eyes wrenched Peggy's gut.

"I suggest you go up your husband's chain of command." Someone there likely knew something. Whether or not they could or would release any information to her was another matter.

"I have. They won't tell me anything."

Peggy understood this woman's frustration all too well. "I can find out who to contact for the local American Red Cross Home Service Corps. They should be able to help you."

"They weren't able to find out anything either. All I'm asking is that you inquire about him to the people you know."

The distress and fear on this woman's pleading face pulled at Peggy's heart. "All right. I'll see what I can do. What's your name?" Not that it would do any good. She didn't know powerful enough people, but the comfort in knowing someone had listened and might do something could be an enormous help. It made those left waiting to feel less alone.

"Wanda Gillespie."

Peggy's breath froze in her lungs. It couldn't be. "Where. . .is your husband stationed?" But she knew.

"Cuba. It is only a short nine-month assignment." The woman's eyes flooded with tears from her anguish. "He is due to be home by Thanksgiving. The children and I stayed here rather than uprooting them. He usually calls every few days, but I haven't heard from him in over two weeks. It's not like him. Nobody in his unit will tell me where he is."

Peggy bit her tongue. She couldn't confess to this woman she knew anything about her husband, even though she knew more than most anyone else. There was nothing she could do for this frightened wife and mother. "How many children do you have?" Polite conversation wasn't much.

"Five, ages four, six, eight, nine, and eleven. We were looking forward to spending the holidays together."

Those poor dear children. They might soon be like her own fatherless daughters, if they weren't already. Peggy pushed back her own tears. She dug in her pocketbook and retrieved paper and pen. "Write down your telephone number so I can call you if I learn anything."

The woman did then tightly hugged Peggy. "Thank you. Thank you so much."

She hated giving this despondent woman false hope.

But it was better than no hope at all.

———— ≈ ————

Two nights later, while the girls were playing in their room, Peggy helped her mother with the dishes.

Mom rinsed a plate and set it in the drainer. "You've seemed more troubled than usual the past several days. Do you want to talk about it?"

Peggy did, and she didn't. "Remember that problem I had last week that you prayed about?" She set the glass she'd dried into the cupboard.

"That thing you couldn't tell me but you did tell the major? Have you heard about it? Did it go well?"

"Yes and yes and. . .no. The military isn't going to do anything." Peggy still couldn't believe they were giving up on those soldiers.

"I'm sorry, but the military people generally know what's best in situations regarding military affairs."

Peggy's anger flamed white hot. "But they don't. They think sacrificing three men's lives is worth the price of maybe—possibly, but no guarantee—peace. Why won't they just let the military go in? I'm sure their families would agree with me." Mrs. Gillespie definitely would. "The risk is worth it to save three lives." She picked up the plate and dried in earnest.

"Wait a minute." Mom stilled her hands in the soapy water.

"You're saying a lot of words and only some of them make sense. I think all of your *theys* aren't the same *they*. Are you saying people's lives are in danger?"

It likely didn't matter if her mom heard the whole story. She knew enough to keep it to herself. Peggy lowered her voice, not that it mattered. "Yes, three US soldiers' lives. The first 'they' is *our* government. The second is Cuba."

Mom furrowed her eyebrows. "So both Cuba and the US are willing to let our men die without trying to help them?"

"Apparently."

"How will that ensure peace?"

How indeed. "Everyone is afraid of creating an international incident. Well, if our boys die, there will be an international incident. So rescuing them might not stop a clash between our two countries, but it might save three soldiers who have put their lives on the line for this country. What bothers me the most is that our government won't even try. They are giving up before even starting." Had the government given up on George without trying to rescue him? She blinked to clear her vision to no avail.

"What are you going to do?"

"There's nothing I can do." She felt so helpless, she wanted to scream.

Junie rushed into the kitchen. "Don't cry, Mommy." Her baby held up her arms.

Peggy set the plate and tea towel into the drainer and picked up her youngest. "I'm all right."

Junie clamped her twiggy legs around Peggy's waist and her arms around her neck.

Peggy held her daughter close, thinking of Wanda Gillespie's five children. That poor family. They didn't even realize yet that they wouldn't likely ever see their father again.

As she listened to her daughter's breathing and felt the heat of her little one's sigh on her skin, it was almost as though the Lord whispered in her other ear. She knew what she must do and held Mom's gaze. "I have to save them."

Mom wrinkled her eyebrows. "How?"

"I don't know, but I sense God does." The only way a plan that went against two governments would work was with the Lord's involvement. The key would be to find the right people to speak to.

Or get her hands on an airplane.

————————≈————————

As Peggy lay in bed that night, she prayed for a solution to the captured soldiers' problem. Having met Mrs. Gillespie made her more determined to plan some kind of rescue attempt.

All the key people in positions to execute a rescue operation had already denied permission with no hope of changing their minds. Since she didn't see how she could convince anyone to her way of thinking to free the men, she would have to go herself. But how? She didn't have an airplane at her disposal, and the military would never approve the use of one for an unauthorized mission.

Nothing came to her until the next day when she gazed out beyond the edge of the tarmac to the Graveyard where the derelict aircraft waited to be scrapped or decay into dust. Perhaps she could find one which wasn't as bad off as the others and cobble together enough parts to make it fly.

Later that day, Peggy met with Jolene and Brownie outside the hangar. "We now know the situation with the captured soldiers is real, and that the coordinates are accurate. We merely need a way to get to Cuba and back without anyone stopping us or finding out."

Brownie pointed at Peggy. "And you have a plan."

"Not exactly a plan, but an inkling of an idea. An idea, mind you, that probably won't work." Peggy didn't want to get their hopes up, but it was something that might bloom into an actual good idea.

Brownie's eyes gleamed. "Let's hear it."

"We can't exactly 'borrow' a military aircraft, and none of us has an airplane or boat at the ready, which leaves us with few options."

Jolene grinned. "But you have an idea about that."

Peggy returned the smile. She'd been thinking of this since arriving at work. "The Graveyard is full of aircraft the military doesn't care about. They wouldn't notice if one went missing for a few hours."

Jolene shook her head. "They call it the Graveyard for a reason. Those planes don't fly."

"Not yet. I bet we could scavenge enough parts from the various birds to get one of those old girls in the air again."

"You think so?" Brownie's enthusiasm was heartening.

Peggy nodded. "There is a Northrop Delta on the edge of the Graveyard which might be in pretty good shape. Of all the aircraft there, it appears to be the closest to being flyable." At least from the outside. "Nobody liked those poor planes, so I doubt anyone would miss it."

Brownie grinned from ear to ear. "Let's do it."

Jolene raised a hand. "Hold your little horses, cowgirl. Let's see what kind of shape this aircraft is in first before we go flying off into the sunset in a condemned plane."

Peggy agreed and stood. "Let's go investigate her."

The trio climbed into Peggy's Ford, and she drove over to the Graveyard.

On the way, Brownie pointed out the open window. "What about that one? It appears serviceable."

"Too small. I think we should take a crew of at least two plus the three men we'll have on the return trip. A small transport plane would be best."

Brownie piped up. "Crew of *three*. You're not leaving me behind."

"Your foot is still healing." The young pilot couldn't be serious.

"It aches but there isn't any danger of my bullet wound breaking open or anything. I'm going. If I don't, then neither do the pair of you. You know the mission will have a better chance of succeeding with all three of us."

Peggy eyed her. "What about your limp?"

Brownie scrunched up her nose. "I don't limp."

Did she truly not realize she still did?

Peggy shared a look with Jolene. She couldn't believe the young pilot's determination.

Jolene tilted her head. "I hate to admit this, but I think she's right."

Peggy had felt a third would be beneficial as well, but with Brownie's injury, she hadn't wanted to involve her or pull in anyone else. "If you want to go and think you're healed enough, it would be helpful."

What an honor to be a comrade-in-arms with these valiant women.

At the Northrop Delta, Peggy stopped her car, and they all got out. It was a short, stubby aircraft with a single engine in its wide flat nose. It reminded her of a chubby, roly-poly baby. The wings sat under the fuselage. "Big enough to carry six people, yet small enough to hopefully go unnoticed."

Brownie kicked one of the tires. "The wheels on this seem decent."

Jolene nodded. "She appears serviceable."

"Let's evaluate the exterior." Peggy had done a quick assessment the first time when she had scoured the Graveyard to see if any aircraft here were even a remote possibility for use. If she hadn't found this one, the plan to free the soldiers would be a bust.

She walked around the craft examining more closely than she had before. Jolene and Brownie did the same. Once they had all circled the plane, Jolene rested a hand on the wing. "The outside seems solid. If the inside is in half as good of shape, I think we have ourselves an aircraft."

Brownie patted the underbelly. "This one wasn't used as a bomber, so the inside probably wasn't fitted with a rear gunner either. That will mean more space and likely the seats are still present."

Peggy hoisted herself onto the wing. She then grabbed the handle on the door and pulled. It was stiff and only barely budged. She yanked harder, and it creaked open, becoming easier the wider it got. "We'll need to grease that. We wouldn't want the door sticking when we're in a hurry."

Jolene widened her eyes. "Nor do we want it making all that racket."

Peggy scrambled inside. The interior had been gutted. Not only was there no rear gunner apparatus installed, but the seats which had been in this aircraft had been removed at some point. As Brownie and Jolene climbed in, Peggy moved to the front. "The pilot and copilot seats are missing too. You want the bad news, the really bad news, or the good news first."

Jolene came up behind her. "Worse than having to stand up to fly this thing?"

"The whole control panel has been pulled out."

Brownie spoke from farther back. "Was that the bad news or really bad news?"

"All the wiring has been stripped out."

"Are you kidding?" Jolene said.

Both Brownie and Jolene peeked around her. "What's the *good* news?"

"None of the windows are broken." Peggy gave a grimacing smile.

Brownie, the smallest of the three, squeezed past and pointed. "Both earphone sets are here and their cords look to be in reasonable shape."

Jolene shook her head. "I don't know about this."

At her comrade's discouragement, disappointment slapped Peggy. "Don't you think we have the skills between the three of us to return this majestic craft to its former glory?"

Brownie laughed. "I don't think anyone has ever called the Northrop Delta *majestic* before."

Jolene narrowed her eyes at Peggy. "I have no doubt we possess the skills, but can we find all the parts we'll need and get it ready quickly enough to rescue those soldiers?"

That could be a problem. "We won't know until we try. The first thing to do is make a list of what is sound and working on this bird."

"Working?" Jolene shook her head. "Nothing."

"Not true." Brownie pointed behind her. "The door worked. We got inside didn't we?"

An optimist. Always good to have one on their team.

Peggy needn't reply to either of their comments. "We'll also make a list of the repairs in order of importance and the supplies and parts we'll require."

Jolene nodded. "A list of tools and equipment as well."

Brownie pursed her lips. "We'll have to be stealthy to get all those things without anyone noticing."

It would be a challenge. "We won't borrow any tools or equipment that aren't extras. If we need one that isn't extra, we'll make sure no one is using it or needs it right away." She surveyed the damage in the cockpit again. "My guess is that someone needed a part or two and some of the wiring. Hopefully, that's the main issue. We'll scrounge in the other dead aircraft for as many of the missing parts and supplies we can find."

Brownie dug a pencil and a small note pad from the pocket on the leg of her zoot suit. "Call out the good first. That will help soften the blow of the bad."

Peggy and Jolene named every positive thing they could think of about the aircraft, including the interior paint, which didn't really matter. Then Peggy said, "Let me check to see if the propeller turns." This whole endeavor would be sunk if that didn't at least turn. She climbed out and down off the wing. She took a deep breath, said a quick little prayer, gripped the propeller blade, and moved it back and forth. Good. It wasn't frozen in place. She stretched up on tiptoes and gave the blades as hard of a spin as she could.

Though it was a little stiff from disuse, it rotated all the way around and then some.

Good. That meant anything wrong with it could be greased or repaired. This endeavor was looking more promising all the time.

Time to determine the bad. An hour later, they had a lengthy list of repairs, and those were only the ones they could assess. Thankfully, there didn't appear to be any exterior damage, no popped rivets or busted seams. No windows had cracks and the caulk wasn't peeling away. The intake for the engine and the propeller seemed good. The rudder wasn't seized, the flaps and ailerons appeared to be in working order, and the wings were still intact. This craft had apparently been gutted of its seats and wiring but nothing more. *Hopefully* nothing more.

Once they could commence wiring things up, they might discover this craft wasn't air worthy no matter how much work they put into it. It had been relegated to the Graveyard for a reason. Even in its day, it wasn't a popular machine. Only thirty-two of this generation of the Deltas had been built. Not that there was anything really wrong with them. It was simply that other aircraft could do the job better.

In its heyday, this craft had many redeeming qualities. It could fly at night. It could be fitted with floats, or skies for land, water, and snow, and ice landings and take offs. It could fly low under the radar. Though on the small side for a cargo plane, it had a spacious interior, especially without the seats. Also, its stocky build made it sturdy enough to land on rugged terrain. All things which might come in handy on this mission—that wasn't a mission.

If they couldn't get the old girl to fly—which they likely wouldn't—at least Peggy was doing something. It beat sitting around on her hands.

Peggy mentally calculated a rough number of hours it might take to get this bird in the air. "This is not going to be an easy undertaking, neither repairing this craft nor attempting to mount and execute a successful rescue. There are so many things that could go wrong. If we are caught at any point along the way, we will be separated from the Women Airforce Service Pilots and could be charged with crimes. If you don't want to do this, I will understand, but I need to know now before we embark on this mission." She didn't want to put a lot of time and effort into this endeavor to have them quit and have this venture all fall apart. She would be sacrificing time with her daughters, so this needed to be worth the effort they would be putting forth. "We could be killed or captured ourselves."

Jolene put her hands on her hips. "We are every bit as dedicated as any of the male soldiers or airmen. We will see this mission to the end. If any one of us were being held, we would want someone to be planning a rescue. We would need to hope our fellow comrades would come for us in order to have the will to survive. We can't abandon those men. This is why we are WASPs. To serve our country and aid the men who are fighting for our country in any way we can."

Brownie held the tablet of paper with all their lists on it. "My brother is fighting in the Pacific. If he were captured, I would want people to go get him. And I know my brother would join a rescue mission without consideration for his own life. I will do no less."

Pride for her brave fellow WASPs filled Peggy. "Let's scout out the other aircraft in the Graveyard and see what kind of parts we can scrounge up. Focus first on wiring. If we can't wire this up, there isn't much point in getting anything else." The wiring was the most obvious and pressing need and would tell them which systems on the Northrop Delta worked.

What would Major Berg think of this endeavor she was about to embark on? Would he think her idea held merit? Or would he deem her a fool?

⋛CHAPTER 20⋚

Peggy climbed out of the Delta. The challenge to make a working aircraft from derelicts was going to be fun. "In my trunk are tools." She opened the back end of her Ford.

Brownie reached in for one of the tool belts. "How do you always think of everything?"

"It's part of being a mother. I always have to stay one step ahead." She probably wouldn't have before having children, leaving it to her own mother to remember mundane details.

She split off from her comrades, each taking a different direction in the Graveyard to scavenge for parts. The variety of planes would hopefully afford them everything they would need. She chose a C-46 Commando to harvest from, bigger than the Delta but not the largest in the Graveyard. The outside had major damage, from cracked and missing windows to popped rivets and a broken wing which sagged to the ground. Also, the landing-gear supports had given way, causing the craft to rest on its belly.

Where the access door should be, an opening yawned wide. That would make getting inside easier. She hoisted herself up and climbed aboard. In addition to the other damage, the seats were missing, except one in the rear of the fuselage lying on its side. Peggy crossed to it to see if it would be worth returning for.

Tipping it upright, she noted the bent frame, which caused it to sit lopsided. Though damaged, it wasn't completely. . .unserviceable. They could likely repair it well enough to be useful if they needed to, provided they didn't find any other seats.

She headed to the cockpit. The instrument panel appeared to still be installed. Hopefully, the wiring remained intact. As she got closer, she realized the dashboard sat a little askew. Her hope dipped.

With her screwdriver, she removed the handful of screws left holding the panel in place. Someone had evidently tried to put it back but didn't bother to replace all the screws. Once she removed the last one, the whole panel shifted down with a clunk. She grabbed the corner and pulled to glimpse behind it. Though most of the wiring was absent, there were a few stragglers left.

After harvesting the remaining wires, she made notes on a paper scrap from one of her pockets of the condition of the gauges. If they needed a replacement, some of these appeared to be functional.

She found and removed additional wiring in other parts of the plane. Then she headed back to the Delta to deposit her treasures. She wasn't the first to return. On the floor of the craft sat a bundle of wires and a seatbelt harness. She deposited her finds with the others and sought out another aircraft.

After more than an hour, all three convened on the Delta, climbed inside, and surveyed their bounty. Peggy eyed the impressive pile of wires and random other pieces. Did they have everything necessary to make this craft fly again? Time and a lot of work would tell. "I think we have enough to get started."

The other two concurred with nods.

Jolene pointed from the heap to the cockpit. "We should start with wiring a few of the vital instruments and controls to see if we should bother continuing this undertaking."

Brownie nodded. "We'll need to remove the battery and charge it before anything will work." Two other batteries sat in the pile of salvaged goods.

"Smart thinking." Peggy had chosen the right people to work with on this.

After a half hour and very little progress on the wiring, they each hoisted a battery and climbed out of the Delta to head to the car and back to the hangar.

As they entered the large building, Major Berg pulled up in a car and met them. "Hello, ladies."

Oh, dear. Peggy had been so focused on the mission, she had forgotten to keep tabs on where officers and other key people would be who might stop them. She stood at attention the best she could while holding the heavy battery in both hands. "Good afternoon, sir."

He quirked an eyebrow. "It's evening. What are you three doing working this late?"

How to explain their presence? "It's war, sir. The enemy doesn't rest, so neither can we."

"Commendable, but you don't want to wear yourselves out. Then you'll be of no use."

Peggy's joints ached. "Yes, sir. Permission to relieve ourselves of these burdens."

His eyes widened as though startled. "Oh, sorry. Yes, please put them down."

Jolene and Brownie hurried away to set their batteries on the workbench. As Peggy put hers on a nearby tool cart, Jolene said, "I'm going to get the charger."

"I'll go with you." Brownie trailed after her, leaving Peggy to deal with the major.

So much for the pair of them being brave. Peggy forced a smile. "Is there anything I can do for you, sir?"

He paused before answering, as though considering his words. "I was surprised you ladies were still here. I want you all to go home or to the barracks as soon as those batteries are on to charge."

"Yes, sir."

With a nod the major walked away, climbed into his vehicle, and drove off.

Peggy heaved a sigh and allowed her shoulders to relax.

Brownie and Jolene rushed out to her, and Brownie said, "That was close."

Jolene squinted after the major's retreating vehicle. "Do you think he suspected anything?"

"He didn't seem to." Peggy hoped not. "He's not a mechanic, so I doubt he would know if we were doing something slightly off."

They needed to keep the major and anyone else from wondering what the three WASPs were up to for a day or two, until the aircraft could be deemed sky-worthy or not. "He said for us to all go home or to the barracks as soon as we put these on to charge. Though I would have liked to work a little longer, I think we should quit for the night. We don't want to draw undue attention to our actions."

"You have to drive into Maryland. You go on home, and we'll take care of the batteries." Jolene pointed to the workbench where two of the three cells sat.

Brownie pulled out the paper with the things they needed for the Delta. "We'll polish this list and make one of what we gathered today. We'll see if we can figure out what else we might need."

Jolene pointed to Brownie's list. "We'll also make a schedule of what needs to be done and in what order."

"That would be good." Peggy nodded. "We can leave it hidden in the aircraft as a checklist so any one of us can see the progress and what still needs to be done. It's probably best if we don't all work on the Northrop Delta at the same time. It might raise too many questions."

"I agree." Jolene waved her hand in the direction Major Berg had gone. "Now that the major has seen us all together this late, if he witnesses us together or all missing at the same time, he might get nosy."

Peggy waved. "I'll see you both tomorrow." She headed to her car and drove home.

What would Major Berg think of her actions if he knew what they were doing? Foolish? Or valiant? She had to admit they were a little of both.

⊒ CHAPTER 21 ⊑

The following morning, Howie sat on the bed in his TLF quarters. He really should find an apartment to rent, but he liked being close to work. What was more convenient than the building next door to his office?

He couldn't stop thinking about Witherspoon's, Nightingale's, and Brownie's behavior yesterday evening. They seemed to be up to something, yet nothing appeared to be amiss. They were good people and fine workers. He would hate for any of them to get into trouble doing something foolish. Especially Peggy. He shouldn't be thinking of the WASP by her first name, but he couldn't help it.

He drove out to the hangar where Nightingale and Brown should be working today. Witherspoon had the day off. Too bad. He looked forward to anytime he got to see her. Her mother hadn't covertly invited him to supper since the first time. He wasn't surprised. It had been a bad idea to fraternize with a subordinate. If asked again, he would have to turn down the invitation. He couldn't help that Peggy Witherspoon had the most appealing family. Her mother was nice and easy to get along with, and her two little girls were as cute as could be.

After the stock market crash, he'd decided he wouldn't marry and start a family until things improved. They never did, so he'd made his career and his life in the military. He gave up on the idea of having a family. And he'd been perfectly content with that decision.

Until Peggy had come along. First her grit and bravery in landing a wounded aircraft without seeming concerned at all. She had such confidence. More than he felt he possessed most of the time. Then she'd flown in the line of fire to save a fellow pilot. That took guts.

What had really melted his heart was her little girl. Having Junie on his lap and reading to her had been more enjoyable than anything he could have imagined. It made him long for a wife and children of his own. Made him wonder what he had been missing by foregoing a family. He hadn't realized there had been an emptiness inside him.

Though he had cursed being injured at the time and since, maybe it had been a blessing after all. It had allowed him to meet Peggy and her daughters. He hadn't known what he would do once discharged. Life seemed hollow and unfulfilled. The Army Air Corps gave him purpose. He couldn't really picture what life would be like after the military. Now he could and hoped it involved a family of his own, or more precisely Peggy and her family.

At the hangar, several WASPs, most of whom he didn't have much interaction with, worked on an aircraft. Nightingale had some sort of engine part in her hand, battling it with a wrench. At least Howie assumed it was something off an engine. He got out of his car and approached her. "How are those batteries doing?"

Setting aside the part, she wiped the greasy wrench with a rag. "Two of them appear to have charged. The other is a lost cause." She put the wrench in the tool box with a clank and retrieved a pair of vise grips.

"Are Brown and Witherspoon around today?" He'd half expected them all to be huddled together even though it was Witherspoon's day off.

Nightingale's eyes narrowed ever so slightly, almost undetectable. "Peggy's off today, but that doesn't mean she won't show up. That one is more dedicated than a mongrel with last week's ham bone. I believe Brownie is in cartography. She should be back later. Do you need them for something?"

This didn't support his theory that these three were up to something. "No. Carry on."

Howie walked to the office where the sergeant in charge was shuffling papers. "You busy?"

Sergeant Kent swiveled in his chair and jumped to attention. "Always, there's a war going on, but any excuse to put off paperwork is welcome. What can I help you with, sir?"

"At ease. What do you know about Nightingale, Brown, and Witherspoon?"

The sergeant relaxed his stance. "Those are three of the most dedicated soldiers we have. I know they aren't technically soldiers, but they might as well be. All the WASPs work hard."

Howie felt the same. "Do the three of them, in particular, spend a lot of time together?"

"No more than any of the others. However lately, I have seen that trio together more. Their heads together about something or going off together."

"Lately? How long?"

"A couple of days."

"Anything odd about their behavior?"

"Naw. Like I said, they work hard. They always have their duties completed on time or early, so I allow them the freedom to do whatever needs getting done."

Howie was satisfied until that word *freedom*. If those three weren't watched as closely as others who needed more scrutiny, then they could veer off the flight plan without notice. "Do you know where Brown is?"

"She was scheduled in cartography, then asked if she could take care of some personal business."

What kind of personal business could a single gal have who bunked in the barracks and worked less than a mile away from where she lived? Not likely a date. Jackie Cochran frowned upon those as a way to protect her WASPs. Not church, it wasn't Sunday. A phone call home perhaps? "Thanks, Sergeant."

"I think I saw Witherspoon's car heading out toward the Graveyard."

"The what?"

Kent pointed in the general direction of the tarmac. "It's where old aircraft are parked until they can be dismantled or scrapped."

A bad feeling spun up inside Howie's gut. They couldn't be planning something, could they? "Any of those planes functional?"

"Naw. That's why they're out there. Beyond repair. They aren't worth much. Most of them are doing nothing more than turning to rust if you ask me. Sometimes soldiers, pilots, and WASPs like to go out there to get away from regular duties in their off time."

Most of the planes, but not all of them. Though the sergeant had eased Howie's worry, he would check to make sure. "Thanks." When he strolled back through the hangar to his car, Nightingale was no longer there. He wouldn't read anything into that, give them the benefit of the doubt. Even so, he drove out to the Graveyard.

Indeed, Witherspoon's car sat parked near a derelict Northrop Delta. Hopefully, she was merely trying to get away as the sergeant had suggested. He climbed out and headed for the open aircraft door. A bicycle leaned against the wheel housing of the bird.

Voices came from within. Female voices, but it didn't sound like a usual female chin-wagging session.

He crept up to the open door and listened. A short folding ladder stood below the wing allowing individuals to climb up onto it and then inside.

Witherspoon spoke. "Catch your breath. We can wait."

We? Likely Brown was here, and the one needing to catch her breath he would guess was Nightingale.

Nightingale finally spoke. "Major Berg stopped by the hangar asking about the two of you."

Yep. He'd been right. The three in question were gathered here like a brood of hens.

"What did he want to know?" Witherspoon asked.

"Where you were? I told him it was your day off but you sometimes came in, and that Brownie was in cartography."

"Did he believe you?" Witherspoon again.

Mostly. Although, he had suspected there was more, and he was right.

"Why shouldn't he? Those were both the truth. Your day off and the last time I'd seen Brownie, she was headed to map heaven. I think we're safe."

Irritation rose in him. What were these women plotting?

There was silence for a moment, then Witherspoon asked, "Are the batteries charging?"

"Two of them," Nightingale said. "The other is shot. How are the repairs coming?"

"Good. We have several of the instruments wired up."

He knew it. They *were* up to something. He climbed the ladder and hefted himself up onto the wing, which made a noise, causing the women to hush.

As he reached the door, Witherspoon appeared, framed in the gap. "Hello, ladies."

Witherspoon sucked in a breath. "What are you doing here?"

"I could ask you the same thing. Permission to come aboard?"

Her eyes were as wide as he'd ever seen them. "You don't want to do that. It's dirty in here. We were just leaving. We'll come down and meet you at your car."

He held his ground. "I would like to come in. Please step aside." If nothing nefarious was transpiring, then there shouldn't be a problem.

Witherspoon shifted away from the opening.

Nightingale sat on a blanket which appeared to be attempting to hide a pile of wires and seat harnesses and whatever else was sticking out from under the edge.

Brown stood against the wall. She hadn't likely been in that spot a moment ago would be his guess, so he took stock of what was around her. Two rolled up long papers lay on the floor between her feet and the bulkhead along with a notebook.

He glanced around and headed up to the cockpit. The dashboard hung loose and a chaos of wires spiderwebbed all over the place. Was the backside of every control panel in that much of a disarray? He spun around. "You ladies wouldn't be removing wires and things from this aircraft, would you?" That would seem uncharacteristic of them.

"Removing stuff?" Nightingale sounded indignant. *"No."*

Conflicted, he both believed her and didn't. How could that be? "Something is going on here. I need you ladies to tell me what that is."

Brown lifted her hands palms up. "Like what?"

He crossed over to her and grabbed one of the rolls of paper. He pinched the straight edge and let it unfurl. Tipping his head sideways, he tried to decipher the markings on it. "This is Cuba. What are you doing with a map of Cuba?" This wasn't a coincidence. He made eye contact with the ladies one at a time.

No one answered him.

He locked gazes with Brown. "You could be in a lot of trouble for removing a map from cartography."

Witherspoon stepped forward. "She did no such thing. She drew it from memory."

He swung his gaze back to Brown. "Is that true?"

The young pilot nodded.

He snatched the other rolled up paper. It was a map from a farther out viewpoint, which included Florida and part of the eastern seaboard of the US in addition to Cuba. "You drew this from memory too?"

Brown shrugged. "A hobby of mine."

That was some memory. "Are you three spies?" He didn't believe it even as the words came out of his mouth.

Witherspoon's eyes widened. "No. Never."

"How else do you explain these maps?"

Nightingale stood. "The jig is up. We might as well tell him."

Brown nodded her consent.

Witherspoon took a deep breath. "As we told you, there are three soldiers afraid for their lives being held against their will in Cuba by a band of German sympathizers or Germans themselves. If it were us or a family member, we would want someone to attempt to free them."

They couldn't be planning a rescue op, could they? "How do you think you can possibly accomplish that?"

Witherspoon straightened her shoulders. "We have been scavenging parts from other aircraft out here in the Graveyard to repair this one. It doesn't appear to be in too bad a shape. Once we have replaced the rest of the wiring and put the battery in, we'll know more. We may not even be able to get it to run, let alone get it off the ground."

"That's why you were charging batteries? Why three?"

Nightingale spoke. "We got them from a couple of the other planes. We didn't know if any of them were good or not, so we thought we would try three of them."

"So if you got this airborne, you thought you could simply fly to Cuba and pick up these men and fly home as though it were a Sunday drive?" He thought these women were smarter than that. No, he *knew* they were smarter than that. However, they just might be careless enough to attempt it.

Witherspoon shook her head. "We know there's more to it than that. Once we are sure the Delta is running and sound, we'll formulate the rest of the plan. Show him, Brownie."

Brown picked up the notebook and opened it. "We fly from here to Tampa or Miami, Florida, refuel, then head down to Cuba. That way we are sure to have enough fuel for the return trip, but we will have used enough to not be overweight once the men are on board."

He studied her notes. On first inspection it had merit, but there would be a whole lot more to planning this type of mission to have any chance of a favorable outcome. "Have you considered different contingencies? What time of day will you execute this rescue for highest potential for success? How will you locate and get our men away from their captors? How will you take off from *here* without anyone noticing? And a hundred other questions that need to be answered long before you ever consider taking off. You can't just hop in a plane and retrieve these men as simply as running to the grocery store to pick up eggs and bread."

"We know." Witherspoon gave him an imploring look. "We're trying to figure out those details."

"I know you mean well." He did admire their pluck. "But this is reckless. You promised me you wouldn't do anything."

Witherspoon squared her shoulders and leveled her gaze at him. "Technically, we didn't. You said the *army* wasn't going to rescue them and that your hands were tied. Are you content to sit around and do nothing to help those men? Let them die?"

No, he wasn't content, but there was nothing he could do. It wasn't like *he* could fly down there. He was restricted from piloting military aircraft for the indefinite future. He had barely been approved to drive a car. "You all could be killed."

"Those men could be killed." She wasn't going to yield.

"Planning out a potentially successful mission takes a lot of skill and knowledge without any guarantee you will achieve your goal." They still didn't get it. "You have to consider weather conditions both on the ground and up in the air, fuel usage and capacity, best time of day to execute the mission, how long it will take. Then you have to be a mind reader to predict what *might* happen in the future so you will have contingencies for that. You have to think like your enemy to factor in what he might do and make plans for that. Have any of you had even one course on the science of mission planning? War strategy?"

They all stared at him mutely.

"Of course, you haven't." Maybe now they would give up this foolish idea.

Nightingale straightened her shoulders. "It sounds like you have. You could help us with the planning."

He held up his hands. "Oh, no. Don't try to rope me into this." It was his job to see to their safety, and this mission was far from safe. It was doomed to fail and would cost them all their careers if not their lives as well.

Brown stepped away from the fuselage hull. "We aren't hurting anything. These aircraft have been junked. We aren't taking anything from the good planes or things that are destined for the good ones. We are using only junk from other junk to make a junked aircraft not junk anymore."

After a moment of silence, Witherspoon spoke. "Are you going to turn us in?"

He should. That would nip this fiasco in the bud right now, but they would also be dismissed from their jobs. He should tell them to stop, but what harm were they doing? He felt a connection to those soldiers he'd never met. Once a person had been trapped in enemy territory, like he'd been, it created a connection with anyone in a similar situation. "Since I don't believe you're going to get this bucket of bolts to run let alone off the ground, I don't see much point." No sense getting them in trouble over nothing.

Brown clapped. "Yay."

This was *not* a cheering matter. "I could order you three to stop."

Witherspoon spoke in a plaintive voice. "Please don't."

Her determination and bravado were endearing. Logic or compassion? Those were his choices. "See to it you don't shirk your normal duties."

"We won't."

"I have one more question." He pointed toward the cockpit. "Is that what the backside of an instrument panel looks like with all that scatter of wires?" Kind of scary if it was.

Witherspoon shook her head. "We had to improvise with the wires we could salvage from the other scrapped birds."

Improvise? This whole operation was an improvisation. An enterprise doomed to fail. These poor ladies were in way over their heads and didn't even know it.

⌕CHAPTER 22⌕

Wednesday 11 October 1944

Tropical disturbance in the Atlantic moved
into western Caribbean Sea.

Peggy wired the last of the instrument panel. She was grateful the major had allowed them to continue repairing this craft even if he didn't think it would actually fly. She had to believe it would. To toy with any other outcome would make everything they were trying to accomplish futile. "Ready to test the flaps."

Jolene stood from where she had been sitting on the floor in the rear compartment untangling and inspecting seat harnesses. "I'll go out and look." A moment later, she called, "Ready!"

Peggy sat in the pilot seat Jolene had located in one of the other aircraft and turned on the power. The battery had held the charge. She moved the flaps lever.

Jolene hollered, "They work!"

"You sound surprised." Peggy had to admit she was also amazed. "We have a top-notch crew working on this old girl, you know."

"Oh, don't I know it. Let's test the rudder and ailerons, now."

They worked as well, so all the oiling and greasing of parts had paid off.

The fuel gauge registered under an eighth of a tank. Enough to test if the engine would turn over and a bit of taxiing but not much else.

Jolene poked her head in through the doorway. "Do you want to try to start her?"

"We might as well." That would allow them to calculate how much more potential work they had ahead of them.

Brownie dashed to the door. "Wait until I'm outside." For being shot in the foot, the young lady hadn't been slowed down much. She still limped but showed no other indication of the pain it likely continued to cause her.

Peggy waited until both ladies stood off to one side in front of the plane. She made sure the brakes were set and prayed they still functioned. She slid open the side window, stuck her arm out, and held out her fist with her thumb pointing up.

Brownie and Jolene returned the gesture.

After priming the engine, she blew out a quick breath and pushed the ignition switch. The engine groaned, made a whirring sound, as well as clicking, but didn't turn over. She stopped and leaned her head out the window. "It's no use. It won't start."

Brownie called back, "But she wants to. I can tell."

An hour later after the three of them tinkered with the engine, Peggy tried again. It coughed and sputtered and choked, but it turned the propeller. Then it died.

All three women cheered. "We did it!"

After yet another hour of tinkering with the spark ignitor, greasing various components, and cleaning other parts, they were ready for another test.

As Peggy went to climb back into the Delta, Major Berg drove up. She waited for him to stop and get out. Jolene and Brownie joined her. Jolene leaned a little closer. "What do you think he wants?"

"Don't know." Had he gotten word of their progress and come to order them to stop? She had been surprised he hadn't already given that order.

As he approached, Peggy snapped to attention and saluted. Jolene and Brownie followed suit.

He saluted back. "As you were." He seemed uncomfortable with them saluting him. Was it because they were women and he was old-fashioned? It didn't really matter. "How is it going?"

"We were about to fire her up." Peggy realized she sounded a little smug, but she didn't care. She was proud of all they had accomplished. A working aircraft out of junk and nothing.

He studied the craft. "You got this bucket of bolts running?"

"More or less."

"More or less isn't running."

It was all in how one defined running. "Stand clear, and we'll see." As Peggy climbed the small ladder onto the wing and then moved inside, she prayed. *Please, Lord, let her start. Our intentions are good. We only want to have a shot at saving those men's lives.*

She settled into the pilot's seat and resisted the urge to automatically strap in. She jutted her fist out the window with her thumb up.

Her friends returned the gesture. Major Berg refrained.

She went through the checklist Brownie had created one item at a time. The moment of truth. She paused, then pushed the ignition.

The Delta chugged and groaned, and then found her feet and rhythm. The propeller looped around once, twice, three times, then the engine puttered to life.

It works! Peggy could hardly believe it.

Outside, Jolene and Brownie cheered.

Major *Doubter* stood with widened eyes. They had made him a believer. But would he stop them now? Make them return to their humdrum lives of being support to the men who really mattered?

Peggy revved the engine to increase the revolutions per minute. It sounded good. Well, good for a derelict, junked craft. She and her WASP friends would be able to make her purr.

Major Berg made the motion for her to cut the engine.

Peggy did. She'd wanted to keep it going, but it would be wise to conserve what little fuel they had. She climbed out of the Delta and joined the others on the ground.

The major shook his head. "I can't believe you got this thing running. Did you seriously only use parts from other aircraft in the Graveyard?"

"Mostly." Peggy shrugged. "We also rescued some used oil from the hangar that had been drained from an aircraft being repaired. Though not too dirty, it wasn't going to be put back into the plane. We asked if we could have it."

The major's eyebrows twitched down. "What did the sergeant think you were going to do with it?"

"He was busy and didn't ask. Probably grateful not to have to deal with it."

Major Berg studied the Delta. "Amazing. I didn't think you could get this thing to run."

"I know." Peggy had sensed his doubt. Men often underestimated the abilities of WASPs.

Jolene put her hands on her hips. "Why? Because we're women?"

He swung a skeptical gaze to her. "No. Because this aircraft was deemed unserviceable. Junk. You three saw potential in this beast and breathed life back into it. You ladies are resourceful in ways I never would have imagined."

He really *did* seem impressed.

Peggy was too but knew her team was up to the task. "There was so much good still left in her."

He pointed at the nose of the Delta. "You realize just because the engine came to life doesn't mean it will fly."

Brownie faced him and squared her shoulders. "She'll fly." She arched her arm over her head. "I dub this aircraft *Princess Possibilities of Second Chances*."

Jolene's mouth spread into a wide smile. "I like it."

It was a bit long, but Peggy nodded anyway. "Me too."

The major chuckled. "Do you seriously trust this plane enough to go up in the air in it?"

Peggy, along with Jolene and Brownie, all said, "Yes," at once. Then Peggy gave half of a shrug. "It's better than some I've flown. I know the ins and outs of this aircraft and how everything functions together, which gives me confidence I wouldn't have otherwise. By observing the engine's performance, I'll be able to identify if it has any issues and what effects they might have on the aircraft. Then I can determine if it's something critical or merely inconvenient."

"I can't even begin to understand what all you WASPs do." After a moment, he motioned them toward the plane. "I have something to show you. Let's go inside."

At least he hadn't told them to cease and desist. He allowed Peggy and her comrades to climb aboard ahead of him. A moment before he entered, he gave a quick glance back. Strange. Why had he done that?

He motioned toward the floor. "Shall we sit."

Peggy and her friends had no trouble. The major struggled a moment with his noncompliant leg as he eased himself down with a wince, but he managed without a complaint. He sat across from them all in a line.

He unfurled a large map of the Caribbean from the middle of the Atlantic coast of the United States down to the northern tip of South America. Flight paths of different routes from Washington DC to Cuba and back crisscrossed it. Scrawled numbers peppered the edges of the paper and the middle of the Atlantic Ocean. Some were latitude and longitude, others were distances, some fuel, some winds, some altitude, some temperatures both on the ground and in the air. Calculations with different times of day.

Peggy studied him. "What is all this?"

He dropped a notebook in the middle of the map. "Oh, I was playing with the idea of taking a vacation to Cuba—after the war is over, of course—and thought I would chart a few things out to see what it would require. I might want to take a few people with me and bring some others back, so I calculated for those scenarios."

Was he doing what she thought he was doing? "Is this—?"

The major jerked his hand up. "I'm planning a vacation. Nothing more. If someone uses this for other purposes, I can't help that."

"I thought you didn't want us to do this. That it was too dangerous."

"I don't, but I thought hard and prayed about it. Looks like you are going to go anyway. You're right, those soldiers deserve to be brought home. Their families deserve to see them again. There has already been too much death in this war." He pointed to the map. "This reminds me of what I risked my life for, what we are all fighting for. Freedom. Those men deserve a shot at freedom. Let me tell you about my leg." He patted his thigh and relayed his experience of being shot down over occupied France. "In part, I understand how those men feel. The mix of hope, fear, resignation, wanting to be rescued, but also not wanting others to risk their lives. Being afraid to hope, but knowing if you don't, you will die. Because they are on

Allied soil, they would have assumed someone would have come for them by now. After this amount of time, they know no one is coming. What little hope they have is fading fast."

Peggy's eyes teared up. Had her George felt all those things?

Major Berg scowled. "If you are going to be emotional about this. . ."

Peggy blinked to clear her vision. "No, sir."

He gave her a slight smile. "The time for emotions will be when those soldiers are home safely. I'll even buy each one of you on this remarkable crew a brand-new fancy handkerchief when you get back so you can cry all the tears you want." He made eye contact with each of them. "Are you three still crazy enough to do this? I won't think any less of you if you decide to back out. No one will be the wiser."

Peggy shot to her feet and saluted. "No, sir. I'm ready to go, sir."

Jolene and Brownie did the same.

"Ready, sir."

"Ready, sir."

Major Berg studied each of them. A look Peggy would describe as pride. "We are all risking our jobs for this. I could be court marshaled, and you three could be jailed. Are you ready for that?"

Peggy had already considered her little girls. She'd be putting their futures at risk, as well, but she wasn't called Mama Bird for nothing. Yes, she would protect her babies by standing up to tyranny. She would do this for her children. She would do this for George. "If it saves those men's lives, I can do no less."

Jolene and Brownie nodded their agreement.

The major wrangled himself to his feet. "You understand that I'm not condoning this mission, right?"

Of course, he couldn't officially encourage or help them with an unsanctioned rescue.

Peggy tilted her head and said in a light voice, "What mission, sir?"

His broad grin indicated that he understood none of them would say anything.

Peggy continued. "We only have one small problem. Well, it's actually a big problem."

"What's that?"

183

"The Delta—"

Brownie gave her a sharp look. "*Princess Possibilities of Second Chances.*"

Peggy nodded. "The plane is out of fuel. We can't even test fly it."

His beautiful mouth pulled up into an enchanting smile. "I convinced General Hawkins to sign off on a minimal amount of funding for a pet program I want to test. It's to see if there is any worth in the old aircraft in the Graveyard, and to see if there are enough salvageable parts to create a working plane. Of course, that airplane will need to be test flown to determine if the program is a success or not."

Peggy couldn't believe it. The other day, he was against them doing this. Now he was helping them? "Really? Why are you helping us? What changed your mind?"

"As I said, I was shot down. I know of other pilots and foot soldiers who were stranded behind enemy lines. Most didn't make it out. Some, I'm sure, are being held as prisoners of war. I can guarantee, with the utmost certainty, every single one of them had hopes that someone—*anyone*—would come to their aid. You three make me proud to be a United States Army Air Corps pilot." He snapped to attention and saluted them.

What an honor to be saluted first by a superior officer. She saluted back, as did her comrades.

CHAPTER 23

Thursday 12 October 1944

Tropical disturbance turned into a tropical depression;
rough seas reported east of the Swan Islands,
110 miles north off the Honduras coast.

Friday 13 October 1944

Growing system headed north; tropical depression quickly
intensified into tropical storm magnitude six hours after
initial classification; strengthened into a hurricane.

After another day and a half of Peggy and her fellow WASPs tinkering and adjusting, the Delta was ready to take flight. Everything had been done they could think of to get the aircraft in shape. The only thing left was to test this bird in the air.

The major had convened with them at the Delta to check on their progress. Seeing all was in order, he motioned toward the plane's door. "The fuel truck is ready and waiting by the hangar. I'll meet you there." He left.

Jolene held out her hand to Peggy. "Do you want me to drive your car over?"

Peggy dug the key out of her zoot suit and gave it to her. "Thanks."

"I'll ride in the copilot's place." Brownie moved to the cockpit.

Jolene furrowed her eyebrows. "There's no seat for a second person yet."

"I'll stand. We are only rolling across the tarmac to fuel up."

Jolene shrugged and left.

Peggy taxied the Delta to the fueling truck. Once the plane was full and all the preflight checks, inside and out, were completed again, Peggy maneuvered to the end of the runway. With only the one seat installed, Peggy would make this flight solo. The recovered bent seat Peggy had found the first day sat in the hangar with attempts being made to straighten it. The others wanted to go with her, but with no place to sit, it would be safer if they didn't. Also no sense risking more lives than necessary. She was confident in the aircraft, as she had told the major, but if something arose during the test flight, she would feel better knowing they were safe.

She waited for clearance.

"Mama Bird, you are go for takeoff."

"Roger." Peggy primed the pump and set the trim.

Lord, make Princess Possibilities of Second Chances *fly.*

Everyone needed a second chance. And God was the Champion of second chances.

She eased the Delta down the runway. It felt good, so she pushed it to full throttle. The engine wound up and thrust the aircraft forward. G-forces pressed her deeper into the seat. Every nuance of the tarmac vibrated up the wheels and through the frame. Then the wheels lifted off the ground and the ride smoothed out. "Yee-haw!" The Northrop Delta was airborne.

No time for celebrating right now. She needed to assess the craft, so she studied the gauges and listened to the engine.

The major's voice came over the headphones. "How is it looking up there? From down here, the view is great."

"It feels and sounds really good." She couldn't believe it. They had done it! Those soldiers had an actual chance.

If no one stopped them.

After putting it through its paces with no discernible problems, she landed and taxied the craft out of the way of the normal air traffic. She set the brakes and cut the engine. As she climbed out, Major

Berg drove up in a Jeep with Jolene and Brownie onboard.

Peggy met them at the vehicle. "I'll be the first to admit, I didn't think we were going to be able to make this bird fly."

Brownie beamed. "I knew *Princess Possibilities of Second Chances* would do great."

Peggy needed to talk to her comrade about that name.

Major Berg grinned. "As a reward for all your hard work, I have something for you." He walked around to the rear of the Jeep, pulled back a tarp, and waved his arm over the cargo.

Peggy stared. "Are those parachutes?" She hadn't figured out how to procure those yet.

"Yes, ma'am. Parachutes, C-1 survival vests, and Mae West life vests. Seven of each."

Jolene cocked her head. "I understand the parachutes, but why would we need the others?"

"You WASPs don't normally fly over large bodies of water nor on dangerous missions where you could be shot down. Better to have these and not need them, than to be without them and wish you had them."

Brownie fingered one of the Mae West life vests. "I can't see us needing these. I could practically throw a rock from the tip of Florida and hit Cuba. Aren't these merely extra weight?"

Peggy understood both Brownie's concern of all that extra bulk and the major's caution to be prepared for anything. "Contingencies for unexpected emergencies."

He nodded. "One can never be too prepared. If you end up going, you'll be refueling at Eglin Field Military Reservation. There is a lot more water between Florida's Panhandle and Cuba."

"Eglin? Wouldn't it be better to refuel in Miami or Tampa?"

He shook his head. "I have a contact at Eglin. Do you ladies know how to put all this equipment on?"

Peggy nodded. "First the C-1, then the Mae West, then the parachute." In the order they would be needed. . .*if* they were needed.

"Are you going to be able to handle wearing all this gear?" He looked pointedly at Peggy and Brownie, both standing at barely the minimum WASP height requirement of five foot two inches.

"Affirmative, sir." It was a lot of weight, and the WASP didn't normally have need for all of it, but Peggy had geared up in it several times in training. She stared at the mound of equipment. "Why seven? Three WASPs and three soldiers equals six. Are there really four men being held?" Did the major have additional intelligence? "Or are you planning to go with us?"

"I would be honored to fly with you ladies."

Peggy could hear the unspoken but.

He patted his injured leg. "But I would be of little use to you and likely more of a hindrance. You can't afford to have extra weight when taking off from Cuba. It could mean the success or failure of the mission. It's a spare. . .just in case. Some pilots believe it to be a little insurance of a successful mission."

Just in case. Peggy was so grateful for this generous gift that she had the urge to hug him, but that would be completely inappropriate. Instead she saluted.

———≋———

At home that evening, Peggy took her mom aside while the girls brushed their teeth. "Mom, I have something to tell you."

"This sounds serious."

"It is."

"Then we should sit."

"There isn't time before the girls come out."

"All right."

"You can't repeat what I'm about to say under any circumstances. Is that clear?"

Mom nodded. "Of course. I won't tell a soul."

"I told you about the three soldiers being held against their will. The WASPs are going to mount a rescue mission." She tried to make it sound as though this was a well-planned, sanctioned mission, and not some off-the-cuff, fly-by-night affair. "I'm one of the ones who is going." Because she was the instigator. "It's dangerous, but I can't sit by while these men's lives are in peril."

Mom remained silent for a long moment, no doubt digesting the information. "I want to beg you not to do this, but you are too much like your father. If he were still around, he would be the one going."

"So you support my decision?"

"If something bad happens to those men and you could have done anything about it and did nothing and they perish, you would feel deep guilt the rest of your life. No, I don't want you to, but I understand your need to go."

She hugged her mom. "Thanks. I can't tell you how much your support means to me. You'll look after the girls?"

"Of course. I always will."

The tightness in Peggy's chest eased. Now to break the news to her daughters.

When Wendy and Junie ran out after dressing for bed and brushing their teeth, Peggy sat with them on the davenport. "You girls know I love you very much, don't you?"

"Yes," they each said in turn.

"I'm going away for a couple of days. It may be longer." She wanted to prepare them in case things went wrong and the mission had to take a long route home.

"Okay, Mommy. Grandma will take care of us." Junie wiggled closer.

Wendy looked up at Peggy. "Mommy?"

"It's going to be all right. I need to go on a special trip for my work. I'm picking up some soldiers and flying them back here so they can be with their families."

Junie patted Peggy's hand. "That's a good mommy."

Wendy blinked. "Is it dangerous?"

Very, but she didn't want to scare her girls. "Flying can always be dangerous."

Wendy pressed into her side. "I wish you didn't have to go."

She lifted her daughter's chin. "Remember when you said you wanted to become a pilot so you could make the bad men stop being bad?"

Wendy nodded. "Like the ones who hurt Daddy?"

"Yes. Well, that's what my job is, more or less—making the world a better place for all the good people."

Junie tilted her head. "Are you bringing Daddy home? What about Mr. Howie?"

At the mention of her late husband, the constant ache deep inside her flared to life. "No. I'm not bringing Daddy home. I can't. I would if I could." Her daughter had more of an attachment to the major whom she'd only met a few times than her own father. She had been so young. Did she even have any first-hand memories of her father—memories that hadn't been conveyed by other people? If she did, they were likely vague shadowy things hidden by the night. She didn't know what to say about Major Berg. Her feelings for him were confusing. Partly because she knew it was frowned upon for a WASP and an army officer to become romantically involved. Who was she kidding? Her heart was already romantically involved even though she'd tried to squelch any of those types of feelings.

"All right, off to bed you two. I'll see you in the morning."

Junie kissed her and ran off.

Wendy hugged her really tight. "I'm afraid." Her daughter could obviously feel the tension and seriousness of what Peggy was telling her.

Peggy caressed her oldest daughter's back. "Everything will be all right. I need you to be praying for this trip. Pray we bring the men back safely." Her daughter's prayers had always seemed to be stronger than Peggy's. She got answers where Peggy didn't. Even so, Peggy knew God loved her. He merely answered most of her prayers with no. This one would be different.

"I will." Wendy hugged her tightly around the neck, then sulked off to bed.

"I'll be in in a minute."

Mom scooted forward in the living-room chair. "I think they sense this trip is different from the others you go on. They sense the danger."

Peggy had contemplated not telling them but didn't want to disappear like their father without a word. "I know, but every time I climb into an aircraft and leave this planet, there is an element of danger."

"Most of that danger you can control. This is a different kind of danger, one you can't control, far more serious and deadly."

"I have the best crew flying with me. I'll be as safe as I can. I won't take any unnecessary risks."

Mom thinned her lips. "Simply going on this mission *is* an unnecessary risk. I wish you hadn't been assigned to this."

Peggy wouldn't tell Mom this whole thing was her idea and that she had planned it all—well, with the help of her comrades and the major. "If I don't go, then who will?"

"Other WASPs and army men. People with expertise and experience."

The problem with that was the people with experience couldn't afford to ruffle the feathers of an ally without major consequences. "I'm the best shot these men have." By the WASPs going, the US Military and government could disavow any involvement or knowledge of this little incursion into a sovereign country. If things went really bad and the mission failed and they all died, the government could make up any cover story they wanted. Or if Peggy and her friends got caught, they could deny any knowledge, which was true. The government and military—except Major Berg—knew nothing.

If they were successful, the government would deny anything ever happened and report that the soldiers came home by conventional means.

Peggy didn't mind, as long as the men were safe.

ⲌCHAPTER 24Ⲍ

Saturday 14 October 1944

Slow-moving hurricane nearly stationary in the Caribbean.

The following day, Peggy stood with Jolene, Brownie, and Major Berg next to the fully fueled Northrop Delta by the hangar, ready for another test flight. Sergeant Kent and Captain Cooper milled about inside the hangar as well as several airmen, soldiers, and mechanics working on aircraft both inside and outside the hangar and performing other duties.

The bent seat for the copilot position, which had been repaired, had recently been installed in the Delta. In the back portion of the fuselage, six seat harnesses had been rounded up and bolted to the outside walls. That way, if the Delta hit any air turbulence, no one would be thrown about the cabin and get injured. A pile of excess blankets sat on the floor. The accommodations wouldn't be the most comfortable, but after being held captive, the men would appreciate any means of escape without complaint.

The "test flight" plan involved flying to Florida, refueling, and returning. The theory for Major Berg's test program was to see how the aircraft did on a longer mission. He had been smart to include that in his project proposal to the general. The Lord must be with this mission, because the general didn't question the longer test. The leg of the journey not included in the official plan was a little detour down to Cuba after refueling. The calculated fuel consumption allowed for the flight from Florida to Cuba and back up to Bolling

Airfield in Washington, DC without a problem.

Once in Florida, the Delta would develop an issue, causing a delay in the return flight until after sunset. Under the cover of darkness, Peggy would take off as though heading north, then bank around due south toward the west end of Cuba to an area which was mostly unpopulated. A good place to hide hostages without being discovered. She would cruise at a low altitude to be undetectable by US radar. As far as US military intelligence knew, Cuba didn't have radar technology yet. Just in case, she would continue to fly low.

The floats for the Delta had been located in one of the other Graveyard aircraft. Finding water locations to take off and land for the first leg of the journey made them not a good option, as they might raise too many questions. Someone higher up the chain of command could decide this program wasn't worth the effort. So they were leaving the floats behind.

Peggy, Jolene, and Brownie had wanted to land near the lake where the soldiers were presumably being held. Major Berg had explained how the captors would hear the aircraft coming. Therefore, the Delta would be exposed to gunfire during landing and takeoff. Stealthiness would be their best friend, surprise the next best. With the major's help and insights, this mission had a higher chance of succeeding.

In light of his advice, Peggy and her friends would set down on a level strip of land near the shore and hike the mile or so to the lake, free the men, hustle back to the Delta, and take off. Hopefully, the captors wouldn't even realize their prisoners were missing until dawn.

One of the biggest problems was not knowing exactly where or how the men were being confined and the number of captors. An assessment of the situation would need to be made once at the lake. Major Berg had given directions on what actions to take for various scenarios. Though he couldn't convey every possible circumstance that might arise, he'd related enough to give an idea of how to improvise for whatever might come up. He mostly explained general scenarios and ways to handle situations rather than specific ones. Hopefully, all his imparted wisdom would be enough to make this mission a success. She and the others were trained pilots who let disgruntled army men shoot in their direction for target practice, so they could do this.

The major made eye contact with Peggy. "May I speak with you a minute?" Limping with his cane, he walked around the other side of the Northrop Delta.

She joined him. "Are you going to try to talk me out of this?"

He raised an eyebrow. "Would it do any good?"

She shook her head. "I'm not only doing this for those men and their families, but for all the soldiers ever captured or who felt abandoned. For those shot down. For America. The rest of the world needs to know if they mess with us, we won't sit back and take it. We will protect and defend our own."

"You sound like an army soldier or a marine."

"If you were capable and not restricted by orders from the military, would *you* go?"

"Yes." His answer came swift and without hesitation. "The difference is, that's what I've been trained for. You haven't."

"I may not have been specifically trained for this kind of mission, but I'm capable."

"I know. Otherwise I wouldn't have let this get this far."

"We have as good of a chance of succeeding as any team of men." She studied the quandary on his face. "What is it?"

He paused before answering. "Everything within me wants to beg you to stay—no, to order you to stay."

A part of her wanted that too and to stay where it was safe, but she knew she couldn't. She opened her mouth to protest.

He put a single finger to her lips, halting her objection. "But what kind of man would I be to keep you from being who you are, from being who God has called you to be? Courageous. Bold. Selfless. If I stop you, you wouldn't be able to be the woman I've fallen in love with."

The air froze in her lungs. He loved her? His words sealed a hole in her heart, perhaps in her life.

She might also love him. No might about it. She loved him too. How had this happened? While she was busy being a mother, a daughter, and a WASP, she hadn't noticed her heart taking off to fall in love with this man.

He caressed his thumb along her jaw. "If I weren't an Army Air Corps officer and you weren't a WASP, you know what I would do right now?"

Her skin under his touch tingled. She knew and wanted it too.

She clasped his hand at her mouth and gently pulled it away. Then she raised up on her toes and pressed her lips to his.

His arms latched around her and held her close.

She melted into his embrace. Why had she resisted this?

He deepened the kiss.

She never wanted him to let her go but knew she must. Even if the three soldiers out there didn't know it, they were depending on this mission—depending on her. She pulled away. "I have to go."

"I know. Please be careful. Don't take any unnecessary risks."

"This whole mission is one risk after another." There were so many ways it could fail.

She hadn't realized she had been longing for a man's affection so much. She wanted to stay right here in his embrace, never letting him go, but that wouldn't free those soldiers.

The major must have sensed it too and released her. He rested his forehead against hers. "Be safe."

"I will."

"Know that if I could go in your place I would."

"I know." A part of her no longer wanted to go but to stay with him. However, three soldiers out there needed her and her comrades.

She and the major rejoined the other two.

Jolene looked at Peggy pointedly. "Are we still going?"

"Yes. If either of you want to back out, I won't hold it against you."

Brownie held her hand out toward the other two with her palm facing down. "Nerves of steel!"

Jolene covered Brownie's with her own. "Nerves of steel!"

Peggy put hers on the very top. "Nerves of steel!" They felt more like nerves of melting snow.

"You ladies do have nerves of steel. I am so proud of all three of you. If we were on the battlefield, I would want you each fighting beside me."

High praise coming from a military man. Peggy knew so from her husband. He would judge people by whether or not he would want to be in the same foxhole as them in the midst of battle.

A military car with small blue flags flapping on the front corners drove toward the Delta. What was a flag officer doing coming out here?

"That looks like the general's car." The major faced the vehicle and stood at attention as it came to a stop.

Peggy and the WASPs did the same.

When the door opened and Brigadier General Hawkins climbed out, Peggy and the others saluted, keeping their hands to their eyebrows.

The general glanced at them and then at the Delta behind them. He returned the salute. "At ease. Is this the aircraft in your little experiment, Major?"

"Yes, sir."

"You ladies are the ones who built it from scrap planes?"

Since this was Peggy's idea from the get-go, she answered. "Yes, sir. The Delta was still in pretty good shape. We mostly needed to rewire it, clean up the engine, and grease everything."

"I rode in a Delta a time or two. I would like to take a look inside." He walked to the mobile stairs and climbed up and in.

Peggy leaned closer to the major. "Should we go in as well or wait here?"

"Wait here, unless he invites us."

She pictured the interior of the craft and her stomach dropped. "Do you think he'll notice the parachutes and other gear?"

"We'll have to wait and see."

Soon the general came back out and down. "Not quite standard issue in there."

Harnesses bolted to the walls, a pile of blankets, and a heap of survival gear? Not standard at all. Would the general comment further?

Since the major was the highest-ranking person, he answered. "That was the point, sir. Seeing if an aircraft could become serviceable again and sky-worthy by using only scavenged parts."

The general stood directly in front of the major. "You believe a longer trip for this bird is necessary to deem this project a success?"

The major didn't waver. "Yes, sir. A short trip around DC is one thing, but another to test it under pressure."

Oh, dear. Was the general going to cancel their mission, their test flight?

The general nodded. "You can tell the real mettle of a machine or person under pressure."

"Yes, sir. The only way, sir."

"The soldiers in meteorology have picked up a low-pressure system in the Caribbean. A ship in the area reported rough seas last night. Maybe you should postpone this mission."

Why had he told them about something that was so far from the known flight plan of this trip?

Peggy couldn't remain quiet this time. "That system shouldn't affect us, sir." Her team was aware of the turbulent weather pattern and could abort anytime if it should threaten the mission.

"See that it doesn't." The general kept his gaze on Peggy for a long moment. "I look forward to a full report when you ladies return." He headed toward his car but turned at the open back door. "Safe flight." He got in, and the car drove away.

Peggy let out a captive breath. "For a minute there, I thought he was going to ground us."

Brownie piped up. "Why did he tell us about the weather? Does he know?"

"If he knew, wouldn't he have grounded us?" Peggy looked to the major for the answer.

"It's hard to tell. By not coming right out and saying he knows what we are doing, he has plausible deniability. There isn't a man in the US military who doesn't want to race down there and rescue those men, but our hands are tied."

"And ours aren't?"

One side of his mouth cocked up. "You wouldn't believe how much more freedom you three have than the average soldier simply because you are civilians."

Peggy hadn't felt as though she had any freedom at all. "Time to saddle up, ladies."

The major frowned. "How are you ladies at flying in winds?"

Peggy answered for all of them. "We've all had training and did well. We'll be in and out quick as a firefly on a summer's night."

"If it looks too rough or the hurricane turns toward Cuba, promise me you'll abort."

"We will." But the storm would need to be nearly on top of them before that would happen.

Major Berg nodded then saluted Brownie. "Good luck, soldier."

Brownie saluted.

He did the same to Jolene who saluted back.

Then he turned to Peggy. "You are the commander of this mission. See to it you bring them all back safely, soldier."

"I will, sir." She appreciated him calling each of them soldier. It showed he viewed them as equal with the men.

He saluted her. She returned the gesture. His gaze held pride and a hint of fear.

Peggy followed the other two up and inside the Northrop Delta. She took the copilot's position next to Nightingale in the pilot's seat. Time to start using—and thinking—their call signs.

Peggy read through the preflight checklist as Nightingale performed the necessary tasks in turn.

Nightingale fired up the engine.

Time to taxi. Peggy glanced out the window to the side. Major Berg had been joined by two other men, Sergeant Kent and Captain Cooper, who all stood holding a salute.

How many people knew about this *secret* mission? Hadn't it been kept under wraps?

Nightingale taxied to the end of the runway and was given immediate clearance to take off. She didn't wait to be told twice and pushed it full throttle. Faster and faster until the wheels left the ground.

The G-forces pressing Peggy into the seat both exhilarated her and revealed the lack of sufficient padding in the repaired seat. *Lord, protect us and make this mission successful.* God's presence seemed to wrap around her. As He had promised in the Bible, He would neither leave nor forsake her.

Peggy glanced over her shoulder. "You all right back there?"

Brownie replied, "It's not the puffy couch in my parents' living room, but I've sat on worse."

Once out of DC airspace, the three WASPs would basically be on their own until they flew back over American soil. The major had set up the refueling arrangements in Florida, but he wouldn't be able to help if someone questioned them or chose to detain them.

Her fellow WASP would fly halfway to Eglin Field Military Reservation in the Florida Panhandle, then Brownie would take over and land for refueling. Peggy would serve as copilot for both, then she would take the Florida to Cuba leg of the journey—as she had the most experience and confidence with night flying—and the return to Florida airspace. Once back over American soil, one of the other two would take the controls.

An hour and a half later, Peggy peered out the side window at the white sand beaches juxtaposed against the emerald waters of the Gulf. Too bad this wasn't a pleasure visit.

Brownie radioed the base. "Eglin Field, this is Northrop Delta four one five. Do you copy, Eglin Field?"

The radio remained silent.

Brownie attempted to contact Eglin Field again. "This is Northrop Delta four one five. Do you copy, Eglin Field?"

After a pause, a voice crackled over the headset. "This is Eglin Field. Is this a *woman*?"

Brownie shot Peggy a disgruntled look.

Peggy merely rolled her eyes, but her insides coiled up tighter than a rubber band on a toy airplane. This aspect of the mission made her more nervous than any other, even landing in Cuba. It was the single most important element next to the actual freeing of the prisoners. If they weren't allowed to land and refuel, the rest of the mission would have to be aborted. Any number of things could go wrong. Men who didn't think women should be flying military aircraft could stand in their way of taking off again. Major Berg wasn't here to run interference. If someone hassled them, it was up to their own ingenuity to get out of it.

Brownie took a deep breath and pressed the talk button on the hand mike. "As a matter of fact, I—"

Peggy snatched the mike before her young comrade said something they would all regret and anger ground control. "Eglin Field, Northrop Delta four one five requesting permission to land. Over."

"I don't think we can allow ladies to land here. This is a military base. Do not approach. Over."

"We are WASPs under the direction of the United States Army Air Corps. May we land? We are scheduled to refuel at Eglin. Over." If they were denied landing approval, they would have to reroute to an alternate location. Major Berg had covered such a scenario, but another airfield wasn't prepared to receive them, and it could take too long to gain the proper permissions to get fueled up.

"Clearance to land on runway two. Taxi straight to hangar Charlie. Over."

Peggy heaved a sigh of relief. "Roger." She returned the mike to its clip. Hopefully, taking off again wouldn't be a problem, and the men here would be glad to be rid of a few WASPs.

CHAPTER 25

Brownie landed the Delta and taxied as directed. "I'm scared someone will try to stop *Princess Possibilities of Second Chances* from leaving."

Evidently, Peggy wasn't the only one thinking it. "They might, but we have orders from Major Berg, and he has approval from a general. If we have to, we'll tell anyone who gives us trouble to contact Major Berg."

"I hope it doesn't come to that."

Peggy hoped so too. "About this name you've given the Delta, it's a bit long."

"I know. I kind of thought the major would have said something about it, like"—Brownie deepened her voice—" 'You can't name an aircraft that.' Instead, he almost looked as though he was going to smile. How about *Second Chances*?"

"Sounds good."

From the back, Nightingale called, "I like that better too. I didn't want to hurt your feelings by saying anything."

As they approached the hangar to refuel, Peggy racked her brain for a plausible excuse to stay until after sunset. A tailwind had caused them to arrive ahead of schedule. Possibly one of them could feign illness to delay them, or better yet, a simple repair.

Brownie stopped the Delta several yards from the hangar and shut down the engine.

Peggy and Brownie headed to the hatch where Nightingale released the catch and swung open the door. Five mechanics clad in coveralls stood with their arms folded. Their grim expressions told her this welcoming party wasn't pleased with the presence of WASPs.

Nightingale removed her leather helmet, fluffed her hair, and leaned toward the opening, a smile in her voice. "Hello, boys."

The man on the end wolf whistled. The one next to him backhanded him across the midsection with a hard wallop. The whistler jerked forward and huffed out a heavy breath the other had knocked out of him.

The middle soldier held up his hand to Peggy and her comrades effectively stopping them. "Stay where you are, ladies. You are *not* to leave the aircraft. We will have you fueled up and ready to leave in no time."

That would never do. If they took off now, they would reach Cuba in daylight and anyone could see them approach, including the captors and the Cuban government. These men didn't want to detain them but get them out of here as soon as possible. They needed to delay a little so it would be dark by the time they got close enough to Cuba to be seen.

Peggy inched toward the door. "Can we at least use the lavatory?"

"Don't let 'em, Sarge."

"We don't want them here."

The lead soldier held up his hand to his men. "Let me clear the hangar. Keep the door closed until I return." He waited, obviously not trusting them to obey his order.

Nightingale pulled the door closed. "Weren't they a friendly bunch."

Peggy had hoped the ground crew would have been neutral toward them. "We need to remain here for a couple of hours at least."

Brownie shook her head. "They aren't going to let us. They would push *Second Chances* down the runway to get rid of us."

"That's why we need to come up with a repair that will keep us on the ground as long as we need."

Nightingale pointed toward the front. "I can unhook something in the cockpit. Being silly females, it will take us ever so long to discover the issue." She batted her eyelashes.

Peggy chuckled. "Perfect."

Nightingale went to the front.

Soon a knock sounded at the door. Peggy opened it.

The sergeant stood on the ground with a short set of steps. "The lavatory is straight back and to the right. Be quick about it. Your aircraft should be fueled by the time you return." A fuel truck pulled up to the Delta.

Peggy wanted to leave one of them with the plane but doubted the sergeant would agree. He escorted them across the tarmac and into the hangar.

Peggy went first then waited with the sergeant who stood close by with folded arms while her fellow WASPs took their turns. "Thank you for your kindness."

"No kindness whatsoever. Orders." He pinned her with a hard gaze. "Women flying is unnatural. It upsets my men. The sooner I get you off my flight line the better."

Peggy needed them to stay for at least a little while. They had nixed their other option of landing in the Gulf of Mexico when they decided to leave the floats. Also, landing and taking off again would consume too much fuel. Major Berg had said to do everything possible to avoid that. Too many things could go wrong, and they would likely be spotted. "We were having a little trouble in the cockpit. We need to run a few diagnostics and repair it before we can takeoff."

He narrowed his eyes. "I don't know what your real mission is, but I can make a pretty good guess."

Peggy swallowed hard.

"Why they chose WASPs for this when I could have recommended a hundred men who would have gladly volunteered *and* succeeded, I'll never figure out. Females are the wrong choice."

Females had been the only choice, but they weren't even that. As the major had said, the military's hands were tied. An unauthorized mission was the only hope for those soldiers. "WASPs make it possible for men to do the more difficult jobs of going into battle."

He harrumphed and led them out of the hangar.

A staff car pulled up, and a full-bird colonel climbed out of the back.

The WASPs and the sergeant all snapped to attention and saluted.

Oh, dear. Was this officer going to stop them from taking off again? With a single order, this mission could be grounded. Or sent away.

The colonel approached and saluted back. "Sergeant, what's the problem here?"

The sergeant smirked. "These females think they can take over the place. I told them they will have to move this aircraft immediately."

The colonel looked straight at Peggy. "WASP Witherspoon?"

He knew her name? *Oh, dear.* "Yes, sir."

"You have some issue with your aircraft?"

"Yes, sir, we just—"

He stopped her with a look. "Are those repairs going to take about"—he glanced at his wristwatch—"two and a quarter hours?"

"Give or take, sir." That was almost exactly the length of a delay that would be best.

The colonel turned to the sergeant. "I don't want anyone disturbing these WASPs or interfering with them while they see to their aircraft."

"Sir? That'll mean they will be flying after dark. Is that wise? They are only. . .*women.*"

Peggy had as many night-flying hours as most of her male counterparts.

The colonel leveled his gaze at the sergeant. "Night maneuvers. Everyone needs to be prepared. I want their plane fueled at once. If anyone gets in their way, they will be scrubbing the latrines for a month with their toothbrushes. Am I understood?"

The sergeant stiffened. "Yes, sir."

Peggy got the impression the colonel knew the true purpose for the WASPs being here.

"Dismissed, Sergeant."

The man's gaze darted about as though unbelieving, and he marched away.

The colonel motioned toward the Delta. "Shall we?" He walked them to the foot of the steps. "You shouldn't be bothered until you're ready to leave."

Should she ask him if he knew the true nature of this mission?

He would likely deny any knowledge. "Thank you, sir." She boarded and took her place in the pilot's seat.

Brownie took the copilot's. "Do we just sit here for two hours?"

Nightingale settled herself on the floor between the two seats and pointed. "We need only plug in that wire." She swung her gaze to Peggy. "So when Major Berg asked to talk to you *alone* before the general showed up, did he kiss you?"

Peggy's mouth swung open. "What gave you that idea?"

"It's obvious he's sweet on you."

Brownie echoed. "Obvious. And now you're blushing."

Nightingale nodded. "He's a good man. I think you should snatch him up before someone else does."

Peggy knew he was a good man. "That sort of thing is frowned upon between army and WASP."

"The war won't last forever."

Had these two been talking to her mom? "I am *not* going to entertain such thoughts." But those thoughts had already been waltzing around in her head. "We have a mission to accomplish. I suggest we run diagnostics on every system while we wait." That should keep her friends from asking any more questions on the subject of Major Howie Berg.

Once the repairs were completed, Peggy, Nightingale, and Brownie stepped out of the airplane to do the exterior inspection to make sure nothing had come loose in the flight down, a standard procedure. Being now dusk, they used flashlights. Heavy breezes tugged at their flight suits. It all looked to be in fine shape. It may be unloved, but the Delta was a good, sturdy little craft.

The colonel advanced towards them as they prepared to board. "Looks like a storm approaching. Do you think this mission should be postponed?"

The wind *had* picked up but nothing which would come close to grounding an aircraft. Would he stop them? "I don't think that would be wise." The captives had already been held way too long. Because they were in a friendly country, the soldiers probably realized if no attempt had been made so far, no one was coming at all. She prayed the severe weather would stay away from where they were going.

He gave a nod. "Understood." A half a second before Peggy and her comrades saluted, the colonel did. Was that in anticipation? Or was he trying to salute first? "I'll inform General Hawkins when you take off."

Peggy froze for a second. He did know. Or had the general merely wanted to have an update on their progress because they were women? She didn't want to stick around to find out. "Thank you, sir."

"Safe flight, and may the Lord sustain you."

She hurried aboard and commenced donning her survival gear. First the C-1, then the Mae West, and finally her parachute. Though the equipment was heavy and bulky on her small frame, she took the pilot's seat this time. Brownie sat as copilot and Nightingale secured the door. "Ready back here."

Brownie read off the checklist while Peggy performed each task.

"Last chance to abandon this." Peggy didn't want anyone to be forced if they were having second thoughts.

Nightingale called from the rear of the craft. "If you ask that one more time, I'm going to tie you up back here and fly this mission myself."

Brownie raised her hand. "I'll help."

Peggy smiled. "Just checking."

After taxiing to the end of the runway, the tower gave immediate clearance to take off. As Nightingale had done at Bolling Field, Peggy pushed it to full throttle and got in the air as quickly as possible.

She flew low to avoid the radar until they were out of range. They didn't want to be called back. Once well on their way, she doubled back, heading due south over the Gulf of Mexico.

She was really doing this.

Lord, keep us safe and make this mission a success.

———— ≋ ————

Howie paced his small quarters. So many ways this mission could go wrong. The least of which was the storm brewing in the Caribbean. He gave up the idea of even trying to sleep and headed to the Bolling Headquarters Building.

Once inside, he entered the war situation room, much smaller than the one at the Pentagon. Meteorology was located in one corner there. He would be able to find out the progress of the storm. A large world map on one wall had color-coded markers dotting across land and sea to indicate all the happenings of the war, on both sides.

A handful of men at workstations around the room glanced up and the nearest man said, "Room, atten-*hut*!"

All present stood.

Howie nodded in acknowledgement. "As you were."

Everyone resumed their duties. Not the bustling place it was during the day, but various events in all corners of the world needed to be tracked around the clock.

He crossed to the lone occupant in the meteorology section. "Evening, Sergeant."

"Evening, sir. A bit late for a visit."

It was, but as a major he wasn't required to give a reason for his presence to a subordinate. "Has there been any change in the storm system in the Caribbean?"

"Winds are increasing. I expect it to be upgraded to a hurricane within twenty-four hours."

Someone called out in a stern voice, "Room, atten-*hut*!"

Howie, as well as the others around the room, stood at attention.

General Hawkins had entered the room. "As you were." He made eye contact with Howie, then moved to the incoming intelligence station. Others went to him with updates in their fields of expertise.

Howie continued his conversation with the meteorology sergeant. "What is the storm's trajectory?"

"At the last report, it was heading mostly west but hardly moving."

That would be good for Mama Bird, Nightingale, and Brownie. "Are commercial flights still traveling to and from the area?"

"Yes, though Pan-American is expected to start canceling flights to and from Cuba. Commercial pilots always stop long before military ones. Our pilots will fly in most any weather to complete their mission."

If the WASPs could execute their mission swiftly and the storm continued slow and west, they should be safe enough. All three were excellent pilots.

General Hawkins made his way over to meteorology. "Major."

Howie straightened. "Sir."

"I heard from Eglin. The WASPs have taken off. I thought you would like to know."

Did the general know about the ladies' true mission? Howie would guess he did. "Thank you, sir." Should Howie ask him directly? Best to leave it unsaid. Plausible deniability.

"I hope their night maneuvers are completed without incident."

Howie echoed that sentiment in a prayer. "Me too, sir."

With the storm having captured most people's attention, hopefully the ladies' presence would go unnoticed.

———————≈———————

The closer Peggy flew to Cuba, the more turbulence gently rocked the Delta. It wasn't bad yet. They shouldn't have too much trouble depending on which way the storm turned. If it headed back out to sea, everyone would be happier.

It didn't take long to reach the northern edge of the island country. Peggy cut the landing lights and gazed out into the inky blackness. At least she guessed they were about where they needed to be. She flew at an altitude of two hundred feet. "Do you see Cuba?"

Brownie said, "I can't see anything."

From the back, Nightingale called, "I see lights on the port side. That must be Havana."

Peggy saw them too and banked to head along the coast, but not too close for anyone on the island to see or hear them.

Brownie consulted her map and instruments. "We should be at the landing zone in one minute."

Peggy turned the plane's lights back on. With this end of the island being less inhabited, hopefully, no one would see a stray aircraft approaching.

"I'm going to come around. Hold on. It's going to be a little bumpy on this terrain."

She aimed for the field Major Berg felt would be the smoothest while still being solid enough to support the aircraft. She prayed it was the best place and set the Delta down near the coast. She motored to a stop. They didn't seem to have stirred up any commotion, no searchlights or air raid sirens. That was good. Hopefully, they had come in undetected. The desire for this entire part of the mission. In and out without anyone the wiser.

She cut the engine.

Nightingale opened the door.

Peggy unstrapped. She and Nightingale removed their parachutes and Mae West vests but kept on their C-1 survival vest per the major's advice. They never knew when they might need some little thing tucked away in one of the many pockets.

She turned to Brownie, who was staying with the Delta. "Remember, no matter what, if there's any danger of you or this craft being captured, you are to take off. Is that understood?"

Brownie saluted. "Aye, aye." With her injured foot slowing her down—whether she would admit it or not—she was the obvious choice to remain with the aircraft.

Nightingale gave Brownie a handgun. "I hope you don't have to use this."

Brownie took it and stared at it. "I hope you don't have to use yours either."

Nightingale handed a belt holster with a service pistol and sheathed knife in it to Peggy who strapped it on. "I never imagined having a duty which might require one of these."

"Me either." Nightingale offered her another, smaller, weapon. "Put this one in your boot." She patted her own boot to indicate she had one as well.

Peggy hoped they didn't need either. She turned and gave a thumb's up to Brownie who returned the gesture. She slipped out of the aircraft behind Nightingale onto the wing and slid to the ground.

They each had a compass and a flashlight with a red filter over it so they wouldn't be as noticeable in the dark.

Clouds had moved in blocking what little light the sliver of moon might have offered. Too bad it wasn't a clear sky with a full moon. The wind had also kicked up. Must be the edge of that storm system brewing to the south.

Peggy pointed her flashlight down. "Keep your light aimed at the ground."

She headed toward the small river that would lead them to the lake the soldiers were supposedly held near. If they weren't there, this mission would be a bust. They covered the space in short order. The running water would help mask any noise from their approach. The wind rustling through the trees would also conceal them.

Twenty minutes later, Peggy saw a light up ahead, stopped, and switched off her flashlight.

Nightingale did the same.

This was in the right location to be the captors' camp. Peggy would assume so until she learned otherwise. She pointed in the direction of the light, which appeared to be a campfire. A lone shadowy figure stood near it. Four crude lean-tos made of branches stood close by.

Nightingale nodded to indicate she saw and crouched with Peggy.

Peggy put her head close to her comrade's and whispered, "I see four lean-tos. We need to figure out which one our soldiers are being kept in." The camp appeared to be nestled between the river and the shore of the lake, but on the other side of the river from where Peggy and Nightingale presently surveyed from.

Nightingale whispered back, "If I were them, I would split them up. The officer in one and the enlisted in another."

That made sense. But which of the four were they in? "Let's hope they aren't that smart."

Two more men joined the one at the fire.

Peggy kept her voice low but loud enough for Nightingale to hear her over the rustling of the leaves in the growing wind. "Let's go back to the rocks in the river to cross and then circle around behind the shelters."

Nightingale nodded and took the lead.

⩵CHAPTER 26⩵

Sunday 15 October 1944

Slow-moving hurricane took a dramatic turn in a
westward trajectory. Passed south of Grand Cayman.
Sustained winds on island peaked at 96 mph with 118
mph gusts. Air pressure bottomed out at 984 mbar.

Once across the river and positioned behind some trees and bushes
at the rear of the lean-to shelters, Peggy took stock of the situation.

Voices, magnified by the open water of the lake, reached their
concealed location, but she couldn't make out what they were saying.
Were those the captors? Major Berg had been right to caution them
away from landing near here.

She put her finger to her lips in a shushing motion then pointed
to the lake.

Nightingale nodded to indicate she understood that the flat water
would amplify any noise they made.

Peggy listened more carefully, trying to figure out what the men
were saying. She still couldn't because they spoke in a foreign language. If she wasn't mistaken, that was German. Germans in Cuba?
Did the Cuban government know about them? Did the US military
here on the island know?

A rustling in the trees near them halted Peggy's train of thought.

A sentry out scouting for trouble.

Major Berg had warned them that the captors would likely send someone to walk their perimeter or have guards posted, depending on how many there were.

Peggy and Nightingale remained still and hidden. The man—whom Peggy could now see wore a military uniform—passed within a few yards of them. She held her breath.

Lord, keep us concealed.

He moved along without hesitation.

Peggy released her breath as silently as possible. *Thank You.*

This sentry made four captors. Hopefully, that was all of them.

Nightingale whispered close to Peggy's ear, "That was close."

Peggy nodded and noticed a man sitting in a slouched position against a tree. She pointed and kept her voice soft as well. "One of ours?"

Nightingale squinted as though having a difficult time determining who he was then nodded.

Which meant, their soldiers weren't being kept in the tree-limb shelters. This was indeed the right place.

Peggy leaned closer to her comrade. "I'm going to crawl up behind him and cut his ropes."

Nightingale jutted her chin to the left. "I think I see the silhouette of another tied up over there. I'll make my way to him."

Peggy agreed and slunk from their hiding spot to behind one of the lean-tos. She lay flat on the ground and slowly belly crawled until she could see the campfire and the men around it.

The fourth man had joined them. As they spoke, they tilted their heads skyward and pointed. Possibly talking about the growing storm. Hopefully, the swishing of the wind in the trees would mask any sound she or Nightingale might make.

Peggy slithered toward the back side of the swaying tree the US soldier was tied to. Once there, she stopped and listened for any difference in the captors' conversation. They continued as they had before.

The US soldier appeared to have a gag in his mouth. She softly made the *shh* sound before whispering, "Don't make any sudden moves or sound."

The man didn't move at all.

Had he heard her? Was he asleep? She wanted to touch his hands to let him know she was there but feared it would startle him into crying out. Even a little sound could garner the German soldiers' attention and give her position away. She had to risk being spotted in order to get him out of here.

She retrieved her knife from the sheath on her gun belt. When she reached for his hands and touched them, he grabbed her finger and squeezed. He knew she was here. Good. She sawed through the rope.

He moved one hand slowly to his face and pulled down the gag. "Give me the knife to cut the one at my ankles." His voice sounded weak.

She slipped it to him.

He freed his feet, crawled around behind the tree where she was, and handed her the knife. "You're a woman?" Scarcely a whisper.

"A WASP. Are there only three of you being held?"

"Affirmative."

"Follow me." Peggy belly crawled back to behind the lean-to and then to the bushes and trees she had been hiding in with Nightingale.

The soldier leaned against a tree with labored breathing and whispered, "Please tell me you didn't come alone." Silver captain's bars sat on his shoulder epaulets.

She pointed. "My partner is checking out someone tied up over there."

"That would be Sergeant Gillespie."

Peggy sighed. What a relief. Wanda Gillespie's children would have their father back for the holidays.

The captain glanced about. "Is it just two of you on this rescue mission?"

"A third is in our aircraft." Peggy scrutinized the man in the almost darkness. Was that blood on his face? "Are you injured?"

"Don't worry about me. I can make it." He pointed. "Private Nelson is being held on the far side. They kept us separated so we couldn't work together to escape. But we need to move quickly to free the others before they make another check of us." He nodded toward her gun belt. "You wouldn't happen to have an extra firearm I could use?"

She handed him her holstered weapon then patted her boot. "I have another." *Thank you, Nightingale.*

The captain took the lead.

When they reached a place near but not too close to the private, Nightingale and a sergeant met them.

The sergeant hurried to the captain's side. "Are you all right, sir?"

"I'll be fine. Free Nelson."

Nightingale said, "I'll do it."

Sergeant Gillespie held up a hand. "Pardon me, ma'am. It might be better if I do it. Won't be so startling to him."

Nightingale nodded and handed her knife to him as well as her spare pistol from her boot.

He took them. "I'll be right back."

An eternity later, which was probably only a couple of minutes, the sergeant returned with another soldier.

The private stopped short. "Are those women?"

"We are." Nightingale put a hand on her hip.

"We were rescued by women? Where are the men?"

Oh, he was one of those who thought women were incapable. "No men. Only us."

The sergeant put his face close to the private's. "You better shut up or I'll leave you out here in this Cuban jungle."

The sound of the private gulping was unmistakable. "Yes, sir."

The sergeant quickly crouched. "Shh."

A rustling sound rippled near them.

Sergeant Gillespie held up his hand and slunk away.

The swishing got closer until it was upon them. Soon a German soldier glared down at them and reached for his weapon.

Just as quickly, an arm wrapped around his throat from behind and a hand covered his mouth.

Peggy held her breath.

The German struggled, trying to get away from the sergeant, until he went limp.

"Is he dead?" Peggy swallowed hard.

"No. Merely a chokehold until he passed out." Gillespie removed the Luger from the German's gun belt. "Can you ladies help the captain?"

"What's wrong with him?" Peggy assisted the senior officer to his feet and draped his arm over her shoulder.

"I think they broke some ribs when they tried to beat information out of him. They failed." The sergeant's words held pride. He handed Nightingale's small spare weapon to the private. He apparently liked the bigger one.

Nightingale propped up the captain's other side.

The sergeant waved the Luger. "Is your pilot going to be able to fly in this wind?"

"Yes, sir." Peggy had no choice. The Delta was the only way off the island for them.

"Which way?"

"We follow the river all the way to the coast."

He gave a nod. "Lead the way with the captain. Nelson and I will take up the rear and head off any trouble."

Peggy hurried in the direction of the Delta. She held up her compass. "Shine your light on this."

Nightingale flicked on the flashlight for only a moment.

"If we head straight west rather than following the winding river, it might be faster."

Gillespie replied. "Take the straighter route. The Germans will expect us to stay close to the river."

Peggy moved as quickly as the captain could travel. He had more weight on her than she expected him to which meant he was injured to a greater extent than she'd realized.

Suddenly, shouts came from behind them.

The sergeant said in a semi-loud sort of whisper, "They've discovered we're missing. Move faster. Ladies, no matter what happens, keep going and don't look back. Get the captain to your airplane."

Surprisingly, Captain Williams sped up, even though he held his sides and hunched as though in pain.

They met the river at the point where it turned from traveling north to heading west and out to the coast.

Peggy said to Nightingale, "We'll follow this to that one sharp bend and cross there, then a straight shot out to the beach."

"Roger," her comrade said.

At the place where they planned to cross, the sergeant and private caught up to them. Gillespie said, "They are almost on us. Where's the plane?"

"Why?"

"They are gaining too fast on us. Nelson and I are going to hold them off while you two get the captain to the plane."

Peggy understood. "Cross here and head due west."

The sergeant took one side of his superior officer and spoke to the private. "Grab the captain's other side."

He did. The soldiers splashed through the water to the other bank faster than she and Nightingale could have. They were practically carrying the captain.

Peggy removed the walkie-talkie from her belt and turned it on. She had kept it off to avoid inadvertently giving away their position. "Brownie, start the engine. We are coming in fast."

The radio crackled. "Roger. I'll be ready. You got them?"

"Yes, but we've been discovered."

"Roger."

Shots rang out.

The men relinquished the captain to her and Nightingale. Gillespie waved his arm. "Go! We'll hold them off here." They ducked behind a boulder.

She handed him her compass, and Nightingale gave the private her flashlight.

Peggy and Nightingale took off as fast as they could with the captain in tow.

He spoke in a raspy voice. "You are the bravest ladies I've ever met."

Peggy felt anything but brave. Terrified was more like it.

Lord, please protect the sergeant and private. And all of us.

The report of the gunfire echoed over the wind in the trees.

Soon they broke out into the opening near the beach. The Delta sat slightly north of their location.

Brownie was right where she was supposed to be and had turned the Delta around so it was ready to take off. That would make for a faster getaway. The Delta's engine roared to life. Good. Brownie had

had time to get through the preflight checklist.

"Just a little farther, Captain."

He answered with a nod. He was likely using all his energy to keep moving.

At the Delta, Peggy and Nightingale boosted the captain onto the wing. Nightingale climbed up and helped the man inside.

The report of gunshots echoed closer and closer.

Nightingale waved her hand. "Get in here."

"What about the others?"

"They're coming. You need to get in the pilot's seat. I'll watch out for the sergeant and private."

Peggy scrambled aboard. The captain lay on some of the blankets. She couldn't fuss over him right now and hustled to the pilot's seat. "How is everything?"

Brownie nodded. "*Second Chances* is purring like new. Is that gunfire?"

"Yes. We need to be ready as soon as the others get here." Peggy called to Nightingale in the rear of the craft. "How is it looking back there?"

"They're coming. Running hard. Be ready to take off as soon as they get here."

Peggy gripped the yoke. "Ready. Brownie, go help her."

"Are you sure?"

"Yes. We have to get them on board."

Brownie unstrapped and went to the rear compartment.

Closer gun reports echoed in the air. A chink sounded against the side of the Delta.

Peggy glanced over her shoulder.

One man's head and shoulders vaulted through the doorway, and he scrambled inside. Nightingale leaned out the door and shot her pistol.

Brownie grabbed the arm of the second man. "We got them! Go! Go! Go!"

Peggy punched it full throttle, and the Delta bumped over the uneven ground.

Gunfire ricocheted off the fuselage.

Peggy pushed the plane to top speed.

The compartment door slammed shut.

"We are all in!"

"Get everyone strapped in." Peggy eased the yoke back, and the Delta lifted into the air. Soon the gunfire no longer hit the fuselage.

They had made it. The mission was a success.

However, the Delta wasn't responding properly. Was that merely the wind buffeting them around?

No this was more than a little weather.

The bullets they took had done some damage. Hopefully, nothing fatal. How much was bullet damage and how much was fighting the increasing winds?

Brownie returned to the copilot's seat.

Peggy aimed the aircraft northeast toward Florida. "Is everyone strapped in?"

"Yes."

"How is the captain?"

"He's pretty beat up. The private got hit in the arm, a flesh wound. Nightingale is bandaging it."

So, they had succeeded. Then this was all worth it. Now, just the flight home. She would say smooth sailing if it weren't for the Delta behaving oddly.

"What's wrong?" Brownie asked.

"We took a few bullets. I think one damaged the rudder."

"Are we going to be all right?"

"I think so. If we have to, we'll land at Eglin Field in Florida." Or any other airport they could get to respond to them.

A few minutes later, Peggy knew Eglin was out of the question. "Brownie, make sure everyone has a Mae West and parachute on."

"What's the damage?"

They had packed seven chutes, one for each of them and an extra for good luck.

Peggy pointed. "They hit the fuel tank. At the rate it's dropping, we'll be fortunate if we make it to the tip of Florida."

Brownie unstrapped again. "Parachutes. The plane was hit. We're losing fuel." She sounded like a drill sergeant.

Peggy fought the Delta in the turbulent air current and grabbed the hand mike. "Mayday, Mayday." No distinctive hiss or crackle came over the line. It must have been hit too. How could four men shooting blindly in the dark do so much damage?

A few lights, dotting the western seaboard, clued her in to Florida's location. She wasn't going to be able to get the Delta to an airfield nor be able to radio one. "Get ready to jump." She climbed as best as *Second Chances* could so there would be sufficient altitude for the parachutes to deploy in time.

Someone opened the side door.

The sergeant came up to the cockpit and laid a parachute and Mae West on the floor next to her. "I'll take over. You jump with the others."

The yoke jerked around in her hands as she fought the turbulence. "Are you a pilot?"

"No, but tell me what to do." He sounded earnest.

He couldn't be serious.

"No time. You are jumping. No arguing. Your wife and children are looking forward to spending the holidays with you. Go!" She didn't have time to convince him.

In a soft voice, he said, "Thank you." Then he saluted her.

She gave him a nod. "When I say the word, everyone needs to bail out."

"Roger."

"Do you think Captain Williams can make it?"

"Yes."

She wasn't sure if that was, *He would make it fine and survive*, or *Regardless, this was the only option.*

CHAPTER 27

Peggy kept her eyes on the horizon for the Florida coast. It was up ahead but not close enough for her passengers to bail out and drift down to land. They would end up in the Gulf of Mexico. Or worse, the Everglades with both alligators and crocodiles to greet them.

She retrieved the radio hand microphone. "Mayday, Mayday. Army aircraft Northrop Delta four one five. Badly damaged. Passengers and crew bailing out. Mayday." She listened for a response that indicated anyone had heard her.

Nothing.

She sent her distress call again.

Still nothing.

Nightingale came up to the cockpit. "The sergeant is going to jump with the captain and keep him in his sights to see to it he lands all right. I can take over the Delta so you can bail out with the others."

No. This mission had been Peggy's idea from the start. "I've got it. Look out for the others."

Her comrade paused as though reluctant to comply. "I will."

"It's almost time."

Nightingale hesitated. "You are going to jump once we're all out, aren't you?"

"Of course. I need to make sure the Delta has a safe place to crash."

"You don't think you can land it?"

"The fuel is spent." There wasn't time to discuss this. "You have to go *now*. Watch out for the wind. It's getting pretty strong. Tell everyone to jump."

Nightingale stared at Peggy a long moment.

Peggy hoped her comrade didn't tell her it had been an honor serving with her, because that would mean she didn't think Peggy would make it. Peggy had to make it.

Finally, Nightingale said, "See you on the ground."

Peggy hoped so. "Go."

Nightingale turned to leave and spoke to the others. "Now! Jump!"

Soon Nightingale said, "I'm the last one. Jumping now."

Peggy glanced over her shoulder as Nightingale disappeared through the black open doorway. Peggy's heart sank. She was alone.

"I am with you."

Was that the Lord? It had to be. A comforting peace that made no sense wrapped around her. She had done the right thing in pushing to rescue those soldiers regardless of what happened to her. Mom would take good care of her girls if she didn't make it, but there was no reason to believe she wouldn't.

Now, to head this plane on a safe trajectory to crash where it wouldn't endanger anyone. In the still darkness and not being able to see much below, the ocean was the best option. If she got the aircraft high enough, it would make it to the Atlantic Ocean before going down.

The wind battered the Delta around. Rather than bank back toward the Gulf of Mexico and fight the wind, she would let the current push her across the southern end of Florida so the plane could crash in the wide, open ocean.

She made sure the aircraft was at a high enough altitude for her to safely parachute out and tried to engage George, the autopilot, but it was being stubborn and wouldn't engage, even after several tries. One more thing the bullets had damaged. It was imperative to stay with the aircraft a bit longer to ensure it didn't go down into a populated area.

She sent out the Mayday distress call one last time.

Jumping out of an aircraft on a calm sunny day and being at the mercy of nature as she drifted down aimlessly had never appealed to her. In a storm was worse. The thought turned her stomach. She chuckled to herself. She felt less trepidation about staying in the "safety" of a doomed craft than jumping into the empty nothingness of the firmament. Not a fan of that weightless feeling. The endless falling. Her feet preferred to remain firmly planted on something solid, which seemed odd for a gal who loved to fly.

She unstrapped herself, stood, and slung the Mae West and the parachute over her shoulder and the C-1 survival vest. After strapping them on, she checked the instruments and looked out the windows to ensure a safe crash. The Delta pitched to and fro as she stumbled her way to the open doorway.

Everything seemed to slow down.

Blackness. Where did the blackness of the air end and the blackness of land or water begin? If her calculations were right, she would drift down on the eastern coast of Florida's peninsula.

Deep breath.

Blow it out.

Jump, Peggy. Jump. Do it for your girls. They are waiting for you.

"*I am with you.*"

Peace washed through her as her legs finally obeyed and pushed her body away from the aircraft.

Down.

Down into the abyss of space.

The winds tossed her and the Delta, and aircraft's tail whipped around and hit her shoulder, spinning her wildly like a dry autumn leaf spiraling in a dust devil.

Which way was up? If she wasn't facing the right direction, her chute wouldn't deploy properly. In a panic, she wildly scrambled, clawing at the air. The heavy winds didn't help.

"*I am with you.*"

She closed her eyes.

Plummeting, she felt for the air current. It was coming from her side then her head, then feet and to other side. Tumbling head to toe, over and over, she moved her arms to counter the spinning. No longer out of control, the air that rushed past her came from her feet as though she were standing up. An adjustment of her body brought her face down with her arms and feet out where she checked for the right airflow. Though hard to determine with the hurricane winds adding to the air's direction, she believed she was correct. She gripped the handle of the ripcord with a prayer and yanked to release her parachute.

The silk shot out of the pack. When it fully extended, it yanked her upward, but in reality, it was her speedy descent which had been swiftly halted. The jolt of it jerked her banged shoulder that had been slammed into by the plane's tail. A sharp pain stabbed through her shoulder and radiated across her chest and back. She reached her other hand over to grip her injured arm. Hopefully, it wasn't broken, only dislocated.

She was at the mercy of the winds now. And they weren't blowing in her favor. Weren't there a few islands off the eastern coast of Florida? Maybe she would land on one of them if she missed the coast altogether.

The wind swung her to and fro from the strings of the parachute.

After pulling out her flashlight from her belt, she switched it on then pointed it down. Where was the ground? She must determine the terrain before she landed. But how, with no distinguishing topography? Salt hung heavy in the moist air. Hopefully, that was because the ocean was close and not because she was over it. Or worse yet, the Everglades.

She wished she was down already. This unbearable waiting frazzled her already frayed nerves. Parachuting was detestable for this very reason. No control.

Lord?

"Prepare your chute."

Prepare it for what? Was she going to land in trees? That could be worse than a water landing. If she got tangled up in branches off the ground and left dangling, she could hang there indefinitely and slowly perish. Or worse—but maybe not worse—she could get mortally injured in the branches and bleed out.

Please, Lord, let the others have found safe places to touch down.

Was that some slight differentiation in the surface below? She moved the flashlight back and forth. Not a difference in a solid surface, but waves on a liquid one, and it rapidly approached.

She needed to release herself from the parachute harness before she hit the water or when her chute landed and became saturated immediately, it would sink and pull her down.

Her fingers fumbled with the buckle holding the parachute harness on her. The catch wouldn't release. In her struggle, the flashlight slipped from her grasp and plopped into the water. It sunk below the surface. Down and down. Each inch dimmed the light more and more.

Her boots touched the water, and a gust of wind dragged her along the ocean's surface with her feet and shins trailing through the cold water. Still, she couldn't release the harness to free herself from the chute.

Thank You, Lord, for this extra time to get the buckle released, but it's not letting go. Help me.

The problem was, with the wind carrying the chute along, it pulled the harness too tightly and had no give for her to unbuckle it. She would have to wait until the chute landed in the water to have enough give to release it. It would have to be done quickly to avoid getting pulled under. Or if the wind changed, that could allow enough slack for her to free herself. Either way she had to be ready.

The cold ocean eagerly swallowed her a little at a time. Up to her waist now. Soon she would be free. Hopefully it wouldn't be too late.

As though by the hand of God, the wind filled the chute and pulled her up out of the water. Then almost as quickly dropped her, causing her to submerge all the way below the surface. She held her breath and worked the buckle free. Then she swam up and up until her hands and arms tangled in the cords of the chute. It was coming down around her, encapsulating her like a large wet blanket, holding her down.

Freedom eluded her. The silk of the chute itself rested over her. She pulled at it and pulled and kept pulling in one direction, hoping to reach the edge of the fabric before she ran out of breath.

Her lungs burned.

Freedom lost.

Time had run out.

Her girls.

Sweet and innocent.

If she could only see their faces one more time. Let them know everything would be all right and that she loved them.

Something bumped her side. Suddenly, cold air on her face caused her to gasp in a huge breath. Free of her chute, she grappled for the CO_2 canisters on either side of her Mae West life vest to inflate it. She managed one all right which inflated half of her vest, causing her to tip sideways. Her injured shoulder didn't allow her to use that arm, so she tried reaching across herself to open the other canister but couldn't with all the gear. One side would have to do.

Her shoulder hurt nearly as bad as the twenty-one hours of labor giving birth to Wendy. She had been sure the baby inside her was going to tear her in two.

After drawing in several more deep breaths and bobbing in the choppy waves, she surveyed the inky water to assess her circumstances. With the blackout calls along the East Coast, no dots of light indicated which direction Florida lay in. Good thing she'd been flying away from the storm or her predicament could be a lot worse.

Lightning flashed in the distance illuminating three dorsal fins circling in the water.

She gasped. *Please don't let me be eaten by sharks.* There couldn't be a worse fate.

If she could get the one-man life raft out, inflate it, and climb aboard, she could be relatively safe. She reached for it, but the pain in her shoulder made it impossible to pull out with both hands, so she struggled with one. A shark bumped her hip, and it slipped from her hand. She grappled for the folded raft and snagged it. Were the sharks toying with her?

Don't panic, Peggy. That will do you no good.

She tucked the edge of the raft in the hand of her injured arm and, with her good arm, proceeded to unfold it. Fingering the CO_2 canister, she pulled the toggle, removed the pin, and turned the top to the left. The raft further unfurled and inflated. As it did, the kinetic energy pulled on her injured arm. She latched onto the edge of it with her good one.

Another distant lightning flash. Two fins moved through the water a few feet away. Where was the third? No time to figure it out now. *Climb into the raft. It's your only hope.*

From only one briefing on these life rafts, she knew to board it on the narrow end. She shifted the vessel around but couldn't lift her injured arm over the edge, so she attempted to hoist herself with her good arm.

From under the surface of the water, the shark lifted her, successfully aiding her into the raft. She scrambled in, pulling her legs out of the water. That couldn't have been a shark or else it would have eaten her.

A soft splash as though something surfaced alerted her to the beast's nearness, then the chatter of a dolphin. Were all three dolphins? They had brought her up from beneath the surface, stayed with her, and helped her to safety. "Thank you."

Shifting around, she laid back in the three-foot-long space inside the boat with her knees bent and gazed heavenward. "And thank *You*." Not even a star in the sky.

Water surrounded her outside the raft as well as inside it. First order of business was to bail it out. Somewhere in here was a collapsible bucket the size of a soup bowl. She located it and removed most of the water.

With a compass and the night sky, she should be able to figure out which way to paddle. Without her flashlight to read a compass, Peggy had no hope of finding her way in the dark. Morning was only a couple of hours away. She could get her bearings then and be able to at least see her compass.

No, wait. Sergeant Gillespie had her compass.

She would have to figure it out in the morning and hope for a Dumbo mission to find her. Not likely since no one knew she was somewhere in the Atlantic Ocean. Leaning her head against the inflated edge of her raft, she allowed the rocking of the ocean to lull her toward sleep.

———— ≋ ————

Peggy shivered and realized she was wet. Had she fallen asleep in the bathtub? That would be foolish but not unheard of. She had evidently been in so long the water had grown cold. Very cold. Something bumped her from below.

After forcing her eyes open to daylight, she scanned the vicinity.

Water surrounded her. The ocean. She startled and splashed her hands outside her little boat.

Five dorsal fins circled the small vessel. Her dolphin friends were back, or maybe they had never left her. Like guardian angels looking after her.

They seemed to be taking turns bumping the raft. Not bumping it but rather propelling it. Where were they taking her? Hopefully toward land. But if they had been doing this since she fell from the sky, shouldn't she be on shore by now? How far off course had the storm taken her parachute?

She studied the sky in all directions. All clear ahead of her, blue with a few fluffy clouds. An agonizing twist to see behind her revealed angry clouds churning in a brewing torrent. That must be the tropical storm. Or had it turned into a hurricane?

Taking a bearing from the position of the sun—provided she hadn't slept most of a day—she determined the dolphins, who seemed to be taking turns pushing her, were heading her north-northeast. But why? Land should be west. They were taking her out to sea.

This is not the way she needed to go. "Whoa. Can you all stop?" How did one get marine life to understand what she wanted?

▤CHAPTER 28▤

Howie remained in the War Situation Room throughout the night. He wouldn't be able to sleep until he received a report that the mission had been successful and everyone was safe. General Hawkins had left with instructions to contact him at home as soon as Howie received any news.

Howie had drifted off a time or two early on, sitting in a chair. Now more than just his leg ached. As the hours ticked by with no word from the rescue party, his agitation grew. They should have returned by now. He wanted to drop to his knees several times during the night to pray for the mission but didn't want to make a spectacle of it. Instead, he'd wandered the corridors, praying for success and safety, especially for Peggy.

She always insisted upon protecting everyone else before herself. *Lord, don't let her do anything stupid.*

He remembered his first encounter with the feisty pilot. She had refused to follow his order to bail out and ditch the airplane. Though that situation had eventually turned out well, he prayed, if she needed to, she would play it safe and bail out. He hoped the mission didn't come to that. The parachutes were merely a precaution.

At dawn, he headed for his office and telephoned the general to let him know he hadn't heard anything. "I hope I didn't wake you, sir."

From the other end of the line came General Hawkins's voice. "No. I was up. Give me an update."

"No word, sir."

"That doesn't mean it wasn't successful."

But it didn't bode well in that direction. "Yes, sir."

A little after 0800 hours, Howie's desk sergeant knocked on his office door and entered. "There's an operator on the telephone wanting to know if we will accept a collect call from Jolene Horner."

Howie didn't have time to bother with such nonsense. "No. And I don't want to be distur—" That name seemed familiar. Nightingale?

Howie snatched up the phone. "Who did you say was calling?"

The operator said, "A collect call from Jolene Horner. Will you accept the charges?"

"Yes." Why was *she* calling instead of Mama Bird? Had Peggy been injured? Or worse?

Nightingale's voice came over the line. "Major Berg?"

"Nightingale? Is that you?" Relief that they had made it back from Cuba flooded him mixed with fear.

"Yes. We are on the southern tip of Florida. Can you send transportation to pick us up?"

"Of course. What is your exact location?"

Nightingale told him.

"Is everyone safe and sound?"

"I have Brownie and the three soldiers with me. The captain is pretty beat up and the private got winged by a bullet."

Bullets? Howie swallowed hard. "What about Mama Bird?"

"We got separated when we had to bail out. She hasn't called you yet?"

"No." *Bail out?* Things must have gone terribly wrong. And Witherspoon had a stubborn streak when it came to leaving an aircraft she was piloting if there was one small chance she could land it. "I'll arrange for transportation to the nearest base and have you flown here."

Lord, please let her have bailed out, and keep her safe.

At dusk, an aircraft landed at Bolling Field with Nightingale, Brownie, and the three rescued army soldiers but still no word from Witherspoon. General Hawkins requested to personally debrief the soldiers who had been held captive.

Howie walked from the cargo plane with Nightingale and Brownie. "Any word on Mama Bird?"

Brownie shook her head. "Since she jumped last, she could have landed miles from us. She hasn't contacted you or anyone at Bolling Field?"

"No." If she had made it all right, wouldn't she have communicated with him or someone? "I'll call her mother to see if she's heard from her. The storm has ramped up to a hurricane. It's heading west and looks as though it will thread right between Cuba and the Yucatán Peninsula in Mexico into the Gulf.

Nightingale nodded. "Then it was a good thing we went when we did. Even a few hours later would have made the mission impossible, and we would have had to wait days, if not weeks, before trying again."

Howie nodded. Nonetheless, the increased winds could have carried Mama Bird far from her intended target. That was if she indeed jumped. He held the door to the main building for the WASPs. "I'll meet you in the briefing room with the others." He hurried to his office and dialed the Witherspoon residence.

Peggy's mother answered. "Good evening, Witherspoons'."

"Mrs. Deny?"

"Yes? Who is this?"

"Major Berg."

"Oh." Her voice brightened. "You can call me Muriel. What can I do for you?"

There wasn't any surreptitious way to ask this. He would need to simply blurt it out. "Have you heard from your daughter?"

"Oh, dear. No." Panic painted her words. "Did something go wrong?"

He tried to keep his voice light, not wanting to cause the woman needless distress. "Not that we know of. We merely thought she might have contacted you."

"She hasn't, but if she does, I'll let you know."

"I would appreciate that. Please don't worry. It's not unusual for a pilot to be out of communication for a while." However, this mission had been different than any other one a WASP had been on.

"Thank you for saying that, but the fact you are even asking tells me there is cause for worry. I'll be on my knees praying she's fine and that she gets in touch with someone soon."

"Thanks. Goodbye." He hung up. So where was Peggy?

He headed down to the debriefing room.

Captain Williams had been taken to Bethesda Medical Center to check his injuries. Jumping from an aircraft in the middle of the night hadn't helped his condition. Fortunately, he'd seemed well enough coming off the plane and would likely recover. The small medical clinic on base was attending to Private Nelson's gunshot wound.

In the briefing room stood Sergeant Gillespie, Brownie, Nightingale, Barbara Poole, the head WASP here, and Jackie Cochran. The general hadn't arrived yet. The sergeant was shaking the ladies' hands. "I speak for the captain and private as well, there are no words to express our gratitude for what you have done for us."

The sergeant immediately crossed over to Howie. "Any word on the lady pilot?"

Howie shook his head.

Nightingale joined them. "Her mother hasn't heard from her?"

"No. I tried not to worry her. I need you to be honest with me. Do you think she bailed out as she should? Or would she have gone down with the Delta?"

The worry line between Nightingale's eyes deepened. "She promised me she would bail out. She just needed to get it on the right course so it wouldn't risk people's lives on the ground. Then she would have set the autopilot and jumped. She wouldn't have stayed with the Delta."

In theory, but she had a stubborn streak in her to protect others. "Unless she felt she had no other choice to ensure it didn't pose a hazard to anyone."

Brownie shook her head. "No. She could have easily aimed *Second Chances* for the Atlantic and still had time to jump." She pinned Howie with her brown eyes. "She jumped."

He hoped so.

Sergeant Gillespie barked out, "Officer in the room. Atten-*hut*."

Howie snapped to, as did the others.

General Hawkins said, "At ease. Please, everyone, sit."

They all sat around the large conference table.

General Hawkins took the seat at the head of the table. "What is spoken of here in this room is not to be uttered again. Is that clear?"

"Yes, sir," echoed from one person to another around the table.

"Major Berg, any update on the status of WASP Witherspoon?"

"No, sir."

The general seemed disappointed with that answer. "I received word that the hurricane has made a sharp turn to the north and will make landfall on the western end of Cuba in an hour or two."

Sergeant Gillespie said, "That means if these heroic ladies hadn't come for us, we would have been swallowed up in the storm." He shifted his gaze from the general to the ladies. "Thank you again." Then he looked back to the general. "General Hawkins, sir. I would like to lead a search-and-rescue mission for Witherspoon."

"Thank you, Sergeant. We have people in Florida searching. We hope to locate her soon."

However, if the hurricane had turned north, then resources would need to be diverted to evacuations and helping people in the hurricane's path, which could include Florida at this point.

General Hawkins continued. "In the absence of Captain Williams, Sergeant Gillespie, will you brief me on the events leading up to you, the captain, and the private being captured? Who were the men who took you and why?"

"They were German spies, sir. Their U-boat was sunk near Cuba. They were trying to gather intelligence on the US." He continued to relay the story of the captain and him being driven by the private to Havana for a social gathering to grease the wheels of goodwill in Cuba. Upon leaving the event, they were accosted and driven to the place they were held. He conveyed how they were tortured for information. Mostly the captain as he held the highest rank among them and was presumed to have the most sensitive information of the three. "We thought no one was coming for us."

Howie knew the feeling. The hopelessness.

The sergeant continued, "The Cubans wouldn't likely admit they had Germans or German sympathizers on their island. Likewise, the US couldn't mount a rescue without appearing as though we were invading Cuba and causing an international incident. We had come to terms with our fate. Then out of the jungle came these brave women. Thank you for sending them."

The general raised his eyebrows. "The US military did not send them. They took this mission up all on their own. With the help of Major Berg."

The sergeant turned to Howie. "Thank you."

Howie knew the general had done all he could covertly to help them. "It was their idea. I figured they were going to go with or without permission, so it was my duty to do what I could to give this expedition the best possible chance of succeeding. Since it wasn't a sanctioned mission, they rebuilt that aircraft with salvaged parts from the aircraft graveyard."

Gillespie rubbed the back of his neck. "Oh, man. The women? By themselves? Never would have guessed." Pride colored every word.

Every step of the way, those WASPs had impressed Howie over and over. That this operation succeeded was extremely impressive. They had the determination to achieve their goal, which had been the most important element.

The general focused his attention on Nightingale. "WASP Horner, tell me about the mission from the moment you took off from Florida."

Nightingale recounted the events step by step. Brownie popped in with what she was doing along the way as well as when she was waiting in the aircraft and turned it around then getting the walkie-talkie call that they were coming in hot. They were being shot at, and as they took off, the Delta was hit, and several systems including the fuel tank were damaged.

Nightingale finished her story with bailing from the Delta then falling through the night sky. "I found Private Nelson right away. He had seen the direction the captain and sergeant had landed. We headed that way. When we arrived, WASP Brown had already found them. We searched the night sky but couldn't locate WASP Witherspoon's parachute."

Nightingale continued. "We walked for a mile or so until we came upon a residence. We used their telephone to call Major Berg. He sent transportation to take us to the nearest military installation where we were flown here."

The general addressed Brownie next. "WASP Brown, do you have anything else to add?"

"No, sir."

"Aren't you the tow-target pilot who got shot in the foot a few weeks ago?"

"Yes, sir."

"Impressive. I take it your foot has healed well."

"Yes, sir."

Nightingale interjected. "Don't let her fool you, General. It still bothers her, but she's a trooper."

The general gave a nod of acknowledgement. "You ladies have performed above and beyond the call of duty. The United States Army and the Army Air Corps thank you, but not publicly. No one can ever know about this mission. Is that understood?"

"Yes, sir," Nightingale and Brownie said in unison.

Howie agreed that the ladies' actions all throughout the planning and execution of this mission were exemplary and outstanding. As fine of soldiers as he had ever worked with.

⪫CHAPTER 29⪪

Monday 16 October 1944

Storm abruptly turned north along the 83rd meridian west; continued to gain strength; slowly accelerated north.

Tuesday 17 October 1944

Major hurricane, passing over western portion of Cuba.

Wednesday 18 October 1944

Hurricane reached peak intensity with 145 mph winds on northern coast of Cuba; pressure of 937 mbar, lowest measured pressure of the hurricane; maintaining peak strength, it crossed west of Havana, narrowest section of the island, causing the winds to diminish slightly before emerging into Gulf of Mexico; the eye passed over the Dry Tortugas, producing two hours of calm on the islands; winds estimated at 120 mph; storm grew considerably with a radius of maximum winds almost twice the size as climatologically expected.

Howie stood at attention in General Hawkins' office. It had been three days since the WASPs and soldiers had returned without Witherspoon. Mama Bird. Peggy.

Captain Williams had been released from Bethesda Medical Center and would recover fully. All three soldiers had been denied permission to join the search for Peggy. The military wouldn't risk their lives with a hurricane bearing down on her last known position.

The general had his hands folded in front of him on the desk. His full attention on Howie. "At ease, Major. Have a seat."

Howie sat.

General Hawkins studied him a long moment. "We have a matter to address."

Mama Bird.

"Permission to go to Florida and lead a search and rescue operation for WASP Witherspoon."

The general shook his head. "Sorry, Major. We had people searching as long as we could. We had to pull them off in preparation for the hurricane to make landfall in Florida. On its current trajectory, the storm is predicted to move up the coast in this direction. All our resources down there as well as along the eastern seaboard are tied up with this hurricane, both with preparations beforehand and the mess that will be left in its wake. It's time to notify her family."

No. He didn't want to give up. If anyone was going to survive, it was Mama Bird. She had to have made it.

General Hawkins continued. "Her family deserves closure. Do you want to inform them, or should I assign someone?"

Anyone else but him would be too impersonal. "I'll tell them." If they had to be told, it should be from a friend. Though he wasn't technically a friend, but Mama Bird's superior.

"I thought you would want to. Take the rest of the day if you need to. Dismissed."

With a heavy heart, Howie left the general's office and headed off Bolling Field to Oxen Hill in Maryland, praying the whole way for the right words to say. He parked on the street, got out, and grabbed his cane. He studied the vile thing. If he hadn't been half crippled, he would have gone on the mission with the ladies. He could have protected Peggy. He could have seen to it she returned safely. He tossed the cane back into the car and slammed the door.

As he strolled up the walk, Junie opened the front door and ran to him.

"Mr. Howie!"

He steadied himself in preparation for the little girl to bump into him.

She did and wrapped her diminutive arms around his waist. "Mommy's not here. She went on a trip. We expect her back any day. Maybe today. We don't know."

He picked her up and held her close. Tears gathered in his eyes.

Mama Bird had performed with as much bravery as any man. All the WASPs had.

Howie concentrated hard to walk the rest of the way to the door without stumbling. Though his injured leg was still weak, he made it without risking the little one.

Smiling, Mrs. Deny—Muriel—met them there. When she locked her gaze on him, she gasped and bit her fist.

Howie didn't have to say anything for her to know.

Peggy's mother took Junie from Howie and set her inside the door. "Go play in your room."

"Grandma, what's wrong?"

"I'll tell you later. Now do as I say."

"But I want to be with Mr. Howie."

"Not right now. Please go."

The girl pushed out her bottom lip in a pout and sulked off.

Muriel closed the door. "She's not coming home, is she?"

"I'm so sorry." Howie ached for her and the girls. "As of now, she is still only classified as missing in action. We will continue searching for her." At least he would.

The older woman's eyes held unshed tears. "Was her mission a success?"

Howie didn't know how to answer that. This woman wasn't supposed to know that there *was* a mission. He longed to tell her everything. "Though I can't divulge any details, I can tell you your daughter is one of the bravest people I have ever met."

"She's so much like her father. Did she help save those men?"

She did know.

Muriel put her hand on his arm. "Don't worry. She didn't really tell me anything, just that three men's lives were in danger. If I had told her not to go, she probably wouldn't have, but then she would have regretted it the rest of her life. I couldn't make her live with that kind of remorse."

Obvious where Peggy got her selflessness from. "The men are safe. And just in time." It didn't hurt to say that. He hadn't said where the rescue took place and not even that they were soldiers. In spite of that, Muriel could probably guess.

Tears rolled down the older woman's face. "Then her sacrifice wasn't in vain." She swiped at her cheeks, with one palm and then the other.

"No, it wasn't."

"Her father and I are very proud of her. Even though he's gone, he would have been so proud of his little girl."

Who wouldn't be? "The bravery she exhibited went beyond what most men have. Would you like me to help you tell her daughters?"

"You don't have to do that." She gave him a sad sort of smile. "Unfortunately, I've had a bit of practice at this sort of thing."

Not having a clue as to how to inform children of the death of a loved one, or in this case missing in action, relief swept through him chased by guilt. "The hurricane in the Caribbean will make landfall in Florida imminently and likely come up the eastern seaboard. Do you and the girls have a safe place to wait it out?"

She nodded. "We do. We know what to do."

"If you need anything, let me know."

"I will."

"Then I'll leave you to it." He strode back out to his car, climbed in, and cried. Why couldn't he have met Peggy long before now? He would give just about anything to trade places with her.

Wherever she was.

≡CHAPTER 30≡

Thursday 19 October 1944

Gradual weakening storm accelerated north-northeast.
Lessened hurricane as it made landfall south of Sarasota, Florida.
Due to large size, it weakened and slowed over Florida peninsula.
It passed east of Tampa Bay and over Central Florida later in
the day. A pressure of 967 mbar recorded at a weather station
in Tampa, Florida. In the afternoon, the large hurricane finally
weakened to tropical storm south of Jacksonville, Florida.

Peggy's head pounded. Eyes closed, she felt as though she was being tossed to and fro. An atrocious stench nauseated her. She struggled to force open her eyes. What she saw didn't make sense. A dingy interior with rust stains on the steel walls. Where was she? How did she get here? The small room moved. Or was she merely dizzy?

She closed her eyes again and took a few deep breaths. The motion didn't stop.

What was the last thing she could remember? She had flown a rescue mission to Cuba, the plane had been damaged, and everyone bailed out. Had the others landed safely? She remembered the pod of dolphins pushing her out to sea. She had drifted for well over a day. Maybe more.

She forced her eyes open once more. When she moved to sit up, pain shot through her shoulder. With her other arm, she worked herself into a sitting position. This wasn't any place she recognized.

She was still in her zoot suit. Strangely, that comforted her.

The rocking and the bulkhead construction led her to conclude this was some sort of boat. How had she gotten here? And who ran this ship? Were they friendly or foe? Whoever they were, she owed them a debt of gratitude. She vaguely remembered hearing men's voices. At the time, she'd believed it was her imagination.

After swinging her feet over the edge of the bed, she waited a moment before standing. She pushed herself up and off the bed. Her legs felt weak and almost buckled, so she gripped the side of the bunk.

Peggy cradled her elbow in her hand to support her injured shoulder.

The waves battered the boat about, causing Peggy to stumble her way to the door. Hopefully it wasn't locked. She turned the knob, opened the door, and stepped into a narrow corridor.

A sailor staggered down the passageway of the pitching vessel. "Miss. Get back inside. The seas are too rough to be walking about."

He sounded American. That was good. "What vessel is this?"

"The *Sea Princess*. We are a fishing boat."

That was the strong smell. "Where are we?"

"The Atlantic. East of the hurricane."

The boat pitched, throwing Peggy against the wall into her injured shoulder. She winced and moaned.

The sailor came up to her. "You're hurt?"

She nodded. "My shoulder."

"Go back in the cabin. When we are out of the worst of this, we'll have Zeus look at you."

Peggy wouldn't be able to get around the ship safely with her injured arm in these rough seas, so she returned to the cabin.

At least the crew seemed friendly.

Thank You, Lord.

Friday 20 October 1944

Hurricane straddled Georgia coast before moving inland over South Carolina. Storm became more baroclinic, transitioning into a fully extratropical cyclone.

Peggy remained in the cabin for the next day or so, sleeping off and on. She wanted to help the crew out, but with her bum arm, she would be useless. She assessed her shoulder and arm. To the best of her knowledge, nothing was broken, possibly dislocated, but she wasn't sure.

The waters had calmed from the previous day.

Two sailors came in where Peggy sat on the bunk, one a white man with a scruffy beard and an unlit pipe clenched between his teeth, the other a burly black man.

"I'm Captain Fredrick." The bearded man motioned toward the other man. "This is Zeus. He tends to all our medical needs. Morris said your arm was causing you pain."

"Yes. When I bailed out of my aircraft, the winds tossed me back against it like a rag doll. The tail collided with my shoulder."

Fredrick nodded. "When we brought you aboard, it was dislocated. Zeus put it back in place." He inclined his head to his companion.

Zeus stepped closer and spoke in a deep baritone voice. "May I take a look?"

He didn't look like any physician Peggy had ever met. "Are you a doctor?"

The captain answered. "Though not formally trained, he has tended to a vast array of injuries. Everyone aboard this vessel would trust him with their lives."

Since the men on this boat obviously thought highly of him, so would Peggy.

She nodded. "It has this burning ache. When I move it, there is a sharp, stabbing pain."

"I will be as gentle as I can." He gingerly touched her arm at her elbow and worked his way toward her shoulder.

Though it hurt, she knew it was necessary to assess the damage.

"Can you remove the clothing from this shoulder so I can get a better look?"

She moved to unfasten the front of her zoot suit and winced. "I don't think so. Do you have scissors?"

The captain rifled in a desk and handed a pair to Zeus. She cringed as the doctor cut from the neck opening across to the sleeve hole and down to the cuff, freeing her arm from her zoot suit. That was a lot of hard-earned money in shreds, but it couldn't be helped. Underneath, she had on a sleeveless undershirt. Fortunately, no one insisted she remove that. She gasped at the angry purple bruise on her shoulder.

With a delicate touch, Zeus prodded the area. "It has come out again but not as far as before. This is going to hurt."

Peggy nodded. "It still needs to be done."

Zeus nodded to the captain. "Hold her steady."

Fredrick sat next to her, gripped her uninjured arm at the elbow, and put his other hand around her waist for support.

"Ready?"

Peggy wasn't but nodded.

With a quick pull, Doctor Zeus popped her shoulder back into place with a sharp pain. The captain moved off the bunk to give the doctor more room to work. Zeus wrapped strips of cloth around her shoulders and down to her waist, pinning her arm to her side and across her front to keep it immobile.

Though it still ached quite badly, it didn't hurt as much. "Thank you. That feels better already."

Captain Fredrick set a fawn-colored, button-up shirt and dark brown trousers with leather suspenders on the bed. "For you to use since your coveralls are ruined."

"Thanks."

"I don't have any females aboard to help you put those on."

"I can manage. I'm going to wait a little bit." She scooted back on the bunk and leaned against the headboard. "How did you find me? The last thing I remember was landing in the water and a pod of dolphins pushing me along."

The captain nodded to Zeus. "That's all for now."

The doctor left.

Then the captain sat in a chair near the bunk. "The seas were getting rougher. A dolphin found us. It kept chattering. One of my men thought it wanted us to follow, so we did. Another joined the first, but that one seemed to come and go. Finally, we saw your life raft in the distance. We closed the distance at top speed, hoping we weren't too late. Three more dolphins were pushing you in our direction. They're smart animals. Once we got you on board, one of them—I think the one who came to get us—chattered at us again. Then, they all dove under the water and disappeared."

"Speaking of water, where in the Atlantic are we?"

"We have been moving out of the path of the hurricane. First, we headed north but when it kept coming in our direction, we swung wide around it and went to where it had already been. Right now, we are somewhere off the coast of South Carolina, I'd say." With a nod, he left.

It took a great deal of effort and much finagling, but Peggy managed to get the shirt on her good arm, wrapped around her, and one button to keep it from falling off her injured arm. The trousers were easier, in that she didn't have to unfasten them to get them on. The one suspender over her good shoulder was enough to keep them up, allowing the other strap to hang loose.

Amazing how God had worked this all out. From the dolphins to the fishing boat with kindhearted men.

A few months ago, she would have viewed recent events as ways God was working against her yet again. But this time she could easily see God's hand in it all. From her overhearing the men in Cuba talking about the captured men, which led to a rescue mission, and eventually to a pod of dolphins and kind fishermen willing to help her, and everything in between. *Thank You, Lord.*

Saturday 21 October 1944

The extratropical remnants maintained the system, emerging over the Atlantic along the coast of the Mid-Atlantic states, heading north, and passing over Nova Scotia later in the day.

Zeus checked Peggy's shoulder and rewrapped it to be held against her body. "That should do until you can get to a real doctor."

"I couldn't have asked for better care. Being a doctor is more than a formal education."

The large man allowed a brief grin. One he seemed to reserve only for her.

The fishing boat docked in Charleston, South Carolina.

From there, Peggy contacted the Charleston Army Air Field. They sent a car for her. As the driver maneuvered through the streets, he had to swerve around fallen debris of branches and building parts. So much destruction. "Did the hurricane go all the way up the coast?" *Please let my family be safe.*

"As far as I know, it's around the DC area now."

Please let them be safe. Please.

"It has lost some of its strength."

"What was the path it took?" When the general had told them about the brewing storm, it was south of the Caribbean.

"It developed into hurricane status south of Cuba. Made landfall on the western end of Cuba on the eighteenth. Crossed over to the lower portion of Florida and made landfall there on the nineteenth."

Peggy and her comrades-in-arms had rescued those soldiers just in time. They would have been swallowed up by the hurricane. Her friends and the rescued men had dropped down into the storm's path. Hopefully, they were able to leave Florida before it hit.

When she arrived at the airfield, she requested a telephone first thing.

"The lines are down all over the place. You're not going to be able to make any calls."

"I need to let people know I'm all right. Are there any aircraft due to fly from here to Bolling Airfield or close to there that I could hitch a ride on?"

"Let me check. On the other hand, why don't you come with me to the hangar? If something is taking off, we'll see if there's room for you."

"Thank you."

At the hangar, crews were apparently finishing up clearing the tarmac of trees, branches, and other debris.

The sergeant who had brought her out to the hangar spoke to a colonel.

The colonel approached her. "I'm Colonel Crocker. Riley says you want to go to DC." He sounded skeptical. "You understand we aren't a commercial airport, don't you?"

She straightened to attention. "Yes, sir. I'm WASP Witherspoon and am stationed at Bolling Airfield, sir." Not looking like a WASP in the oversized fishing clothes, she nodded toward her coveralls folded in her good arm. "I'm merely trying to return to my command."

Sergeant Riley said, "This is the WASP Florida was searching for before the hurricane hit."

"You're the one?"

"Yes, sir." Knowing people *had* been looking for her was comforting.

His demeanor changed. "All right then. We have a B-17 scheduled to head to Bolling Field. It's fueled and ready. It takes off in forty-five minutes. If you want a place on it, we can squeeze you in."

"Tell me when to board, sir."

Forty-five minutes later, Peggy sat in a cargo-net seat with several soldiers in matching seats. The cargo they were transporting was secured down along the center of the fuselage.

As the B-17 lifted off and rose into the air, so did Peggy's hope and joy. She would be home in a little while and be able to see her family.

And Howie—er—Major Berg.

She replayed his kiss in her mind. After that kiss, it didn't seem quite right to refer to him or think of him as *Major Berg*. He was Howie. She needed to be careful not to slip up in front of others.

Howie sat in his office with a heavy heart. It would be some time before he could look for Peggy. If the whole world wasn't at war, he would resign his commission and search full-time.

His desk sergeant knocked on his door. The phones were still down. "Come in."

"Sir, there are some WASPs here to see you."

"Send them in." He needed to stop wallowing and be useful to this command. He stood.

Nightingale and Brownie entered, standing shoulder to shoulder. "Sir, we have something for you. It came in on the B-17."

He wasn't expecting anything. "So the tarmac got cleared enough for it to land?"

"Yes, sir."

It was good to know progress was being made. He studied the women but couldn't see anything in their hands. Then he noticed someone standing behind them. He raised his eyebrow for them to get on with it.

With huge grins, they parted. In the space between them stood Peggy, in a light-colored shirt and dark pants.

He rounded his desk without the aid of his cane. "You're alive!" He reached out to hug her but thought better and dropped his hands to his sides. Too many witnesses. "You'll have to tell me everything that happened."

Nightingale raised up on her toes and back down. "We'll leave the two of you alone."

As they exited, Brownie winked and pulled the door closed.

He crossed the short distance between them and hugged Peggy. "Ow."

He stepped back. "What happened?" That was when he noticed her left arm wasn't in the sleeve of the shirt but tucked inside the front.

"Injured my shoulder."

"Is it broken?" There was no cast.

"Only dislocated and bruised as far as I know."

"As far as you know? You need to go to the medical clinic right away."

"The only thing I want to do is see my mom and daughters. I can't drive with my arm bandaged. Could you take me?"

"Of course. Does the general know you're here? He'll want to debrief you."

"Can that wait? My family is probably worried about me and fears the worst. I would call them, but the telephone lines are down."

"Of course. I'll have Sergeant Miller inform the general you have returned safely and that I'm taking you to let your family know you are all right."

"Thank you."

As he headed along the corridor with her after informing his desk sergeant, General Hawkins came down the walkway toward them. "I heard you had been found, Witherspoon. I'm very pleased to see you are hail and hardy."

"Thank you, sir. My arm is a little banged up, but other than that, I'm good, sir."

"I'm glad to hear. You go home and see your family. In the next day or two, we'll conduct the debriefing. Things are a little hectic. I'm sure much of it is what I already heard from the others. The information will be what happened after they all bailed out."

"Thank you, sir. I appreciate that."

"Major, see to it she gets home safely. She shouldn't be driving with an injured arm."

Exactly Howie's plan. "Yes, sir." But now it was an order, so he could do it without anyone wondering where he was or why he was escorting her home.

———— ≈ ————

Peggy's insides flitted about as Howie turned down her street. A lot of debris littered the roads and the yards. When he pulled into her driveway, her heart nearly leapt out of her chest.

He held up a hand. "Let me get the door for you." He scrambled out.

At the house, the front door swung wide, and Mom stood in the opening.

Peggy's breath caught. There had been a point when she thought she might never see her family again.

"Major Berg?" her mom said.

"I have something for you," Howie moved around the front of the car.

Peggy pulled at the door handle, too impatient to wait.

Howie arrived at her side in time to open the door. He gripped her hand and helped her stand.

Her mom squelched a scream of delight. "Girls!" She ran from the house to Peggy before Peggy even reached the front of the car.

Mom extended her arms as though to hug her, hesitated, then gave her a gentle hug. "You're injured."

"I'll be fine."

Peggy's daughters ran out of the house screaming. "Mommy! Mommy!"

As they got closer, Mom said, "Be careful. Your mother is hurt."

Junie appeared to not hear and threw her arms around Peggy's waist. "We thought you might not come back. But you did. I prayed for you to come back."

Peggy caressed her daughter's back. "Thank you. God heard your prayers." She had felt her little one's prayers and God's hand upon her.

Wendy stood nearby with tears in her eyes. "We were so worried about you."

Peggy held out her good arm for her daughter to come closer for a hug.

Wendy shook her head. "I don't want to hurt you."

"It's my shoulder. We can hug on the side."

Her daughter stepped closer, leaned into Peggy, and sighed.

As her daughters moved her toward the front door, Howie cleared his throat. "Witherspoon, I'll return the day after tomorrow to take you to Bolling Airfield for debriefing. You rest up today and tomorrow."

Peggy patted her daughter's arm. "You three go inside. I'll be there in a minute." She walked back to the car. "Thank you. I'll be fine to come in tomorrow to be debriefed."

"You heard the general, a day or two. We are going to be busy with cleaning up the area from the storm. Take it easy for the time being. Your shoulder will thank you for the rest. Trust me." He climbed into the driver's seat.

She studied him a moment, unsure if she should speak her mind. "I missed you too."

He squeezed her hand. "I thought my heart was going to burst when we had to accept you were dead."

That warmed her all over. She leaned into the open car door and kissed him. He'd initiated their last kiss by bringing up the subject, but this time, she threw all propriety aside. She wanted the major to know she felt the same about him.

He hooked his hand around behind her neck and deepened the kiss. When they finally parted, he said, "We're going to have to talk about your breach in protocol just now."

She smiled. "I look forward to it."

She hadn't imagined having these kinds of feelings for another man after George had died. But here she was having them. . .and loving it.

⊒ CHAPTER 31 ⊒

Three weeks later, Peggy stood in the briefing room in her dress blues. Nightingale and Brownie had also been told to show up in their dress uniforms. None of them had been informed as to what this was about. Her stomach knotted as she waited.

Brownie bit her bottom lip. "Do you think they are going to separate us even though we saved the lives of those soldiers? Because we didn't have permission?"

Nightingale thinned her lips. "If that's the way they want to treat heroes, they don't deserve pilots like us."

Peggy felt the same. Her shoulder still ached, but she wouldn't do anything different. She would still go rescue those men. Knowing now about them being in the path of the hurricane, she would have been even more motivated to go. "If they plan to separate us, would they have had us wear our dress uniform?"

Her comrades both shrugged.

The door opened, and a line of commanding officers paraded in. Brigadier General Hawkins, Major Berg, WASP Commander Barbara Poole, the founder and leader of the entire WASP program Jackie Cochran, and the three soldiers they had rescued.

Peggy and her comrades snapped to attention and saluted even though they were indoors. They held the salute.

All four superior officers and the men they had rescued saluted them back.

The general stood in the front of the room at the center, the others stepped off to the sides. "What is about to take place and anything said here today does not leave this room. If anyone here speaks of it, they will be court-martialed. Is that understood?"

Peggy joined her comrades and all the others in the room in a single response. "Yes, sir."

Captain Williams, whom they had rescued, seemed to be fully recovered from his injuries. But then Peggy appeared to be recovered as well, even though it would be a while before her shoulder returned to its former function without pain.

"WASPs Brown, Horner, and Witherspoon, you are civil servants and do not qualify for any military recognition. However, you three have shown through your bravery to exemplify what it means to be a military soldier. Though no one outside this room may know the deeds you have performed in the service of your country, your actions have not gone unnoticed."

Peggy couldn't believe it. They were actually being praised for their actions.

"WASP Brown, please step forward."

Brownie marched forward to stand directly in front of the general. The general motioned for her to turn around.

She did a brisk about-face.

"For your bravery and going above and beyond the call of duty, the United States military awards you the Distinguished Service Cross."

The highest award that could be bestowed on a civilian.

Private Nelson, whom they had rescued, walked up holding a rectangular, flat, military-medal case. He opened it, and Commander Poole removed the medal and pinned it on Brownie's dress uniform jacket.

Poole shook Brownie's hand then and so did the private, the general, the sergeant, the captain, Cochran, and Major Berg.

Brownie stepped back in line with Peggy and Nightingale.

The process was repeated with Nightingale, but it was Cochran and the rescued sergeant who presented her the Distinguished Service Cross.

Then Peggy's turn. The rescued captain and Howie presented hers.

She moved to return to her place with her fellow WASPs, but the general stopped her.

"Not so fast."

This time it was the founder of the WASP Cochran who held a case box which normally held a military medal.

General Hawkins studied her with what appeared to be pride. "WASP Witherspoon, your selflessness saved three soldiers' lives and the lives of your fellow WASPs. Your actions were above what we expect from our military soldiers—they are what we hope for in every soldier but few rise even close to that level. In the course of you putting your life on the line for your fellow countrymen, you sustained bodily injury which you never complained about and which I imagine hurts still."

Cochran opened the medal box.

The general reached in and retrieved a Purple Heart. "I award you this Purple Heart for your services to your country."

"Hooah!" the sergeant said and then looked penitent, but not really.

The general smiled and continued. "Ladies, even though these medals are well earned, you must hide them away where no one will find them. You may not even tell your closest family members. Understood?"

"Yes, sir."

The unsanctioned mission could never be made public.

Peggy gazed out at the faces around the room. *Thank You, Lord, for giving me the honor to serve with all these fine men and women.* She couldn't be more proud.

≣ EPILOGUE ≣

December 25, 1944

At mid-morning, after the presents had been opened—they had each gotten one—Peggy sat on one end of the davenport with her feet curled under her, sipping on a mug of hot chocolate. Life was about as perfect as it could be. Last Christmas had been almost unbearable with George gone. As they say, time heals all wounds.

Well, time and the love of all the special people in her life. Though her wounds weren't all healed. Yet.

This year, an additional loved one had been added to her life. Howie had told her he loved her, and she had told him of her love too. A giddiness swirled within her every time she thought of him. Even with the war still going on in Europe and Asia, the war with God inside Peggy had come to an end. She no longer blamed Him for the losses she'd experienced, but instead could see His grace and mercy in the events of her life. Her spirit was at peace for the first time since her brother and father were killed in the First World War.

Junie bounded onto the davenport and crawled up next to her. "Mommy, read me a story."

Peggy wrapped her arms around her youngest daughter. "All right. What story would you like to hear?"

Wendy held out a folded sheaf of papers. "This one."

Peggy gazed up at her oldest daughter. Had she written a story? She scooted Junie over to make room for Wendy on the other side of her and took the thin booklet.

Wendy sat next to her.

Mom sat in the adjacent chair, looking like the cat who'd caught the canary and roasted it up for Christmas dinner.

Something was up, but Peggy couldn't put her finger on it.

Peggy held the book so both girls could see it. *The Happy Warrior.* The cover illustration was definitely drawn by Wendy.

She opened it to see that the left side had a drawing by Junie. Her youngest pointed to her artwork. "I drew that. Do you like it, Mommy?"

"I do." It appeared to be five people, each drawn in a different color. All had smiles except one. Someone with a sword, whom Peggy guessed to be the warrior in the story. The person had no mouth at all.

Peggy pointed to that figure. "Isn't this person happy?"

Junie held up a crayon stub in her fist. "We don't know. Read the story."

Something was definitely up.

On the facing page were several typed paragraphs, so she began to read aloud about a warrior who fought many battles. When the warrior came home, the warrior was given many awards. "But the warrior was missing the best award of all. The warrior didn't have. . ."

Peggy flipped to the last page but nothing was there. "How does the story end?"

A male voice came from the other side of the room. "The warrior didn't have a special person to grow old with." Howie crossed the room and knelt in front of Peggy, holding out a silver ring. The top of it had a dual-blade propeller conformed to the curve of the ring with a blue topaz in the center. "Will you marry me?"

Peggy wanted to shout yes but felt she needed to discuss this with her daughters first. She glanced at them.

Junie tugged on her arm. "Answer him, Mommy."

Mom responded. "Everyone else in this room has already agreed. You are the only person left to say yes."

Junie beamed at Peggy. Wendy gave her an encouraging nod.

Love and happiness exploded inside Peggy. "If everyone else has said yes, then I'm happy to make it unanimous." She held out her hand, and Howie slipped the propeller ring onto her finger. Better than even her secret Purple Heart.

Howie leaned forward from his position on the floor, and Peggy closed the distance toward him. Their lips met for a brief blissful moment.

"Yay!" Junie slipped off the couch, knelt at the coffee table, and drew a smile on the warrior.

It was then Peggy realized *she* was the warrior.

And she was indeed happy.

AUTHOR'S NOTES

I researched a wide variety of topics for this book. Everything from Women's Airforce Service Pilots (WASP) to WWII military aircraft to survival gear and surviving bailing out over the open ocean to fifth grade spelling bee words to meatloaf and so much more. Every time I worked on a new scene, there was something new to research including WWII food ration books, radar technology, and aircraft wiring.

In 1942, two independent female flying organizations were created, the WFTD (Women's Flying Training Detachment) and the WAFS (Women's Auxiliary Ferry Squadron). Each spearheaded and led by two different female pilots. In August 1943, these two organizations combined to form the WASP (Women's Airforce Service Pilots). During the war, 1,074 of these skilled female pilots became the first women to fly American military aircraft and underwent vigorous training. They took off from 126 airbases across the US to relocate combat aircrafts and flew 80% of the ferrying missions. WASPs flew just about every type of US aircraft used by the military during WWII. They delivered more than 12,000 aircrafts, flew over sixty million miles, and freed around 900 male pilots for combat duty. Thirty-eight WASPs died in the line of duty, and one disappeared while on a ferrying mission. Her fate is still unknown.

During WWII, besides ferrying airplanes from factories to bases where the male pilots were stationed for training and deployment, WASPs also tested airplanes, trained male pilots, were airplane mechanics, transported cargo, and towed targets for live anti-aircraft artillery practice. Yep, green soldiers learning to fire large artillery weapons with live rounds shot at some of these brave WASPs as they flew in the wild blue yonder. One WASP wouldn't likely perform all the duties I have Peggy do, but to highlight the vast range of tasks WASPs did, I gave her many of the jobs.

Though they worked for the Army, they were still civilians. They were paid less than the men who did the same job and without any benefits. They had to pay for their own travel expenses and purchase their own uniforms. The WASP arrangement with the Army ceased

December 20, 1944, when returning male pilots took over the ferrying duties.

Partway through writing this story, a stray thought skipped into this west coast gal's head. Hmm? What about hurricane season? So, I researched the 1944 Atlantic hurricane season. Did I want to move my story's timeline or location to avoid hurricane season? At first, I wanted to avoid hurricane season at all cost. I didn't want to research hurricanes. But then…I found the *perfect* hurricane that fit beautifully into my story to make the difficult stuff my heroine was already going through even harder. Enter the Cuba/Florida hurricane (October 9-24). I also had to make sure that any other hurricanes during my timeline that might affect my story setting at least had a mention. Enter the Great Atlantic hurricane (September 9-15).

Though Cuba was part of the Allied forces during WWII, I went with the supposition there could be Axis (German) sympathizers in Cuba or even some Germans. I needed someone closer to home to want to hold Americans captive, but there didn't seem to be any Axis countries on this side of the ocean. So for this story, I created a fictional group of Germans hiding out in Cuba to hold my three US soldiers captive. I believe that in any country around the world, there are likely sympathizers for both sides in any conflict or war regardless of where the country as a whole stands.

One thing that surprised me in my research was the amount of gear a pilot needed to wear and still fit into the cockpit of a fighter plane. They, of course, had their flight suit with some underclothing beneath it. Over that went the survival vest with more than thirty items: everything from an inflatable one-man lifeboat with hand paddles, emergency rations, matches, fishing kit, sewing kit, first aid kit, signal flares, fire starting tabs, matches, water purification tablets, knife, .45 caliber pistol with bullets, toilet paper, sun goggles, signaling mirror, compass, collapsible canteen, insect repellant, smelling salts, and more. Next came the Mae West vest. This was a life vest with CO_2 canisters to inflate it. Last but not least, the bulky parachute. These items were in the order the pilot would need them in the event he or she had to bail out of their aircraft.

I thoroughly enjoyed researching and learning about the wide variety of topics I needed for this story.

 **MARY DAVIS** is a *Publishers Weekly* Bestselling, award-winning author of over thirty novels and novellas in both historical and contemporary themes.

Mary is a member of American Christian Fiction Writers, is the past-president of a local ACFW chapter, and is active in critique groups.

She enjoys walking, being with her family, playing board and card games, rain, and cats. She would enjoy gardening if she didn't have a black thumb. Her hobbies are quilting, porcelain doll making, sewing, crafts, crocheting, and knitting. She enjoys going into schools and talking to kids about writing. She loves creativity in various forms.

Mary lives in the Pacific Northwest with her husband of over thirty-six years, has three adult children, three adorable grandchildren, and one cat.

Visit her author pages on Amazon and Facebook at Mary Davis and join her Facebook readers group, Mary Davis READERS Group. You can also find her on BookBub and GoodReads.